Lieutenant Brittle put a gentle hand on her head, and without a word, pulled back the coverlets.

He was still fully dressed, but he lay down next to her, gathering her close as Laura threw her arm across his chest and cried. He held her until she stopped crying and sat up again. He stayed where he was, practically asleep himself.

Careful not to disturb him, she watched his face relax. She loosened his neckcloth, sliding it slowly from him. As he breathed evenly and deeply, she unbuttoned his shirt, then removed his cufflinks. Her breasts grazed his chest as she did that, but he did not even stir.

She hesitated a moment, then decided in for a penny, in for a pound, and unbuttoned his trousers. You'd be an easy man to seduce, she thought, smiling at the idea. She knew she should retreat downstairs, but she didn't. She lay down, then backed up against the surgeon, who responded by turning sideways, draping his arm over her and breathing steadily into her ear. She'd never slept better.

* * *

The Surgeon's Lady
Harlequin® Historical #949—June 2009

Carla Kelly
the SURGEON'S LADY

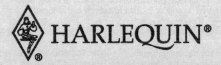

HARLEQUIN®

TORONTO • NEW YORK • LONDON
AMSTERDAM • PARIS • SYDNEY • HAMBURG
STOCKHOLM • ATHENS • TOKYO • MILAN • MADRID
PRAGUE • WARSAW • BUDAPEST • AUCKLAND

Recycling programs
for this product may
not exist in your area.

ISBN-13: 978-0-373-29549-4

THE SURGEON'S LADY

Copyright © 2009 by Carla Kelly

www.eHarlequin.com

Printed in U.S.A.

*Available from Harlequin® Historical and
Carla Kelly*

Beau Crusoe #839
Marrying the Captain #928
The Surgeon's Lady #949

The Surgeon's Lady features characters you
will have met in *Marrying the Captain*

DON'T MISS THESE OTHER
NOVELS AVAILABLE NOW:

#947 STETSONS, SPRING AND WEDDING RINGS —
Jillian Hart, Judith Stacy and Stacey Kayne

Meet Clara, Brynn and Constance as they go West. They are
looking for new lives, and three forceful men are determined to
be their new loves! They want to keep these courageous women
where they belong—in their towns, in their hearts and,
most of all, in their beds....
Romance blossoms in the West!

#948 LORD BRAYBROOK'S PENNILESS BRIDE—
Elizabeth Rolls

Viscount Braybrook is paying Christiana Daventry to keep her
wayward brother far away from his stepsister. But when he
realizes he wants to keep Christy *intimately* close, suddenly his
heart is at risk from the one thing money can't buy—love!
The Viscount and the governess...

#950 BEDDED BY THE WARRIOR—Denise Lynn

Newly wedded, Lady Sarah of Remy has a hidden purpose—one
that shouldn't involve being passionately bedded by her warrior
husband! William of Bronwyn also has his own reasons for the
marriage, but his secretive wife is too alluring to resist....
At her warrior's command!

Dedicated to the men of the Channel Fleet,
whose wooden walls kept the Corsican Tyrant
from England's shores

Primum non nocere.
First, do no harm.

—Credited to Galen, Roman physician,
and English physician Sir Thomas Sydenham

Chapter One

Taunton, June 28, 1809

For several months Lady Laura Taunton had avoided the desk in her sitting room because of two letters, one inside the other, she had not the heart to destroy. She had thrown them away one evening, but retrieved them before the maid did her early morning tidying. She shoved them back in the desk before continuing her restless slumber.

Suddenly, the letters mattered. She blamed her change of heart on her nearest neighbor, who had invited her to tea. Lady Chisholm probably had no idea of Laura's feelings. She merely wanted to drink tea and share a happy event.

Laura had dressed with deliberate care for the tea. It was a year since death had released Sir James Taunton from the apoplexy that had turned him into a helpless infant, and made her his nurse for the previous three years. She would dress in gray this afternoon, signaling a departure from black, which she hoped fervently, if unrealistically, never to wear again.

She hadn't missed James for a minute, but no need for

the neighbors to know. A widower thirty years her senior, James had paid attention when her father, William Stokes, Lord Ratliffe, had shared her miniature around his circle of acquaintances and promised her to the highest bidder.

She had been eighteen then, a student at Miss Pym's Female Academy in Bath, sent there by her father for an education, with no idea that he would demand so high a return on his investment.

"My dear wife was never able to give me an heir," James had told her after their wedding. "Your duty is to give me an heir."

During the first year of her removal to Taunton, a country seat near Bath, Laura had asked herself daily why she had not bolted from school at the mere idea of what her father had planned. During those nights when James Taunton heaved, gasped and thrust over her, she cursed her own weak character.

She did not become a mother, for all James's attempts that consumed his energy and left her feeling no satisfaction beyond relief when he finished and left her room. When he suffered a stroke while out riding, his groom carried the baronet back to the house, practically dropping Sir James at her feet like a game bird. She hoped the staff saw her calm acceptance as well-bred courage, rather than gratitude.

Stung by her own faulty character, she had thrown herself into nursing her husband. By year two of his apoplexy, she could have challenged anyone to improve upon her delivery of competent care. She conducted herself with dignity when he died, and dressed in black. Beyond tea at Chisholm, that was her world.

That was a year ago. This afternoon, she had walked to

Chisholm, happy not to be suffocating in black. Tea with Lady Chisholm usually demanded no more of her than to nod and interject the occasional short word. But this afternoon, Lady C had dealt her a blow. Sitting right next to her neighbor and holding her hand, was a slightly younger version of Lady Chisholm.

As Laura had hesitated, Lady Chisholm waved her closer. "Do forgive me, my dear. It's just that…" She glanced at her sister and burst into tears. "This is my sister and it has been so long."

It was simply said, but Laura felt her heart pound from the look the sisters exchanged. *What have I done?* Laura thought. Then: *Can I change it?*

Not wanting to startle her own servants when she returned to Taunton, Laura allowed the tears to slide down her face in silence. She had perfected this art through many a night in her late husband's bed. By the time she reached the estate, hers alone now, she was in control again.

She had a moment of panic when she could not find the letters. She reminded herself that it had been three months since she had retrieved them, and dug deeper in her desk. She sighed when she unearthed them.

She held up the first one, the only one she had had the courage to read in March. *Read this first!* had been scrawled across the folded sheets in Miss Pym's handwriting. Even after eight years and a supreme dislike of Pym, Laura had obeyed.

She read it again, knowing the news still had the power to shock her. She read again of Lord Ratliffe's dealings with the Female Academy and his relationship to Pym, his illegitimate sister. Her breath came faster as she read again Pym's news that she had two half sisters. *You are too old now to remember Polly Brandon,* she read again, *but perhaps you recall Eleanor Massie.* Eleanor was now Eleanor Worthy, wife of a captain in the Royal Navy, who had somehow managed Lord Ratliffe's incarceration in a Spanish prison, as part of a botched hostage exchange.

"Good riddance," Laura said.

The Worthys had gone to Bath because Lord Ratliffe had told the captain, probably to taunt him, Laura thought sourly, his wife was one of three illegitimate daughters educated by Miss Pym. Pym had written,

Eleanor has told Captain Worthy her whole history, and they are here to find her sisters—Polly Brandon, who still resides here, and you, Lady Taunton.

Laura put down the letter and stared at the ceiling, remembering her relief when she read Pym's confession that Eleanor had not succumbed to a fate similar to the one Lord Ratliffe had proposed to her, but had fled Bath with nothing but the clothes on her back.

She had a place to go, Laura thought. *I had nowhere and no one.* Still, it couldn't have been much rosier for Eleanor. She looked at Miss Pym's letter again, with its concluding paragraph, urging her to read Eleanor's accompanying letter.

That was the letter she had not opened, too humiliated by her own circumstances to think anyone, even a half sister, would ever want to contact someone who hadn't her own strength of character. *Why would she want to know me?* This time, though, she took a deep breath and opened Eleanor Worthy's letter.

Her eyes welled with tears. If Eleanor had begun it formally, Laura could have resisted, but she had not. Laura let out a shuddering breath. *Oh, sister,* the letter began. *I want to meet you.*

Laura was on her way to Plymouth by noon the next day. She didn't write ahead, knowing that if she had to put pen to paper, her courage would fail her completely.

Laura arrived in Plymouth when farmers were leaving their fields and shopkeepers shuttering up for the night. Nana Worthy, that was how she signed her name, had included directions to the Mulberry, and the coachman got lost only once. She wished he had been lost another two or three times, because her misgivings had begun to flap overhead like seagulls.

There was the Mulberry, small and narrow, but well tended. The paint on the door and windows looked newly fresh, and she had to smile at the pansies in their pots and ivy making its determined way up the walls. *It must be the inn that won't die,* Laura thought, with amusement.

She told the coachman just to wait, and shook her head against an escort up the walk. There was nothing wrong with her legs, only her resolve. A small sign in the door's glass said Please Come In, so she did, and understood within five minutes what made the Mulberry a fiber in Nana's heart.

Though shabby, everything was neat as a pin. *Nana, where are you?* she thought, sniffing the air which was redolent of roast beef and gravy, something her French chef would rather die than serve. Her mouth watered.

A door down the corridor opened, and an older woman came out. She was small and thin, her expressive face full of sharp planes and angles, but Laura could not overlook her brown eyes. This must be Nana's grandmother.

"Mrs. Massie?" she inquired. "I am…"

She didn't even have to say. The innkeeper grasped her by both arms.

"I wondered if you would come," she said simply. "Nana has nearly given up."

The woman must have realized how presumptuously she was behaving, because she dropped her hands from Laura's arms and stepped back to curtsy. *Don't stop,* Laura wanted to say. *No one has ever touched me kindly.*

There was something in Mrs. Massie's eyes that demanded equal frankness. "I hadn't the courage to come," Laura said. "I could not believe that Eleanor, Nana, would really want to meet me. Not after what I did."

"She was nearly beside herself with excitement when she and the captain returned here from Bath in March," Mrs. Massie said. "'Sisters, Gran, imagine,' she told me."

Laura didn't know how it happened, but the innkeeper had her by the hand and was leading her into a small sitting room off the corridor. "Where is Nana, please?"

She astonished herself by bursting into tears when Mrs. Massie told her the captain had settled Nana in Torquay, a half day's drive east. She astonished herself further by leaning against Mrs. Massie until the woman was grasping her shoulder and murmuring, something like the crooning of parent to child.

Her whole story tumbled out, how her father had sold her to Sir James Taunton to pay his creditors; how her husband had tried to fix a child on her; how she had faithfully tended the old man through his final illness; how humiliated she was by what had happened. Through it all, Mrs. Massie held her close, offering her apron for Laura to dab her eyes.

"It is my shame to bear," Laura said, when she could speak.

Laura stayed in the protecting circle of Mrs. Massie's arms. "No shame. You didn't have a Gran to run to, did you?" she said.

"No, I didn't have a Gran."

"You do, now."

Laura slept soundly that night, burrowed deep in Nana's bed, with its homely sag. The room was light when she woke up, but she contented herself with lying still, hands behind her head. She looked around the room, noted a shaving stand and mirror, and reminded herself that Nana had shared her small bed with a husband.

Well, Nana, you were spooned in with the captain, she thought. *No wonder I am to be an aunt.* Sir James had never been inclined to share her bed, content merely to use her and leave her. Laura doubted that her sister and the captain had separate bedchambers in their home in Torquay.

The Mulberry's keepers waved her off from the front walk and Laura blew Gran a kiss before she settled back in the coach. She wished the road had followed the coastline, but there were glimpses of Devon's lovely coast. A brisk wind blew, so the water sparkled and danced.

Then they were in Torquay, where she could practically breathe in the magnificent sweep of Torbay, with its warships at anchor there, too, and tidy houses rising from the coastline in pastel terraces. As gulls wheeled and scolded overhead, she began to wonder why anyone would want to live inland.

When she reached Nana's home, it was as Gran has described it: two and a half stories of sturdy stone with a pale blue wash and red roof. A captain could see that roof from the Channel, Laura thought. He could probably even keep it in his mind's eye for months on the blockade.

The post chaise came to a stop on the neatly graveled driveway in front of the door. Not wasting a moment, Laura opened the door, put down the step and was knocking on the front door before the coachman barely set the brake. The door opened on a generously built woman rather than a butler, who asked her to state her business, in that soft burr of the Southwest Coast that Laura had detected in Gran's speech.

"Lady Taunton from Taunton, here to visit my sister, Mrs. Worthy."

"Well, well! Come this way," the woman said. "Things are at sixes and sevens right now, what with the news, but…" She was silent then, which from the look on her face, must have been a difficult thing. "Mrs. Worthy can tell you everything."

This is a bad time, Laura thought with dismay, as she entered the sitting room. There was Nana, obviously, sitting between another comfortable-looking woman and a man in uniform who, with his short brown hair and bright blue eyes she could see even from the doorway, must be related to the woman. They had the same air of comfort about them.

Laura knew she was not familiar with naval uniforms, but this one was different than most: plain, with no epaulets and only gilt buttons. The insignia on his upstanding collar was unusual, too, with its double row of gilt-embroidered chains.

"Lady Taunton," the housekeeper announced.

The man in uniform stood up when he saw her and bowed, but Laura had eyes only for her sister, who looked as though she had been crying.

There was no denying she had come at a bad time. Her instinct should have propelled her backward, but not this time, and not in this room, not with her sister sitting there, her eyes widening. Laura stepped forward, her hands out.

"Nana," was all she said.

Nana rose from the sofa as though pulled up by strings. In a gesture that looked automatic to Laura, she put her hand on her belly, almost as a gesture of reassurance.

"Laura?" she said, and there was no mistaking the strength in her voice, even behind the quaver.

Laura felt the world's weight leave her shoulders. *Thank God you have not called me Lady Taunton,* she thought, as she crossed the room.

Nana met her halfway, throwing her arms around Laura. She pressed herself close until Laura could feel the softness of her belly. Nana was shorter than she, so she rested her head against Laura's bosom. The most natural thing in the world was for Laura to kiss her hair, which she did, as she locked her arms around her sister.

"Oliver told me you would come. He said I had to be patient," Nana murmured in that same lilting, West Country burr. "Laura."

Laura remembered Pym's determination to give Eleanor Massie a well-bred accent, and her pique at never quite erasing the burr from the pretty child's voice.

Her words were for Nana only, so she whispered them. "Sister, it took me three months to work up the nerve. What a fool I was."

Nana drew a shuddering breath, then held herself off to look at Laura, from her stylish bonnet, to her impeccable traveling dress to her elegant half boots, then back to Laura's hair, the color of her own. She gave it a gentle tug.

"When we were at the academy, I used to think you were the most beautiful creature in the whole world," Nana said. She laughed out loud, a delightful sound that traveled to every corner of Laura's heart. "I should have known we were related!"

Laura couldn't help laughing. "You're still a scamp," she said, taking her sister's hand.

Just then Nana remembered the others in the room, the man still standing.

"Mrs. Brittle, Surgeon Brittle, this is my sister, Lady Taunton."

Suddenly, it was too much. Laura felt Nana sag, but the man was quicker. In a moment he had seated Nana on the sofa, and stepped back so Laura could join her. He poured a glass of water and handed it to her sister.

"Drink that and lean back," he told her. "Deep breath." Nana obeyed him without question.

Laura looked from the man to his mother, which served to give Mrs. Brittle leave to speak.

"My son is a surgeon," she said. "He's newly arrived from Jamaica."

That would explain the handsome tan. She wouldn't have called him good-looking, but the mahogany of his complexion seemed determined to cover the defects of sharp nose, thin lips and hair so short she wondered at first if he was bald. On the other hand, if Lt. Brittle was not the most handsome man she had ever seen—even in his glory days, her late husband was worth a second look—the surgeon had magnificent shoulders, the kind commonly associated with road-mending crews. Laura was impressed and puzzled, in equal shares.

"They came in force to bring me bad news," Nana said in her forthright way.

"No, merely it-could-be-worse news," the lieutenant contradicted. "The good news is that Captain Worthy can swim." Nana relaxed further under the calmness of his gaze.

Laura watched him, interested, as the sheer force of his personality seemed to steady them. Mrs. Brittle said he was a surgeon. For years, she had seen many a physician up close, but never had she observed a better example of bedside manner, and from a mere surgeon in the Royal Navy. So much for the day's surprises.

"Swim?" Laura asked. "I am in the dark."

Nana took her hand and started to speak, but couldn't. She looked at Mrs. Brittle, who took up the narrative without a pause.

"My husband is the sailing master on the *Tireless,* Lady Taunton," she said. "He sent us a message by way of a coastal ship. The *Tireless* was on the receiving end of a real donnybrook by Ferrol Station." Her voice hardened. "It wasn't a fair fight, but Captain Worthy never backs away. The *Tireless* limped into Plymouth Sound and sank last night."

"My God!" Laura exclaimed, and felt her face go pale. She barely sensed his fingers at her throat, but in a few seconds, the surgeon had removed her bonnet and was waving her with it. "Deep breaths," she said, and he smiled.

"Oliver can swim," Nana said, her voice dogged.

"Apparently even with a wounded man on his back," Lt. Brittle added, returning the bonnet to Laura. "He insisted my father deliver the news to Torquay as soon as possible, so Mrs. Worthy wouldn't hear it from someone else. That is why we are here."

"The others? Your father?" Laura asked. "How are they?"

Mrs. Brittle reached across Nana and touched Laura's hand. "You sound like a West Country lass yourself, to care about jack-tars."

"I care," she said softly.

"You'll watch over your little sister?" the surgeon asked, his voice matching hers for calmness in a way that utterly beguiled her, she who had listened to too many physicians blather.

My little sister. "Aye. I'll watch over my little sister."

Chapter Two

After the Brittles left, Laura and Nana each burst into tears, then started to laugh, which only led to more tears and laughter.

"I could not believe you wanted to see me, so I did not open your letter until two days ago," Laura confessed.

"Silly you."

Nana placed Laura's hand on her belly. Laura held her breath as she felt the tiny motion under her fingertips.

"The first time it happened, I thought it was my imagination," Nana said. "It felt like a butterfly trapped on the other side of my shimmy." She laughed. "Lt. Brittle said to give Baby Worthy a few months, and he, or she, will feel like a prisoner rattling a tin cup along the iron bars of the brig."

"The lieutenant's a common one," Laura said before she thought.

"We're all common, Laura," was her sister's quiet reply.

It was not a rebuke; even on their short close acquaintance, Laura didn't think Nana had a rebuke in her entire body. Hers was a statement of fact; they were a common lot. Laura felt another layer of self-deceit slide away.

"Common we are." She removed her hand. "I think you should lie down now."

If Laura expected mutiny, she got none.

"I agree. The Brittles and I already had luncheon. I expect you haven't, unless travel has suddenly become much more convenient."

"You know it hasn't," Laura said with a laugh. "Direct me to your housekeeper, and I will…" She went to the window. "My stars, I forgot about the chaise."

Nana was already settling herself on the sofa, her hand tucked against her belly. "Send them away, Laura."

"I don't want to inconvenience you…" Laura began.

"I'll be more inconvenienced if you leave." She gave Laura a look that was as calculating as it was a bluff. "Ladies in waiting are to be humored. Lt. Brittle told me so."

"He did no such thing," Laura teased. "He looks far too practical for that."

"All the Brittles are practical," Nana said, perfectly complacent to be found out and corrected. "Do you have pressing business in Taunton demanding your immediate attention?"

She said it so gently that Laura felt the tears start in her eyes again. Since Sir James's death, there had been not one demand on her time. If she showed up next week in Taunton or never again, no one would really care, except the servants she supported.

"I have no business anywhere. I didn't bring many clothes, though."

Nana sighed when Laura covered her with a light throw.

When she replied, her voice was already drowsy. "In the bookroom, Mrs. Trelease will show you, there are paper, pens and ink. Write a note to your staff, tell them to collect more clothing, and hand the note to Joey Trelease. He's a scamp but he loves to post letters quayside. Heaven knows he's posted enough of mine."

Laura hesitated, and Nana narrowed her eyes. "I am she who commands."

"You and who else?" Laura teased. It was the mildest of banter, but she almost shivered with the pleasure of sharing it with a sister.

Nana yawned. "If Oliver were here, you would snap to. He would say, 'Lively, now, madam,' and the earth would tremble."

She began to cry, and there was no subterfuge anywhere, just the raw edge of a wife who has heard her man was in danger, even if safe now. Laura dropped to her knees by the sofa and put her cheek against her sister's.

"Whatever my failings—don't stop me, I have many— I am an excellent guest, and possibly even more of a tyrannical big sister than you ever imagined."

Or than I ever imagined, Laura thought, as she shushed Nana, kissed her and sat on the floor by the sofa until her little sister slept. When Nana was breathing evenly, Laura went outside, paid the coachman and dismissed him.

Luncheon was Cornish pasties so crisp and brown that she salivated as Mrs. Trelease served them. After a leisurely cup of tea in the breakfast room—windows open, seagulls noisy—Laura went upstairs to find her few dresses already on pegs in the dressing room and her brush and comb lined up on the bureau.

Before she went downstairs to find the book room, she walked quietly down the hall, past what must be Nana and the captain's room. She saw the boat cloak thrown across the foot of the bed. *I wonder if Nana wraps herself in it at night,* she asked herself. What must it be like to love a man so often gone?

The next chamber was the future nursery. Already there was an armchair there with padded armrests, pulled close to the open window and the view of the bay. She went to the window, watching the ships swinging on their anchors. At this distance, the smaller boats darting to and from them looked like water bugs.

There was a cradle, too, one that looked old and well-used. Something told her, how, she did not know, that it must have come from the Brittles' house, which must be the pale yellow one next door and a little lower down the hill.

As she stood there, she noticed Lt. Brittle standing on the side lawn, looking out to sea, hands in his pockets. He must have felt her scrutiny, because he turned slightly, then waved to her.

She waved back, knowing Miss Pym would be shocked at such brazen behavior, but not caring in the least. She couldn't keep staring at him, so she looked out to sea again, content to watch the boats come and go. When she glanced at the side lawn again, he was walking inside his mother's house, whistling. The sound made her smile.

Lt. Brittle came to the house again that night after dinner was long over, and Nana was starting to yawn in the middle of sentences. She looked up when the surgeon came into the room.

"Is there a cure for sleepiness?"

"Most certainly," he told her. "In your case, give it about five months. Of course, then you'll be tired because of two o'clock feedings. You're a no-hoper."

How is it he knows just the right tone to strike with my sister? Laura asked herself, as she listened to their delightful banter. *I am in the presence of an artist.*

It was a beguiling thought. Nana, who had been reclining on the sofa, tried to sit up, but the lieutenant shook his head and she stayed where she was. To Laura's surprise, he sat on the floor right by her sister, tucking the throw a little higher on her shoulders against the cool evening breeze blowing in from the Channel.

His eyes on Nana's face, he took a note from his uniform jacket and opened it. Laura noticed the suddenly alert look on Nana's face. Nana took hold of the surgeon's hand as he tried to unfold the note, stopping him.

"It's all right, Nana, it's all right," he said, his voice soothing. "It came to me about an hour ago from Captain Worthy himself. Hey, now. He wanted you to know he'll be here tomorrow, but he also wants you to be prepared."

Laura found herself on the floor by the sofa, too, her arm around her sister in a protective gesture she never would have imagined herself capable of, only that morning in Plymouth.

"He sustained an injury to his ear," the surgeon said. "Read it yourself."

Nana snatched the letter from his hand, her eyes devouring the words. She took a deep breath when she finished. "Listen, Laura: 'My love, I am not precisely symmetrical now, but I trust you will still adore me.' Oh, Phil! What else did he write to you in the other note you are not showing me?"

"You know your man pretty well, don't you?"

"Beyond degree. Confess."

"It was a splinter." The surgeon shook his head at Laura's expression. "Not those aggravating ones you get under your fingernail. This is when pieces of the railing and masts go in all directions during bombardment." He looked at Nana again. "From his description, I think he lost his earlobe and maybe part of that outer rim. Could be worse. If you want, I can look at it before I leave for Stonehouse tomorrow."

"You know I want that," Nana replied. She put her hand on the surgeon's arm. "We're lucky, aren't we, Phil?"

"Unquestionably. My father said Captain Worthy knew the *Tireless* was going down, so he offloaded his most seriously wounded onto a passing water hoy headed to Plymouth and sent a message requesting aid. The rest of the wounded he put into the ship's small boats and towed them behind the *Tireless*, so he would not have to get them out in the general confusion. He thought of everything. No wonder crews like to sail with Captain Worthy. So do you, eh, Nana?"

She burst into tears, great gulping sobs that tore at Laura's heart. Laura cradled her sister, thinking about her own husband's welcome death; how she had closed his eyes without a tear.

The surgeon let Nana have her cry, offering his handkerchief so she could blow her nose. He appeared to have all the time in the world. He took the note from Nana's hand.

"You'll see here he wants me to stay the night. He doesn't know that your sister is here, but I'm still inclined to stay. The sofa in your book room will do."

Nana shook her head. "I won't hear of that. Laura, could you make up the bed in the room across the hall from you? I'm afraid this is Mrs. Trelease's night out."

"Of course I can, dearest," she said.

On Nana's instructions, Laura found the linen, happy to have something to do. Even though it was July, there was a chill on the room which she remedied with a small fire in the grate that the surgeon could extinguish, if he felt too warm. She shook out a bottom sheet.

When she lowered it onto the bed, Lt. Brittle was standing on the other side to straighten it. "I thought I'd leave her alone for a few minutes," he said, as he tucked in his side of the bed, with even more razor-sharp corners than hers.

He noticed her glance and gestured for her to hand him the other sheet. "I'm a surgeon, Lady Taunton," he said. "Nothing exalted like a physician. I've been known to give a good shave and haircut and empty slops. The air isn't too rarefied around me."

There was no mistaking his common touch. True, he was in uniform, but there wasn't anything crisp about him. His hair was short, as short as men who wore wigs usually wore their own hair, but she doubted he owned a wig.

She found a light blanket while he pulled a case onto the pillow and fluffed it at the head of the bed. She held out the blanket and they settled it on the sheets together. When it was smoothed out, she looked at him and chose to say more.

"The air may not be rarefied, but you are a good surgeon."

"Thank you," he said simply.

"In fact, I wish you had been at my late husband's bedside. I…" She stopped, her face warm.

He didn't say anything, but the look of sympathy in his eyes made her brave enough to continue. "He suffered a stroke four years ago, and I nursed him through three years of…"

"Thirty-six-hour days?" he asked quietly.

"Precisely," she said, relieved that he understood. "I listened to all manner of wisdom from his physicians, and…"

She couldn't find the words to continue, but he seemed to know. "…and you wanted someone to give you concrete advice?"

"Precisely so again," she said, and sat down. "I wanted to know how long he would live, but hadn't the courage to ask so callous a question."

"It's not callous. I'd have answered it," he told her. "Typical expectation might be eighteen months. Apparently you are a superior nurse, if he lasted three years."

"He was my husband," was all she said. "Why aren't there more doctors like you?"

He sat down, too. "I don't know what Nana has told you about us, but we Brittles are as common as marsh grass. I always knew I would be a healer of some sort. For a time, when I sailed as a loblolly boy, I pined for proper medical schooling. After that first battle at sea, I knew I could be more useful."

She nodded. There was no denying he looked like the most capable man on the planet. He also was built like a road mender. She had never met anyone like him.

"Did all your education come at sea?"

"No. Surgeons require degrees. Captain Worthy paid tuition, room and board for three years at the University of Edinburgh."

"He strikes again. Nana has been telling me all about her captain this afternoon."

"Contrary to what she has said, he doesn't *really* walk on water. After Scotland, I spent nearly two years as a ward-walker in London Hospital. I should have been another year there, but man proposes and Boney disposes, apparently. I passed my viva voce, got a license—two, in fact—and found myself back at sea, this time with Lord Nelson at Trafalgar. We all know how that came out."

She shouldn't have been sitting on a bed with him. He must have had the same thought, because they both got up at the same time. She wanted him to tell her more about his life at sea, but surely he had better things to do.

Laura looked around the room, then drew the draperies. "Is there anything else you might need?"

"No, you've thought of everything. I'm going to go next door and finish packing, but I'll be back."

"You mentioned Stonehouse." *Heavens, Laura,* she told herself, *let the man be. He's trying to go home.*

He seemed in no particular hurry. "I started my duties there last week after returning from Jamaica."

He must have noticed the question on her face. "Stonehouse is a Royal Naval Hospital between Plymouth and Devonport. By the dockyards. I am one of the two staff surgeons to some eight hundred patients, depending on Boney."

She couldn't have heard him right. "So many! How can you possibly get away?"

"Not often," he said as she walked him to the door. "I did insist on seeing me mum, however. After Jamaica, she was pining after my careworn visage."

"Is there no Mrs. Brittle?"

"Not besides me mum," he said cheerfully, as he walked down the stairs with her. "Any woman I'm to court will have to come to Stonehouse and empty slops."

Laura laughed. "And probably wash smelly bandages."

"Certainly." He nodded to her. "Just leave the side door open. I'll lock it when I come in, if you and Nana have already gone to bed."

When she returned to the sitting room, Nana was awake and knitting by the window. She held up her work. "Soakers. Mrs. Brittle says I can never knit too many. Do you knit, sister?"

She did. They spent the evening knitting. Under Nana's gentle questions, she was even able to talk about her marriage and Sir James Taunton.

"He wanted an heir, and reckoned his first wife had been at fault," Laura said, her eyes on her knitting. "After a year of trying, he had a stroke and left me in peace." She knew that was enough to tell Nana. "I…I do have a lovely estate in Taunton."

Nana didn't look convinced.

"It's lovely," Laura repeated. "If I never see it again, it wouldn't be any loss to me. Life is amazingly dull when you want for nothing."

Nana did smile at that. She leaned back and rested her hand on her abdomen. "Please don't tell Oliver, but life moved faster at the Mulberry, when I was hauling water up and down stairs, placating our few lodgers, and sweeping hearths."

"You'll be busy soon enough."

"So I will." Nana leaned forward and took Laura's hands in hers. "Oliver's all right, isn't he?"

If she hadn't felt so confident in Lt. Brittle's comments, Laura knew she could not have spoken. "I do believe he is, this captain of yours. You're a goose, Nana! No wonder everyone loves you."

Laura shared Nana's bed that night, because Nana insisted she did not want to be alone. She saw that Nana was comfortable, touched by the way she matter-of-factly pulled the boat cloak over her side of the bed and tucked what would be Oliver's pillow lengthwise to her. Laura smiled at that and got her own pillow from the other bedchamber.

She knew her sister was tired, but Nana had another question. "Laura, who raised you before you came to Miss Pym's? I had Gran."

I had no one, she thought. *My mother, whoever she was, had no interest in me.* "When I tell you, you'll understand a little more about our dear father."

Nana gave an unladylike snort. She giggled then. "Laura, I almost said something I've heard Oliver say when he didn't know I was listening, but I would probably lose all credit with you."

You could never do that, Laura thought. "As I was saying, when you so rudely interrupted—there you go again!—our dear father's problems with money began with the fourth Viscount Ratliffe, who was as dissolute and spendthrift as our loving parent. Nana! Your manners!"

"Sorry," came Nana's meek reply in the dark, followed by a barely suppressed laugh, probably smothered in the folds of her darling's boat cloak.

"Lord Ratliffe Number Four was hell-bent on a flaming career as London's greatest ne'er-do-well when one of the Wesley brothers—John, I believe—took him on as a project, after John's return from Georgia. Nana, are you awake?"

"Of course I am," came the sleepy reply.

"I'll move along. Dear Grandpapa renounced his evil ways, turned to Methodism, and set up his own illegitimate daughter—our beloved Pym—as the headmistress of a female academy. I spent my earliest years in a Wesley orphanage."

Nana reached under Oliver's pillow and took her sister's hand. "Laura," was all she said.

"If you don't know any better, what is the harm?" Laura said. "You know the rest as well as I do. After Grandpa died, our father was forced by some curious honor we scarcely knew he possessed, to maintain Pym's school and keep us in it. Of course, he found a way to make us pay, didn't he? Nana, I'm so ashamed I did not have your courage."

Nana pushed aside Oliver's pillow and her voice was fierce. "Laura! Listen to me! You had no one to help you and nowhere to go." She held Laura by the shoulders. "You have us now. You always will." Her grip relaxed. "Heavens, you'll think I'm ferocious."

"You are, sister," Laura said, drawing a shaky breath. "Did you terrify that French officer in Oliver's prison?"

"Probably," Nana said, her tone kindly again. "He deserved it, though, for getting between me and my love."

And that is that, Laura thought, as her sister found Oliver's pillow again and stretched it out.

She thought Nana slept, but then: "Laura, please say you'll stay here. I need you."

"I'll stay." *I need you more,* she thought, as her eyes closed.

* * *

Laura woke a few hours later, because she heard the bedchamber door open. She sat up, alert, to see the tall form of Lt. Brittle—what had Nana called him? Phil?—holding up a lantern similar to one she had used in James's sick room, with its sides slatted to allow only a little light, enough to see a patient by.

He could see that she was sitting up in bed, but he didn't pause at the door. He came closer in stockinged feet, to kneel by her.

"Is she all right?" he whispered.

"She's fine," Laura whispered back, leaning close to him, unwilling to wake Nana. "We've been catching up on our lives."

"You're a welcome distraction," he said. "She needs you." She could see him distinctly now in the subdued light. "I like to ward walk before I sleep. Good night, Lady Taunton."

Laura nodded and lay down again, grateful for his reassuring presence, even if he did nothing more than shine a light and let her know he was there. To her unspeakable pleasure, he tugged the coverlet up higher and patted her shoulder, before he got to his feet and left the room as quietly as he had entered it.

She put her hand where he had touched her, closed her eyes and slept.

Chapter Three

Lt. Brittle left before breakfast. Laura thought she might have to bully her sister to sit still and eat, in her anticipation for the captain to arrive, but admonition was unnecessary. After the meal, Nana went to the kitchen to plan the week's menus, while Laura went to the book room to write a letter to Taunton.

Writing the letter was a simple matter. Laura wondered what her butler and housekeeper would say when they learned she planned to stay in Torquay for the immediate future. She wanted to recommend holidays for them all, but knew that would be a shock to the system for her retainers, none of whom was younger than fifty.

She was sealing the letter when she heard the front door open, then firm steps in the front hall. He's here, she thought. Nana will never hear him from the kitchen. She stood up, wondering whether to go to the kitchen or into the foyer to introduce herself. Shyness kept her from doing either, but it didn't matter.

"Nana?"

Captain Worthy's voice wasn't loud, but it carried, even though probably not far enough to reach the kitchen.

Laura hadn't known her sister long. Certainly she had no reason to appreciate how close a bond between husband and wife could be. She opened the bookroom door just as Nana sped past her, arms open wide.

Their embrace was wordless, but the intensity of it made Laura catch her breath. She opened the door enough to see her sister caught in the arms of a tall man made even taller by the fore and aft hat he wore, which was cocked slightly to the side to accommodate a bandage around his head.

Before he kissed his wife, he removed his hat. Nana's hands were gentle on his neck, careful not to touch his ear as he kissed her, kissed her again, and once more after that, until Nana ducked and asked him when he had last shaved.

That seemed a good note for Laura to open the door wider and meet her brother-in-law, except that she stood where she was, transfixed by what followed. Oliver dropped to his knees and rested the undamaged side of his head against Nana's belly. With a sob, her little sister laid her hands on him like a benediction.

Laura softly closed the door as her heart pounded. All she could think of to do was thank the Almighty for tender mercies and count slowly to one hundred before opening the door again.

She found the Worthys in the sitting room, looking out the window at the bay, the captain standing behind Nana, his arms around his whole family. He appeared to be resting his chin on Nana's head.

I still shouldn't be here, Laura thought, embarrassed. She turned to go, but the captain looked around and smiled to see her. He let go of Nana and walked toward her. She thought he might bow, but he didn't bother. Taking her by both arms, he kissed her forehead.

"Life's too short to stand on much formality, sister," he said. "Start by calling me Oliver."

What could she do but agree? "I am Laura Taunton," she replied, "and most heartily pleased to meet you."

He was handsome in a seagoing way, with a myriad of wrinkles around his eyes that were probably caused by years of facing into wind and water. His lips were thin as a Scotsman's and his nose full of character. Still, none of his features registered as much as his brown eyes, so warm and kind, probably only because he was in the presence of the person he held most dear in the world. On the quarter-deck, she did not doubt he was absolute monarch. At home, her sister ruled, even though she probably did not know it.

Laura took all this in, understanding her brother-in-law completely before she had said more than a sentence to him. How strange life was. In two days she had gone from having no family in the world, to the possession of a sister and a brother. Maybe there really was a God in Heaven.

Nana stood by Oliver now, making him sit down on the sofa, then putting a pillow behind his head.

"My love, would you humor me and let Philemon Brittle look at your ear?" Nana asked.

Laura knew her brother-in-law would refuse his wife nothing. In his world of war over which he had no control, any gesture of kindness to his wife must have felt like the greatest gift he could give. He nodded.

"I'll get him," Laura said.

She took the well-traveled path between the two houses.

So his name is Philemon, and not merely Phil, she told herself. *It has been a long time since I have read that particular book of the New Testament. I wonder if anyone reads it.*

Lt. Brittle came to the door, his shirtsleeves rolled up. "Just helping me mum with the dishes," he said. "Come in. Did I see a chaise pull up with Captain Worthy?"

"You did," she said, walking with him to the kitchen, where Nora Brittle was up to her elbows in soapy water. "Good day, Mrs. Brittle. May I help?"

The surgeon handed his dish towel to her. "You finish. I'll get my pocket instruments and some wadding."

Laura took the plate Mrs. Brittle handed her, wondering when she had last dried a dish. *In the last day, I have been hugged and cosseted, and cried over and touched,* she thought, as her eyes prickled. *People need me. If I am ever alone again, it will be my own fault and no one else's.*

"Are you feeling all right, Lady Taunton?" Mrs. Brittle asked quietly.

"Never better."

After sitting Oliver Worthy in a straight chair, draping a towel around his neck and advising Nana to recline on the sofa out of view of the injury, Lt. Brittle took out a pair of long-nosed scissors from his packet of instruments, then handed the rest to Laura.

"I should ask—are you up for this?"

He seemed to expect no answer but yes, so she did not disappoint him. It wasn't the place, not with Nana looking so anxious, but perhaps later she could tell him that she actually was curious.

Laura noticed that Nana was looking more distressed by

the moment. In fact, she was getting ready to leave the sofa for a look of her own. Obviously, her husband felt unwilling to subject her to that kind of stress.

"Stay there, m'dear," Oliver said. "I am in good hands, as you well know. Laura, you should ask the surgeon to tell you of the time he stitched a teat back on a cow's udder."

Well done, she thought, even as she laughed, and Nana relaxed on the sofa again. "You must tell me, Lieutenant."

Brittle had finished unwinding the bandage. After folding the blood-dappled portion inward so Nana could not see it, the surgeon handed it to Laura. He snipped at the hair around Oliver's ear.

"Oh, that cow. You would remind me, Captain. That was when I voyaged with you as surgeon's assistant on the *Chrysalis,* wasn't it? As I recall, you were a lieutenant, and determined to assure your captain that I could patch a cow's teat."

Laura asked. "On a ship?"

"It's common enough," Nana said. "You'd be amazed what some officers will take on board, as they prepare for a long voyage."

"Pigs, cows, chickens…it's a regular Noah's ark," Oliver said. "Due to my mismanagement, Captain Fitzgerald's little Jersey sustained an undignified injury when a crew under my command swung her into the hold."

"Nana, your husband promised me all kinds of perquisites if I would but take a needle and thread to the bovine," Brittle said as he calmly snipped away.

"Did you succeed?" Laura asked, as the surgeon indicated Oliver's mangled ear, which looked remarkably like liver.

"Succeed? Aye. Earned a prodigious kick to my ass, though."

You are so composed, Laura thought, as Nana laughed. *I can be, too,* she told herself as she forced herself not to show any disgust at the sight before her. After the first inward quiver that evidence of raw mortality seemed to invite, she found herself more interested than squeamish.

"Hmm."

Brittle stood by the captain, hands on hips, lips pursed. "That is not edifying," the captain said.

"Perhaps not to you, sir," Brittle replied. "Your surgeon on the *Tireless* is still Joseph Barnhart?"

"Yes," Oliver said, sounding wary.

"He did a fine job. When it heals, you'll look a little lopsided, but I promise you, you won't frighten children. Not even your own."

Captain Worthy gingerly touched what remained of his ear. "Just as long as I still terrify midshipmen."

"You will, sir. Lady Taunton, observe how well it is granulating." He pointed at the raw rim. "Barnhart threw some nice blanket stitches on the lobe, or what's left of it."

She looked closer, because he seemed to expect it. As she gazed at the injury to her brother-in-law's ear, it suddenly occurred to her that a common surgeon with the preposterous name of Philemon Brittle was treating her as an equal. She thought how appalled Sir James Taunton would have been by her even being in the room, much less in Torquay visiting a sister as illegitimate as she was. The sheer audacity of it all made her smile.

"It *is* funny-looking," Brittle said, which made the captain grin.

"I'm not laughing at your ear, Oliver," Laura protested. "Lt. Brittle, I might tell you later what was amusing me."

"Very well," he said, holding out his hand. "Give me that same pad, please, and then the bandage. I'll reuse it now, but you should replace it tomorrow with a length of gauze I will leave you."

He seemed to take for granted she would tend Captain Worthy. "I will if Nana lets me," Laura replied. "After all, this is *her* ear."

Both Worthys laughed and exchanged glances that told Laura she was going to busy herself somewhere in the house that afternoon, far from their bedroom.

Lt. Brittle finished his work. "Take good care of him, Nana," he said. "If he tries to leave the house in less than three days, you have my permission to shoot him." He replaced the scissors and pocketed his instrument envelope. "Captain, when you return to Plymouth for your court martial, drop by Stonehouse. I'll compound a salve for you. G'day now."

She followed him into the hall. "Court martial? What do you *mean?*"

"Every captain who loses a ship goes through a court martial," the surgeon explained, as she walked with him. "It's routine, and from what my father said in his letter this morning—he'll be here in a few days—the captain was as brave and coolheaded as anyone could wish. He will have another ship quite soon. My da said he already convinced the admiral of the port to keep his crew together and not disperse them to other warships in the harbor."

It was afternoon now, and Mrs. Brittle had mentioned how her son had to be on his way immediately to Plymouth. Still, he seemed to slow down as he approached the door, giving her all his attention. He put his hand on the knob, but just held it there.

"What were you smiling about?"

"I had the distinct feeling that you were treating me as an equal. Sir, I know nothing about medicine."

"I disagree," he replied.

Still he stood there. She put out her hand, which would have astounded her proper butler, and shook the surgeon's hand. "Thank you for that marvelous performance in there. Nana didn't have any choice but to relax, did she?"

"No. Under ordinary circumstances, Mama tells me Nana is as tough and resourceful as a Cornish tin-pit pony," he said, still holding her hand. "Let's just say I like to handle expectant mothers gently." He looked into the distance. "Something I learned at university, and most decidedly not at sea."

"Where you physic cows and cut hair, on occasion?"

"Aye."

She thought he would release her hand, but he tightened his grip instead and his eyes had gone deadly serious. "Nana knows better than any of us that one half inch to the right, and that splinter would have taken off her husband's head."

Laura could think of nothing to say to his candor, but she didn't have to say anything. He stood even closer, his hand on hers, the sheer size of him reassuring her.

"We all fight Boney in our own way, even Nana."

She nodded, absurdly wanting to burrow in close to him, because he seemed so sure of himself, so capable.

He released her hand and opened the door. "Now it's time to kiss my mother adieu and return to the grind. Take a good look at the captain's ear tomorrow, if you please. If there are red streaks or he is feverish, send Joey Trelease for Mr. Milton." He hesitated, then plunged ahead. "When you get tired of being a widow, Lady Taunton, I can offer you gainful employment at Stonehouse. What a cheeky tar I am. Goodbye."

She couldn't have heard him correctly. After a moment to allow her high color to return to normal, she walked toward the sitting room. The Worthys were already at the top of the stairs. Nana leaned across the banister.

"Laura, Oliver declares he will not lie down and rest unless I am there," she said.

Laura laughed and blew them both a kiss. *You would not let him out of your sight, even if he wanted you to, which he does not,* she thought. She went into the sitting room and was standing there, looking out the window a half hour later, as Lt. Brittle left his house, shouldered his sea duffel and started for the harbor.

"I suppose you will take the mail coach," she said out loud, admiring the pleasant swing of his hips, something she had already noticed in Plymouth, while observing the seagoing fraternity. It must be the loose walk of the deep-water sailor, used to shifting balance on a heaving deck. Whatever it was, she watched him until he was only a small speck, heading down the hill. She doubted she would see him again.

Mrs. Brittle didn't seem surprised when Laura knocked on the side door. "Come in, dearie," she said. "I suppose you are a fifth wheel next door right now."

"Decidedly so," Laura agreed. "Have you something useful I can do?"

"I do. Phil told me to give you some gauze and wadding for Captain Worthy."

She followed Mrs. Brittle upstairs to a small bedroom tucked under the eaves. "Watch your head," the woman advised. "My boys can't come home often, but I like to have their beds ready."

She reached under the bed and pulled out a small chest, which contained rolled bandages, and a batt of lint. She set the items on the bed between them, and reached into the chest again, this time pulling out a well-worn case. She opened it, and Laura gasped to see several knives and a saw. Mrs. Brittle touched the dark-stained cloth band on the tourniquet, then closed it again.

"That's the set Phil used on the *Victory,* where poor Lord Nelson, God rest his soul, was struck down. He has a much better set now, but he said he'd never part with this one. I don't know how he does what he does." She shuddered. "Through the years, I patched up four little Brittles for this and that, but I could never…"

Like mother, like son, Laura decided. Without any discernible urging on Mrs. Brittle's part, she found herself telling the woman all about the last few years of her life, as she had tended her ailing husband without respite.

"I was grateful when he died," she finished, "because I was so tired. It was a thankless task."

Mrs. Brittle cleared his throat. "Forgive my plain speaking, but Nana has told me much about herself. Are you the eldest of Lord Ratliffe's daughters?"

"As far as I know. Another thankless thing." Laura replied, trying to keep the bitterness from her voice.

She thought she almost succeeded, except that Mrs.

Brittle covered her hand with her own. "Not thankless at all, if you'll pardon me, Lady Taunton. You have a younger sister who has fought her own dragons, and now there are two of you."

"Does she need me?" Laura asked simply.

"Maybe you need her more," Mr. Brittle replied, just as honest. "Nights can be long, though, when your man is at sea, and there's war. She'll be busy with a baby soon, and I'm next door to help." She patted Laura's hand and then released it.

"Are you telling me I could leave here?" Laura asked, remembering what Lt. Brittle had said before he left. Of course, she may have misunderstood him. Her ears weren't entirely tuned to the soft speech of the West Country.

"Only if you don't go too far."

Nana came quietly into the sitting room when the afternoon shadows were starting to fall deep on the lawn. She sat down beside Laura and leaned her head on her shoulder.

"I trust you made him very comfortable," Laura teased.

"That's never hard," Nana said, her cheeks rosy. "I asked him once if he thought I was a loose woman, since I enjoyed…him…so much. He just laughed and did it again."

Laura couldn't help smiling at her sister's artless disclosure. "I suppose every moment is sweeter than the last, since he is not home so much."

"It is. Sadder, too. I would like to give Boney a piece of my mind."

"You and most of the women of the Channel Fleet."

Dinner was eaten in the breakfast room. Laura doubted they ever used the more formal dining room. Oliver ate like a starving man, passing up nothing. He rolled his eyes when Nana patted his middle.

"Almost as big as yours, love," he said, which earned him a sharp nudge.

It was a curious meal. Between the relaxed banter between the Worthys that Laura found herself envying, Oliver told of the fight off Ferrol Station, when he took on a French ship of the line and received a thrashing, even while sacrificing his frigate so two smaller ships bearing vital dispatches could escape.

"Nana, remember my time in dry dock last November?" he asked. "Well, I think my stern was still vulnerable. The whole rudder sheared off, and we limped here under judicious sail power." He looked at Laura. "We'd be drowned without Dan Brittle, my sailing master."

"Did you conn the helm?" Nana asked.

"Most of the time. I slept a little on deck, when I could." He stood and rested his hands on his wife's chair back as though the room was suddenly too small. "I trust my helmsmen, but I wanted this way to be my blame and not theirs, if we all drowned. I'm sorry, love, but that's how it is. Hard to say what would have happened, if we hadn't reached Drake's Island before we sank."

"That's where the *Tireless* is?" Nana asked, holding his hand against her cheek now.

"Just off the island. I lost everything, Nana." He sat down. "Not quite. I took off the log, charts, orders and dispatches, of course." He reached into his uniform jacket. "And these. Couldn't leave you behind."

He unrolled two small sketches of Nana and anchored them to the table with a glass and a plate.

Nana dabbed at her eyes with a napkin. "Does the Admiralty know what a silly romantic you are?" she asked, her voice gruff.

"Hopefully not. That's our secret."

He rolled up the drawings, but left them on the table. "Fifty men are dead, Nana, and others are wounded."

"Mr. Ramseur?" Nana asked. "He's Oliver's first mate, Laura."

"Hale and hearty."

He stirred in his chair and Laura thought he would get up again, to roam the room. "Nana, Matthew was injured badly in the fight."

She gasped. "You didn't tell me!"

"A splinter on the gun deck took off his arm." He pulled out a handkerchief and handed it to Nana. "He's a powder monkey, Laura. He stayed with Nana at the Mulberry once. He's eleven now." He leaned closer to his wife and toyed with her hair. "He lost a lot of blood, Nana, and I won't say I'm not worried."

Nana blew her nose and gave her husband a defiant look that told Laura that she was not quite the biddable creature her usual deportment suggested. "I must go to Stonehouse at once. Oliver, he has no one!"

Oliver shook his head. "I'll not have you and our baby jouncing over bad roads to tend him in a place that will frighten even you, oh fearless one."

This is easily solved, Laura thought, watching the mutiny in her sister's eyes and the equal firmness on her brother-in-law's face.

"I'll go tomorrow."

Why did I say that? she asked herself immediately, even

as Nana's eyes lightened up and Oliver looked relieved. *I want to help my sister,* she assured herself. *It has nothing to do with Lt. Brittle's offer of employment. I can scarcely imagine being influenced by something so totty-headed. He must think I am truly bored.*

She had occasion to think about that as she composed herself for sleep later. She climbed into bed with her usual feeling of gratitude, even after the past three years, to know that her late husband would never open her door again. It was dark and there was no one in sight to scold her for feeling that way. She could even allow herself a moment to consider Lt. Brittle's startling offer.

Laura couldn't help remembering how Lt. Brittle had tucked up her blanket last night, and patted her shoulder. It was her secret alone: next to Nana's heartfelt embrace, that was the kindest touch she had ever felt in her life.

"I will visit a powder monkey and I will return to Torquay," she said out loud to the plaster whorls in the ceiling. "I would have to be an idiot to even consider what Lt. Brittle is suggesting. No one is *that* bored."

Chapter Four

Perhaps I will see Surgeon Brittle again, Laura thought, as she walked to the administration building. The Marine at the entrance to the complex had pointed it out as a good place to begin searching for one little boy.

Neat walkways, well-tended courtyard… She didn't know what she had expected, but it hadn't been this. She counted ten substantial buildings connected by covered walkways of Italianate style. That's intelligent, she thought. Patients with contagion can be isolated in distinct buildings.

The administration building appeared to be a warren of small offices and cubicles, staffed by a flotilla of clerks. Other than a glance or two in her direction, none of the men she passed seemed interested in offering help, so she continued down the hallway to a large desk, where another clerk sat.

"Good afternoon. I am looking for Matthew Pollock, a powder monkey from the *Tireless*," she said, determined not to feel intimidated by the way he looked at her over the rim of his spectacles.

"Are you a relative?" the man asked.

"No. I…"

"Then there are no visitors."

The clerk turned his attention to the ledger in front of him, as though she had already vanished. When he looked up again and saw her still standing before him, he even appeared surprised.

"I can't disappear like an apparition," Laura told him. She set down her valise. "I still want to see Matthew Pollock."

A door opened down the hall and a man came out, resplendent in blue, with gold bullion and lace on his sleeves and collar. The clerk stood up at once.

She didn't know his rank, but his appearance indicated someone considerably more exalted than the clerk. She wanted to speak to him, but he surprised her by striding directly to her and standing too close for comfort.

"You're a day late." He sniffed the air. Laura resisted a powerful urge to slap his face. "You don't smell of gin, at least. You were to report to the clerk in room 15. Are you illiterate, as well as tardy? Well?"

He was too close. She was a tall woman, but she stepped back, reminded too much of her own father and Sir James, with their shouting and demands. She wanted to turn and run down the corridor and out into the quadrangle. *Not this time, Laura,* she told herself. *Not ever again.* Putting her hands behind her back so he would not see them tremble, she stood her ground, not moving an inch.

"You have me confused with someone else."

The clerk gasped. Obviously no one else had ever contradicted this exalted personage before. *It's high time someone did,* she told herself, even as her stomach began to churn.

"I don't make mistakes." He bit off each word like a dog snapping a bone for the marrow.

"I never knew that the Lord Almighty wore a naval uniform," she snapped back.

She heard a strangled sound from the clerk, but knew better than to take her eyes off the man intimidating her. Maybe this was what she had wanted to say to her own father. Maybe she had stored it up in her heart and mind, waiting for the opportunity.

"I'm sacking you before you even begin!" the officer roared, perhaps thinking he was on a quarterdeck of a most unfortunate ship and she was his lowliest powder monkey.

"You think I came here for employment?" She pitched her voice deliberately low, so he was forced to listen. "I wouldn't work for you if I was starving, and I most certainly am not." She unclenched her hands from behind her back and brought them around to her front, so she could fish in her reticule.

She yanked out a sheet of paper. "My brother-in-law, Captain Oliver Worthy of the *Tireless*, thought I might need this. I told him it wouldn't be necessary, but he insisted. Obviously he knows you better than I do."

With a loud exhalation of air, the officer stepped back, as though propelled by his own breath. With a thunderous look at his clerk, he grabbed the note and read it.

Laura jerked the strings of her reticule together, wishing they would make a loud noise like a thunderclap, instead of a harmless little whish. *Maybe I am like my sister, tough as a Cornish tin-pit pony,* she thought. *Wasn't that what Lt. Brittle said about Nana? Couldn't I use a champion, about now?*

No champion appeared, but none was necessary, not

after Captain Worthy's brief note apparently. As the officer's complexion turned from red to a mottled gray, she felt her own composure returning. She didn't know what Oliver had written, but she suspected the note involved Lady Taunton, rather than plain Mrs. Taunton.

"Lady Taunton, a mistake was made," the officer had the grace to say. It wasn't much of an apology, but couldn't have been easy, not with his clerk right there. "We must be so careful here."

"I understand completely," she replied, in what she hoped was her kindest voice. Then she could not resist. "I imagine there are female spies who attempt to weasel their way into naval secrets by talking to powder monkeys. Wise of you to be so cautious."

She assumed what her late husband used to call her "pudding face," and smiled at the officer, who wasn't quite certain if he had just been held up to ridicule. Pudding face, indeed. Even her late husband—he who only complained—would have been impressed with the bland face she presented to the stuffed shirt in epaulets harassing her now. "Sir, I wish to know whom I have been addressing."

Reminded so gently of his dereliction, he bowed again. "Admiral Sir David Carew at your service," he replied. "I am chief administrator and physician."

She curtsied again, thinking that if he could make a better beginning, she could, too. "Sir David, can you kindly direct me to the office that knows where such a little powder monkey might be found? He serves…served…on the *Tireless*."

The physician indicated a door back down the corridor. "Room 12, my lady," he said. "Let me escort you there."

"I needn't take you from your work," she said, not wishing his escort at all.

"It is of no consequence," he assured her.

She had no choice. She did manage to catch the look that passed between the clerk and admiral; the admiral gave the poor man such a glower that Laura was almost certain that no word of what had just happened would ever leave the clerk's lips. The poor clerk would probably be set adrift in a lifeboat on the Amazon River at the mercy of headhunters, Laura thought, as she reassumed her pudding face.

The clerks in room 12 appeared astonished to see their chief administrator, which made Laura suspect Sir David seldom did his own legwork. *And why should he,* she thought. *He is the Lord Almighty, after all.* She managed to turn her laugh into a cough.

Flip, flip went the pages in a ledger, while another clerk ruffled through a stack of cards in a small wooden box as though his life depended on it.

"He is a new arrival," Laura offered, not wishing to have so many men in pain on her behalf, not with the admiral standing there, looking ready to pounce. "The *Tireless* sank in Plymouth Sound on Sunday night," she added, remembering what Oliver had told them that morning over breakfast.

"Ah, yes," one of the clerks said, and turned to another ledger. He ran a trembling finger down a column. "Ward Block Four, second floor, Ward B, ma'am."

"Just point me in the right direction."

Again, Sir David would have none of that. "I will take you there, Lady Taunton."

In the corridor, she looked down to see her valise,

which—perhaps not wanting to be abandoned in such a place—must have crawled after her or been deposited there by a clerk. She knew this was a dilemma for the admiral. If she were to pick it up, he would be forced to take it from her. And from the looks of him, he did not carry parcels and certainly not valises. She hoped he was not one to carry a grudge, either.

He stared at the valise as though someone had dumped out a chamber pot right at his feet. For the sake of his staff, Laura put him out of his misery.

"Let me leave it here, Sir David. I will fetch it when I leave."

That way he only had to pick it up and set it inside, which seemed to suit him completely. In fact, he even smiled when he offered her his arm again, as though he had already forgotten that earlier scene, and assumed that she would, too.

You, sir, are a pompous fool, she thought as she smiled and took his arm. *Apparently I am to suffer you gladly.*

He did provide some useful information, once outdoors. "The buildings are numbered in clockwise fashion from this block," he said, as they walked along the covered colonnade. "You'll observe they are separate, which helps to keep down contagion and noxious odors."

He stopped in front of Ward Block Four. "Lady Taunton, are you certain you wish to visit this ward? I can have what's-his…"

"Matthew."

"…brought to the administration building."

"I would never require that," she said, shocked at his eagerness to move an injured patient just so she could be accommodated. "I am completely comfortable with this."

He tried again. "Madam, these are uncouth men."

"They are injured men," she replied, and decided on some plain speaking, since she was beginning to understand his degree of discomfort. "I am a widow, Sir David. I recently nursed my late husband through his final illness. I doubt anything in this—block, you call them?—will surprise me."

He shook his head. "These are battle injuries, Lady Taunton. I cannot guarantee you will not be shocked."

"I expect no guarantee, Sir David," she said, trying to keep her voice serene. She took a deep breath, and wished she hadn't. Under a strong odor of carbolic, it was hard to ignore corruption. Take a shallow breath now, she advised herself, but only one or two.

Heads popped out of rooms as they walked to the stairs, which made her wonder how often Sir David visited the wards.

Perhaps he read her thoughts. "Sick and hurt officers are housed in separate blocks," he explained, as they mounted the steps. "That is where I am usually in attendance."

She didn't think powder monkeys often came to his attention. "Who takes care of these men?"

"My surgeons. I have two, and each has four assistants, as well as orderlies."

He took her to the next floor and opened a door. "B Ward, Lady Taunton. Let us find, er…"

"Matthew," she said patiently. *You would remember if he was an officer,* she thought.

"Matthew. I will locate the surgeon. As you can see, we are overcrowded. Let us blame Bonaparte."

She looked around the spacious, well-lighted room with

windows on both sides to let in the sea air. She counted twenty beds, each with an occupant, plus two cots. A thin woman with a permanent frown between her eyes was seated at a desk. Eyes popping out of her head, she rose when she saw the admiral, and smoothed down her stained apron.

"We're looking for Matthew."

"Pollock," Laura said. "He's eleven."

"Go get the surgeon," the admiral ordered. The woman scurried from the room.

Then Laura saw Matthew, the youngest one in the room, lying propped into a sitting position, on one of the two cots. He had looked up when he heard his name, hope in his eyes. When he did not recognize her, he looked away.

It was impossible to overlook the misery in the room. Men had limbs missing, and some were lying still, as if any movement was painful. Some had that inward expression she recognized from tending her dying husband.

She sat on a stool beside Matthew Pollock's cot and touched his good arm. "Nana sent me," she said. "She's expecting a baby, and Captain Worthy didn't want to tire her. I'm her sister, Mrs. Taunton."

The boy looked at her and released a shaky breath, as though he had been holding it for days. He was small for his age, and she had to remind herself that he was a veteran of the Royal Navy. Oliver had said Matthew had been a powder monkey for three years, one of two little boys on the *Tireless* whose sole duty was to carry powder from the magazine to the gun deck.

He was pale, which was no surprise, considering the insult to his system. He didn't look overfed, either, although there was an uneaten bowl of mush on the table by his cot.

His eyes were a crystal blue that made her think what a handsome man he might become someday. The skin was stretched taut across his face, which seemed to throw his nose into prominence.

She could not overlook his empty sleeve, with its blood-stains. It was rolled back to expose the thick bandage that made the rest of his body seem much smaller.

"May I call you Matthew?"

He nodded.

"Speak up, lad, when you're addressed," the admiral ordered. "You don't nod at ladies."

"He's but eleven, Sir David, and wounded," Laura reminded the admiral.

She heard smothered laughter from one of the other beds, and knew she should not have spoken out of turn, not in front of this powerful man. "I'm sorry," she said contritely. "I should not presume to know what is best for him."

She knew it was on the tip of the admiral's tongue to agree with her, but he refrained, perhaps remembering the fool he had made of himself earlier. He was saved from further comment by firm footsteps, and then a comfortable laugh.

"As I live and breathe, Lady Taunton. You're a sight for sore eyes, and we have plenty of those here!"

Laura glanced at the admiral's face, whose sudden relief had just as soon turned to outrage, and then at Lt. Brittle, who came into the room in front of the woman sent to fetch him.

"Lieutenant! I'll have you remember your manners, too!" the admiral exclaimed in a loud voice, which caused two of the bed-bound men to moan and stir restlessly.

Brittle went to one of the men and touched his face,

keeping his hand there until he was still again. He nodded at the other one and winked, which seemed to settle him down.

"Beg pardon, Sir David," he said, his eyes on Laura now. "It happens I know Lady Taunton." He bowed in her direction. "How are the Worthys?"

"I left Nana in complete charge of the captain," she told him.

She couldn't help but notice the interest this conversation created among the invalids. All these men must be from the *Tireless,* she thought. "I'll have you know she is a worse tyrant than your captain," she said, addressing the room. "He hasn't a prayer of leaving that house until she says so."

Several men laughed, and one cheered feebly. The admiral looked around, obviously out of his depth, not knowing if he should reprimand them all or leave well enough alone. He chose the latter, backing toward the door ever so slightly.

To Laura's gratification, Lt. Brittle played his superior like a violin.

"I know Captain Worthy's men are deeply grateful for your kindness in bringing his sister-in-law here, Sir David," Brittle said. "We all know how busy you are. With your permission, I'll see to Lady Taunton now, and make sure these tars behave."

"You do that," Sir David snapped, looking around the room again. He left without another word.

Some of the tension went with him. Brittle nodded to the silent woman standing by the desk and she sat down again. He perched on the edge of Matthew's cot, one knee on the floor, careful not to overbalance it. "Matthew, you're the luckiest tar in the room, as far as I can see, with a visit from a pretty lady."

A series of emotions crossed the powder monkey's face. His lips trembled and he closed his eyes, exhausted with pain. "I wanted to see Nana," he whispered, and then began to cry—not loud tears, but the hopeless kind, the kind she was familiar with.

Laura wanted to touch his face. She glanced at the surgeon, and he nodded his approval. She touched Matthew's face, cupping her hand against his hot cheek, and then moved closer to circle her other arm around his head. Matthew turned his face toward her arm, which told her that she could console him.

In another moment, she had changed places with the surgeon, who moved to the stool. Careful not to bump his arm, she gathered Matthew close and let him cry.

The moment passed quickly. She took the damp cloth Lt. Brittle held out and wiped Matthew's face. "Maybe I can wash your hair tomorrow," she told him, keeping her voice matter-of-fact. "I always feel better when my hair is clean."

She didn't know what to say then, but the surgeon took over. He ran a practiced hand over Matthew's upper arm, feeling for swelling. His eyes on Matthew, he spoke to Laura.

"What a brave son of a gun Matthew is, Lady Taunton. I had to take him to my surgery yesterday morning and smooth away some of Barnhart's work—bless the man, he was even working in the dark at one point, wasn't he, Matthew? I never heard a peep out of Matthew. Captain Worthy only has brave seamen on the *Tireless*."

He knew just what to say. Matthew's eyes brightened as he mentally seemed to reach inside himself and draw up.

I know what they want, she thought. She spoke loud enough for the other *Tireless* crew members to hear. "He's doing well. Lt. Brittle examined his ear yesterday in Torquay, and said that although he was no longer symmetrical, he could still keep all of you in line. He's in good hands, Matthew, and you're kind to ask. I'll send him a letter tonight and make sure he knows how you all are doing."

"He said he would visit us, mum," said a man in the next bed.

"Then I know he will," she answered. She looked back at Matthew, who was watching her face, maybe looking for some resemblance to his beloved Nana.

"We don't look alike, except for our hair," she told him.

"Your eyes are greener than the ocean," Lt. Brittle said, almost to himself. His face reddened, but he did not lose his aplomb. "I *am* observant, Lady Taunton." He returned his attention to Matthew. "D'ye have any questions for me, Matthew? Now's the time to ask."

She didn't think he would speak. She knew these men were trained not to speak to a better unless spoken to, but the surgeon had asked.

"What can I do now?" the boy questioned.

"You can come with me to Torquay, when you are able," Laura said.

Matthew frowned. "Mum, I'm in the navy."

"So you are, Matthew," Brittle said. "I'm not sure yet, but I do know this—you still have your elbow and two inches more of forearm. You can still rule the world if you have an elbow."

"The gunners won't want me now," he reminded the surgeon.

"No, they won't," Brittle said frankly. "Give it some time and thought. When your arm heals, we can attach a device. Maybe a hook." He rubbed the boy's head. "You'll be the terror of the fleet and Boney's worst foe."

He stood up then, looking around the ward. "Can I trust you seamen with this fine lady? I need to patch up a cook on the second floor who's not half as sweet as you darlings."

The men laughed. The surgeon nodded to Laura. "Stay as long as you like. Are you planning on spending the night at the Mulberry?"

"I think I will."

"I'll come back in an hour, and at least escort you to the main gate, Lady Taunton. I'd escort you all the way, but I'm on duty tonight." He touched Matthew's head again. "If you're not too tired, tell her about some of the places you've been, Matthew."

"Aye, aye, sir."

She moved to the stool the surgeon had vacated, watching him stop at one or two of the other beds to bend over and assess the patient, and then spend a moment with the woman at the desk. When he left the room, she turned back to Matthew.

"You're in good hands, Matthew," she said.

She knew he was in pain, but he seemed to relax and wriggle himself down into a more comfortable position. She tugged his pillow down to help, and tucked the light blanket across his middle.

"I'm going to the Mulberry tonight," she told him. "I'll tell Gran, Sal and Pete to come visit you as soon as they can."

Before he left, Lt. Brittle had whispered to her to get Matthew to drink more water. She picked up the cup, but he was looking over her shoulder, his eyes wide.

"Mum, do something!" he gasped.

Startled, she turned around to see what he was looking at and sucked in her breath, then leaped to her feet, spilling the water on the floor.

Sitting propped up with pillows, a seaman clawed at his throat, blood pouring down his nightshirt. The man in the next bed, the stump of his leg encased in a wire basket, reached for him. "Please, mum!" he begged.

Laura looked at the desk, but the woman was gone. *My God,* she thought, *my God. There's no one to help but me.*

She could tell there was no time to scream and clutch her hair, or faint like a lady would—or should. She forced herself to dig down deep into a place in her heart and mind she hadn't even known existed. A life depended on her and her alone. For the life of her she didn't understand it, but her next thought propelled her into action: what would Lt. Brittle do?

Chapter Five

~~~~~~~~~~~~~~~~~~~~~~~~~~~~~~~~

She ran to the patient's bedside. Blood streamed from his neck and mouth and his eyes were wide with terror. Disregarding everyone in the room, Laura raised her dress, untied her petticoat and stepped out of it in practically one motion, then crammed the white muslin against his neck.

"Who can walk?" she shouted.

One seaman tried to pull himself into an upright position, then slumped to his pillow again, exhausted by that puny effort.

"I can walk, mum."

She turned around to see Matthew, wobbly but upright, holding his injured arm with the good one, trying to keep it level.

He could barely stand, but she had no choice. "The surgeon said he was going to the second floor. Find him!"

I won't watch him go, she thought. *I won't think about what he is doing to his own injury. I won't think about anything except this poor man.* He was breathing better, but barely, searching her eyes with his own. Her heart went out to him, someone she didn't know, a man who would probably never, on a normal day, come into her sphere at all. But this was not a normal day. He was suffering and casting all his hopes on her.

She watched his face as she pressed on his neck, praying she wasn't doing him more injury. The room was silent, except for his labored breathing. She noticed then that he was glancing sideways, looking into her eyes, then glancing again.

"You're trying to tell me something," she said.

He nodded, then looked again. She glanced in that direction, toward the small table between the two beds. She saw a pasteboard box with the word *styptic* written on it in large letters. Next to the box was a gauze pad.

"Styptic. Styptic," she muttered, then remembered white powder in a ceramic box by her husband's shaving stand. She leaped up and grabbed the box with her slippery fingers, dumping it onto the gauze and turning back with it to place it over the opening in his neck where the blood still flowed.

He flinched when the caustic touched his skin, and his breathing slowed, which took her own breath away at first, until she realized he was calming down. She pressed gently on the gauze pad, relieved to see the blood was no longer pouring through her fingers.

She spoke to the others in the room without turning around. "If any one of you is near an open window, can you shout for help?"

Someone yelled "Fire!" which struck her as strange, until she realized that someone always comes when you yell fire.

The bleeding slowed. Laura sprinkled more styptic on

the man's neck. Probably only a minute or two had passed since the whole ordeal began, but she had never known time to suspend itself, as it did in that ward.

Then, blessed sound, someone came thundering up the steps. "Thank God," she whispered.

Philemon Brittle couldn't have come in the room fast enough to suit her. He was carrying Matthew, whom he deposited on his cot. With just a moment's observation, he bumped her aside with his hip and sat in her place.

"Hand me that box," he ordered, and she did, aware how bloody her hand was, and how it shook. Some of the powder spilled on the floor. "Get another pillow."

Three pillows flew through the air in her direction. She caught them all and put two behind the seaman's head at the surgeon's command, until the man was sitting upright.

"Pull the nightshirt off his right shoulder. Gently now."

Puzzled, she did as he asked, then noticed the bullet wound there, where blood was also oozing. She looked at Lt. Brittle, a question in her eyes.

"It's the exit wound," he said, his own voice more normal now. "Davey Dabney isn't part of the *Tireless* crew. He was wounded in the battle off Basque Roads. Shot by a French sniper in the rigging of one of their ships."

"That was April, wasn't it?" she asked.

"Aye." He sprinkled more styptic on another gauze pad and handed it to her. "Put it against the exit wound and press. That's right. You have a good touch, Lady T." He wiped his hand on his apron. "You saved his life."

She couldn't help her tears. "I thought I did everything wrong."

"No. You did everything right."

Unbelieving, she gazed at the bloody bed, the patient pale almost to transparency now, and her own arms, red to the elbows. There was blood on the floor, too.

"Physicking is an untidy business, Lady Taunton," he said, which sounded to Laura like the vastest understatement ever uttered. He gestured toward the box, bloody with his fingerprints and hers. "This is Davey's third round of what we call secondary hemorrhage. I've been using persulphate of iron, which I think is better than iron perchloride. A little less caustic."

She just stared at him dumbly, until he reached for her wrist with one hand and felt her pulse, while maintaining his other hand on the neck wound.

"I don't want you to faint, Lady T, because I don't have enough hands."

She managed a laugh that sounded more like a shudder, to her ears. "If I feel faint, I promise to put my head down."

He turned his full attention to his patient, who was breathing regularly now. He continued to talk to her, though, and maybe to the others in the room, the newcomers from the *Tireless*, who were silent and staring.

"David here was shot in the neck. The bullet tore through his trapezius muscle—this one here—and then broke his clavicle before it left. I think it nicked his carotid artery, and that's our problem. It's sloughing."

How can this man possibly survive? she wanted to ask, but not then, not while the patient was listening. She sat where she was on the stool, mainly because she knew if she stood up, she would fall down. She leaned closer, so only the surgeon could hear.

"Did I do Matthew an injury by sending him to find you?"

"No. He's young and healthy. I think he's a hero." He looked over his shoulder at the others in the room. "Maybe when we all feel more like it, we can give Matthew three cheers. You, too."

The men chuckled, and the whole room seemed to relax. The patients tried to settle back again, except for the man in the next bed, the one with the remains of his leg in a basket. He looked at Laura and shrugged his shoulders, and she could see he had gotten trapped by his own blankets when he leaned out of bed to help the bleeding man.

Laura stood up slowly, swayed a little and took several deep breaths before she tried to move. Careful not to slip on the blood, she went to his bed. "What direction should I pull your leg to get you back under the blanket?" she asked. "That way? Put your arm around my neck and I'll tug you up a little. Good."

She started to turn back, but he tugged her skirt.

"Please miss, I need a piss pot." His face was red with embarrassment.

"I think we all do," she said, which made the patients laugh. "Where is it?"

"T'ledge, mum. There by the table."

Laura picked up an earthenware urinal, avoiding everyone's eyes as much as they were all avoiding hers, and brought it back to the amputee's bed. Without comment, she lifted the blanket and slid it toward his hand. "Can you manage now?" she asked quietly.

"I'll try, mum." He tried, then leaned back in frustration.

"I can help."

And she did, holding him in there until he finished. "My late husband was ill for three years, so don't you mind this," she said, keeping her tone light. "I don't think any of you gentlemen can surprise me."

Again there was the murmur of laughter from men too weak or hurt to do more. She removed the urinal and smoothed the blankets around the amputee.

"Well done, Lady T," Lt. Brittle said. He nodded toward the door. "There's a sluice hole in the washroom next door. While you're in there, wash your hands and face."

He spoke to the amputee in the next bed. "Tommy, what happened?"

The man thought a moment. "I was dozing, sir. I heard Davey start to gargle, like he did that time before. As soon as he started to spout, t'old bitch leaped up like a flea on a hot griddle and did a runner."

"She better just keep running," someone else said, the others murmuring their agreement.

Laura let her breath out slowly, and left the room. In the hall, she backed out of the way as two men in uniform ran up the stairs. They stopped in their tracks at the sight of her, so bloody. One of them tried to take her by the arm, but she shook her head.

"There is nothing wrong with me. It's the patient in B Ward. Lt. Brittle is with him now."

"Someone yelled 'Fire,'" he said.

"We were trying to get your attention. Excuse me now."

She went into the washroom, relieved to be alone for a moment. She found the sluice hole and poured out the urinal's contents, then poured water into it from the bucket nearby, swished it around and poured that out, too.

She turned to the row of basins and pitchers and rolled up her sleeves. She wouldn't have noticed the crouching woman, if she hadn't heard her try to smother a sob sound in her apron. Laura whirled around, her heart in her throat.

It was the woman who had sat at the desk, who stared at her with terrified eyes. Laura balled her slimy hands into fists, wanting to smack her. Instead, she turned back to the washbasin, where she took her time washing her hands and face, trying to decide what to do.

She dried her hands and face. She couldn't leave the woman there, not after what she had done. At least there was no one in the other room with the strength to tear her apart and Lt. Brittle was too busy. Suddenly, she felt more sympathy than disgust.

"Do you have any children?"

Wary, the woman nodded, tucking herself into a tighter ball.

"Where's your man?"

"Dead these three months at Basque Roads," the woman whispered.

"If you lose your job, you will all starve," Laura said. "Or end up in a workhouse, at the very least. I'm not certain that would be a blessing."

The woman nodded, tears in her eyes again. She leaned her forehead into her knees and sobbed.

I'm a curious contradiction, Laura thought, as she went to the woman and tugged her to her feet. *A few minutes ago I wanted to stuff her head down the sluice hole. Now I don't.* She grasped her by the back of her dress and gave her a shake, then pushed her into the hall and the ward next door, as the woman shrieked and tried to dig her heels into the floor.

Lt. Brittle was on his feet. "Good God, Laura!" he exclaimed, then was silent, disgust on his face, as he saw who it was making the noise. A low sound like a growl from several of the men made Laura's blood run in chunks, and terrified the woman, who tried to make herself small under Laura's armpit.

At a nod from the surgeon, one of the orderlies grabbed her. She stood there, head bowed, shoulders slumped, her hair in strings around her face.

"What can you possibly have to say for yourself?" Lt. Brittle asked, after a long silence.

"I was afraid," she said at last.

"So was this lady," the surgeon replied, his voice as quiet as hers. "She didn't run, though. Maude, you're sacked. Get out of here before the Marines come running and clap you in irons."

The woman wrenched herself free of the orderly and dropped to her knees. "My children will starve!" she cried.

Laura took a deep breath and stepped deliberately in front of the bedraggled woman. "Don't sack her."

"You can't possibly think she should stay on here," Lt. Brittle said, looking more puzzled than irritated, which gave Laura the courage to continue.

"I certainly do not. She isn't fit to watch kittens." Laura gestured around her. "Does Stonehouse have a laundry? Put her there. Her man is dead at Basque Roads and she has children to feed. I will not have that on my conscience. I think you do not want that, either."

She had him there, and she knew it, as sure as she knew there was no reason for anyone in B Ward to offer any hope. As she looked the surgeon in the eye, and he returned her gaze just as emphatically, she thought of what Sir David Carew would do, or even what her own father would have done, had he been there to pass judgment on frailty.

He was silent a long time. "I'm inclined to agree with you, Lady Taunton," he said, then looked at the woman. "Maude, you should be horsewhipped and never employed at this hospital again."

The woman said nothing, only hung her head lower.

Lt. Brittle turned to Davey Dabney, pale and watchful. "It's your choice, Davey. No one in this room will fault you if you want her sacked."

Maude began to cry, lowering herself even closer to the floor as her tears fell on wood slimy with the seaman's blood. *I can't watch this,* Laura thought, even as she stood there, her hands tightly clasped together. *This is worse than anything I endured today.*

"Send her to the laundry," Davey said, his voice rough and barely audible above the woman's sobs. "And my sheets better come back smooth like a baby's bum or you'll be out on yours."

Lt. Brittle smiled. "That's fair enough." He took hold of Maude's arm and hauled her to her feet. "Go home. Think about this and report to the laundry tomorrow at six bells. I'll clear it for you there. Go on."

Maude left without a word. Laura looked around the ward. She couldn't see any anger on any of the faces of people who had a right to be angry. She didn't think it was resignation, either. *Maybe we all learned something,* she thought, *me as much as anyone.* She looked at Lt. Brittle, who seemed to be gazing into that same middle distance as the men in his care, and realized how close to the bone this scene had played out. She turned to the orderlies.

"Would one of you please fetch my valise? It's in room 12 of the administration building. And you, would you please mop this floor? Lt. Brittle, where might I find fresh linen for Davey?" She looked at her own bloody clothes. "I know I am getting stiff and imagine you are, too, Davey."

"Aye, miss," he said. "We look a pair, don't we?"

It was a cheeky thing to say, something no one of his stamp would, on an ordinary day, ever say to a lady, except this was no ordinary day.

"Aye, we're a pair," she agreed. "Lt. Brittle, I will stay here, now that there is no one to watch this crew of miscreants, rascals and layabouts."

The men laughed, as she had hoped they would. "You're a game'un," someone called.

"Mind your manners, lads," Lt. Brittle said quickly, but there was no sting in his rebuke. "Lady Taunton, that's too much to ask, but I'll not deny we need you now." He touched the strip of adhesive that had been draped around his neck as he ran upstairs, carrying Matthew. "There's a man one floor down who is probably wondering when I am going to close up his arm. He can wait a moment more. I'll show you what you need, Lady Taunton. Come along."

In the hall, he startled her by grasping her shoulder in an enormous hug, and then releasing her almost before she knew what had happened. It heartened her more than anything she could remember.

He opened a door and handed her sheets, towels and a nightshirt. "I'll hold Davey while you strip the bed and remake it, then we'll get him into this." He pulled out an apron. "Put this on first."

"I'm afraid to touch him, for fear he will bleed again," she told him, as she tied the apron strings around her twice.

"But you're not afraid to wash him?"

"I'm not. I did that enough for my husband. I can manage, as long as you wipe around Davey's neck. That does terrify me."

"Fair enough."

She hesitated. He seemed to know what she was thinking; maybe he was thinking it himself.

"You're wondering how much longer Davey Dabney can live."

Laura nodded. He leaned against the linen press and kept his voice low.

"I don't know. I wish I did. I want to try two new things tomorrow." He ushered her out of the room. "I discovered a long time ago that doing the same thing over and over usually gets the same results."

While Lt. Brittle held his patient in his arms, Laura changed the sheets. The orderly brought warm water, and began to wash Davey Dabney. When he stopped to help two of the other patients from their beds to the washroom for calls of nature, Laura took his place, sponging off the sailor and listening to the surgeon's conversation. She wasn't sure if it was designed to put his patient at ease, or her.

"Davey's a foretopman," he said, while she dabbed at the man's thin legs and wondered how someone so pale could live. "I tried climbing the rigging once, Davey, and never got past the mainsail. Davey?"

Laura stopped drying his leg. "He's asleep," she whispered.

"Good."

Davey woke when she lowered the nightshirt carefully over his head, but closed his eyes again as she angled his arms into the sleeves. Lt. Brittle put him back in his bed, situating the pillows behind his head so he was nearly upright. He stood a moment longer over the patient, staring at his neck wound.

"Galen counseled we should do no harm, and some interpret that to mean do nothing," he said, more to himself than to her. "I disagree, but I am always left to wonder how much I can do before it turns into harm." He turned to her. "I'm a churl to ask this, but would you stay here for the rest of the day? It may even be after dark. As useless as Maude was, I'm shorthanded now. I can leave an orderly to work both wards. Am I straining a friendship?"

"I had no other pressing engagements this afternoon," she assured him.

He left, after telling her precisely what needed to be done until supper at the end of the first dog watch. The orderly made himself busy in the room, tidying up the invalids, helping others to the washroom or with a urinal. When he was busy, she filled in with the same duties, maintaining a detached air to keep from causing any embarrassment.

Supper was simple enough: a thin broth for a few of the more fit patients, Matthew among them, and a pale gruel the orderly called "panada," which looked like watery milk with lumps of bread floating in it. *How can anyone regain any strength eating this?* she asked herself, as she spooned the gruel down patients who could not help themselves. *My chef at Taunton would be aghast.*

After more trips to the washroom, the men began to settle down for the night. She sat beside Matthew, trying to draw him into conversation as the shadows lengthened and Lt. Brittle did not return. She decided Matthew was shy, and why not? With the exception of Nana and Gran, he probably never spoke much to females.

She looked around her. Some of the men slept. She was familiar with that kind of exhaustion because she had seen it often enough on her husband's face: too tired to do much except doze, and store up enough energy for the next day.

Others were awake, looking as though they wanted to converse with her, but tongue-tied like Matthew, kept silent by their subservience, these men who had so much talent to work a ship, but who might have lived on the moon, for all that she and they shared the same world. She thought of Maude, a woman with no hope ahead of her. She glanced at Davey. She decided she would not feel so sorry for herself.

She didn't mind sitting in the dark, when the sun finally left the sky. The orderly lit the lamp on the table where Maude used to sit, and put a smaller lamp there, too, like the one Philemon Brittle had used when he checked on Nana Worthy.

"I usually see what I can do on the deck below," the orderly said. "If you need anything, just go to the stairwell and sing out."

She didn't want to just sit there. She went from bed to bed, making sure everyone was covered. Before he left, the orderly had given sleeping draughts to those who were prescribed for it. She sat beside Matthew again, putting her hand against his forehead, which was cool now.

"It hurts, miss, in a strange way," he whispered. "It's like I can feel my fingers, and they're stuck with pins."

"We'll have to ask Lt. Brittle about that," she said.

"Aye, mum."

She thought he would sleep then. He closed his eyes. She started to release her grip, but he tightened his hand on hers.

"Mum, what am I going to do for the rest of my life?"

I am asking myself that same thing, she thought. She sat there until he slept.

Chapter Six

Laura dozed, exhausted from a day that had begun early in Torquay, and showed no signs of ending. She thought of Taunton, with servants everywhere. There was no one in B Ward except herself and the occasional orderly.

She asked herself how she could possibly help the men lying around her. She sat by Matthew, stupefied with exhaustion, wondering why she had ever told Nana she would check on the little powder monkey.

Someone was crying. She thought it was Davey Dabney at first, and who could blame him, but it was Tommy, the seaman with one leg gone, in the next bed. She extricated herself from Matthew's slack grasp and went first to the water basin. She squeezed out a cloth, went to his bed and wiped his face.

"There, now. Can you sleep?"

"The pain's bad, miss." His voice was tight, that of a proud man trying not to cry.

"I haven't authority to give you anything, but I'll tell Lt. Brittle when he returns."

He seemed to understand. She wiped his face again, then held his hand, because there was nothing else she could do. She thought she should close the window, now that the sun was gone, but the sounds outside gave her comfort. Below in the quadrangle, she heard men walking, and farther away, laughter.

"Would you like to be at sea?" she asked, then kicked herself because his sea days were probably over, and she was only reminding him.

He didn't take it that way, to her relief. "Aye, mum. Much rather. I never feel comfortable-like on land."

His voice was drowsy now, without the tension, and all she had done was wipe his face and hold his hand. When he slept finally, she felt the tiniest spark of satisfaction. She did not release his hand. Whether he knew it or not, and how could he, he was giving her comfort, too.

She was nearly asleep herself when she felt a hand on her shoulder. When she started, the pressure increased and kept her silent because she knew who it was. Lt. Brittle bent down to whisper in her ear.

"I'm sorry I am so late. Ward Block Three is also my bailiwick, and there are burn cases from an explosion." He squatted by her stool. "The night orderly is coming now. Let me take your valise and walk you to my house."

"Oh, but…"

"The Mulberry's too far, and are you as tired as I am? I've sent word for my housekeeper to prepare a bath for you, and dinner's probably ready."

"I'm sorry to put you to trouble," she whispered.

"I rather think you were the one put to trouble today."

Standing by the door, she watched him as he went to

every bed, looking, touching, covering, and in one case, kneeling in conversation that ended in low laughter. She remembered the amputee, who slept now, and told him about the man's pain. Lt. Brittle nodded and wrote a note for the orderly, prescribing laudanum, should the man wake before morning.

He carried her valise down the stairs and she followed, still stiff from sitting. On the colonnade, he offered her his arm and she took it. As she walked at his side, she found herself appreciating his height, which made their strides equal. With every step she took, she felt more tired than before. Even then, she knew she could not accept his offer.

"I should find a hotel," she said, as they came to another building in the quadrangle.

"No need. I occupy the end of this building. I have a dragon for a housekeeper and cook. As soon as I leave you here, I'm going back to Block Three. I'll be back in an hour to eat—I know it's late, but that's my life—and then it's back to Three for the night. You won't be in any way compromised."

That was blunt enough. Embarrassed, she glanced at him, and found him looking at her with an expression entirely matter-of-fact.

"You must think I am an idiot," she said. "My concerns are so puny and your responsibilities so huge."

"I think nothing of the kind," he said briskly. "Credit Niall McTavish at Edinburgh University, Lady Taunton. I happened to be paying attention when he said…" He paused on the walk, struck a pose, and continued in a Scottish accent that made her smile. "'Lads, everrryone's consairns are parrramount and it is evarrr thus.' I believe him."

"Verrrra well," she told him, and he chuckled.

By now he was opening the door to the end apartment. "Here is that dragon I was telling you about," Lt. Brittle said cheerfully, as a woman just slightly shorter than he was entered the room. "Aunt Walters, this is Lady Taunton, our guest for the night. Aunt Walters is also my father's older sister, and was never afraid to pound me when I deserved it." Lt. Brittle set down her valise and left the room.

"Dragon, is it?" Mrs. Walters said as she picked up Laura's valise. "He always was a cheeky boy and I can still pound him. Come along, my dear. I have a bath ready for you, and I intend to wash your clothing. I hear you were pitchforked into physicking."

There didn't seem to be any point in arguing. Despite her bone weariness, Laura couldn't imagine arguing with Mrs. Walters. There also wasn't any point in arguing when Aunt Walters scrubbed her back and washed her hair, as she sobbed in the tub.

"He bled and bled. I didn't know what else to do," Laura said when she could speak.

"What you did worked," the woman reminded her. She picked up the sponge and rubbed Laura's back. "Hippocrates and his stupid oath! Those Greeks! I'd pit an Englishwoman against them any day. You did what you could and without flinching."

"I'm crying now," Laura argued.

"The crisis is past so you're allowed to cry all you want. You did what you could," Aunt Walters repeated.

I did, Laura thought, as she let Aunt Walters help her from the tub and wrap her in a towel that was blessedly warm. The woman left her to dress, taking the bloody clothes with her. "I think your petticoat is unsalvageable," she said. "Come down when you're dressed, Lady Taunton. My nephew is coming in a few minutes for supper."

Lt. Brittle was sitting at the dining table when she came downstairs, her hair wet but pinned up on her head. He stood up when she entered the room and pulled out her chair for her. He had removed his surgeon's apron, thank goodness.

The food was plain and ordinary, but every morsel was delicious. She hadn't eaten since tea and toast hours ago in Torquay, and hoped she didn't look like a famished pensioner as she downed sausages and mashed turnips, then sat back, satisfied.

"I don't know when I've been so hungry." She glanced at the clock. "My word, it is nine o'clock. I suppose I will be awake all night, after that feast."

"I doubt it."

"I do not," she contradicted. "When I close my eyes, I know I will see Davey Dabney."

He nodded, but offered no platitudes that would only have made her uncomfortable. Instead, "Was today the worst day of your life, Lady Taunton?"

His question startled her, but she thought about it in a different light. "No, sir, it was not," she said finally, "not by a long chalk."

She was telling the truth. He didn't say anything, but something seemed to snap within her. Maybe it was the sympathy in his eyes.

"It wasn't when my husband died. I shall be honest. I was grateful when that happened." The words seemed to spill out of her. She put her hand to her mouth. "Oh, what you must think," she murmured.

"Go on," he coaxed.

"He had suffered, and I was glad that ended. I will not leave the ill untended."

"I know," he interjected, but quietly, so she would not be too distracted to continue.

"All my husband wanted was a son. He reckoned it was his late wife's fault that he was not a father. He was determined to get a child off me."

How can I be saying this? she thought in horror, but could not make herself stop. "After months and months, he gave up. There never was a woman more relieved than I."

"Understandable," was the surgeon's only comment.

She was looking into his eyes now, for some reason beyond her knowledge, not afraid to speak to this kind man of her trouble. *Do they teach that in Edinburgh?* She asked herself. *I think not.*

"Those were not my worst days." To continue required a deep breath, and she took several. *I am gulping like a goldfish,* she thought. She was hardly aware of the surgeon holding her hand now. She didn't even know when he first touched her, but there she was, clinging to him.

"It was the day my father…" She couldn't help herself; she practically spat out the word. "My Father told me what I had to do to repay him for my education. Nana has probably told your mother, so perhaps you know already."

"She only mentioned her own circumstances."

"Then you know Nana left Bath because she would not let our father sell her to the highest bidder to pay off his creditors."

Lt. Brittle nodded.

"I was the older sister who succumbed. I was almost eighteen and I didn't know what to do."

Her words seemed to hang in the air like a noxious fog. "That was my worst day, sir. I had no advocate and no resources of my own." She sighed. "Nana is five years younger than I. At the time, I had no idea she was my sister. If I had known, I would have told her." Her voice broke. "I could have warned her!"

He continued the thought. "And she would have sent you straight through to Plymouth and Gran."

Laura nodded. "If I had known…" she repeated, when she could speak. She couldn't look at him now. She released his hand. "But I did not, and there the matter will ever remain. I should never have told you."

"It will go nowhere," he replied, and took her hand again. "You really have had worse days than Davey Dabney. If you consider the matter, I doubt you are afraid of anything now."

She had never thought of it in that light. "As to that, I am not so brave. It took me three months to get up the courage to respond to Nana's invitation to visit."

"But you did."

"I did, didn't I?"

She sat back, exhausted, and Lt. Brittle released her hand. He opened his mouth to speak, but the doorbell jangled. He rose quickly, and was gone a long time. Not sure if she was exhausted more from the events of the day, or her avalanche of words, Laura felt her eyelids begin to droop. *I should get up and walk around,* she told herself, but that suddenly sounded like too much exertion. She heard Aunt Walters in the kitchen. *I should help,* she thought, as she moved aside her plate. *I will do that after I rest my arms just a moment. Just five minutes.*

She woke hours later in a dark bedroom, with only the vaguest recollection of someone carrying her upstairs and depositing her on this bed, which was comfortable beyond belief. She was dressed only in her shift, and someone had taken the trouble to put a towel under her head and spread her damp hair across the pillow. She hoped it was Mrs. Walters, but Laura also had the distinct impression someone had taken her pulse. *Dear me,* she thought, as she turned onto her side and closed her eyes again. *I wonder if he takes a person's pulse when she lies down as a matter of course. If he ever marries, he will be the despair of his wife.*

When Laura woke again, she smelled bacon. After a quick wash, she put on her remaining dress and petticoat and brushed her hair. She knotted it on top of her head in a style so casual she was almost embarrassed, but she suspected this was not a household that stood on much ceremony. Besides, there was that aroma of bacon.

Following her nose, she found the breakfast room with no trouble, a sunny spot with windows wide-open. She stood outside the room, wondering whether after all she had said last night, she should be embarrassed to even look at the surgeon, much less eat with him. The bacon won out, finally.

Lt. Brittle, looking worn-out, had already helped himself from the sideboard. He waved his fork in that direction.

"Thought I'd pop 'round for breakfast," he told her. "If I'm lucky, maybe a nap."

She grazed across the sideboard, gathering food until her plate felt heavy. "I should be embarrassed at the amount of food I am eating," she told him as she sat down. He had pulled out her chair from where he sat, but did not rise, which made her feel completely at home. She knew it was proper for a gentleman to always rise for a lady. Indeed, her husband had always done that, even at the breakfast table. Lt. Brittle's complete lack of pretension struck her as more natural. More than that, nothing about him indicated he thought any less of her for yesterday's confession.

He reached behind him and speared another rasher of bacon from the sideboard. "Excuse my manners. I never waste a movement at meals because I never know when I'll be interrupted. And I never know when I'll eat again."

It sounded perfectly logical to her, and she told him so. He returned her comment with a raise of his eyebrows and kept eating. After another piece of toast and more tea, he sat back. In seconds, he was asleep, sitting upright.

Amused, and not a little touched, she continued eating, careful not to clink her fork against the plate. Wondering how long he would sleep that way, she glanced at the clock on the mantelpiece. Five minutes, then five more.

Fifteen minutes after he had closed his eyes, Lt. Brittle opened them, blinked a few times, and looked around. "That was pleasant," he said, not in the least embarrassed. "I hope I did not snore or drool."

"You did mutter the secret formula for curing lice and ringworm," she said with a straight face.

"Lady Taunton, you are a wit! If I should, in future, reveal a cure for malaria during that nap I laughingly call slumber, do write it down. We shall make our fortune."

His remark touched her, because he was implying a future. *I wonder if he even knows what he just hinted,* Laura asked herself as she wiped her mouth and sat back. It was ridiculous, of course, but comforting.

She hoped he would not leap up now and leave. To her delight, he poured himself another cup of tea, and after an inquiring look, poured another for her, too. He leaned forward and drank it, resting his elbows on the table. Miss Pym would have cringed at his manners, but Laura found herself amazingly stirred by the intimacy of his casual ways.

"Two of the burns died last night," he told her.

She was already getting used to the clinical, almost cold way he described wounds. A glance at his eyes told Laura a different story. "The third one?"

"Barring infection, I think he'll make it."

The teapot was near her elbow. He held out his cup and she poured. "Ta," he said.

She almost hated to ask. "How is Davey?"

"Surprisingly cheerful," he said, to her great relief. "He said if he wasn't being a cheeky son of a gun, he wanted to wish you good morning."

He set down his cup. "Lady Taunton, I am going to take a nap now."

"A *real* one?"

"A climb-in-my-rack one. I'm aiming for four hours, but I never know. When I am done, I am going to take Davey Dabney outside into the bright sunlight, tilt his head back and try to see that artery. I just know it's nicked and I want to throw in a stitch or two. The light just isn't good enough inside. I'll try to trim away dead matter, if I can. The chief surgeon will assist, and surgeon's mates will be there."

Then he did a funny thing. He tapped the edge of her shoe with his shoe. It was a low-bred, casual gesture, but it connected them for that brief moment.

"Lady Taunton, Davey wants you to be there to hold his hand. That's all he wants. Call me names, but I assured him you'd be delighted."

She was silent a moment until she knew she could speak without a quaver in her voice. "I was going to visit Matthew this morning, wait for my other dress to dry, and return to Torquay."

"I know."

"Of course I'll be there," she said quietly.

"Thank you." He took her hand and kissed it, then poured himself another cup of tea. He looked at the cup. "No, Lady T, this won't keep me up. I have one more request."

"Ask away. It can't be any more presumptuous than the last one," she said, amused.

"It is! I was quizzing you two days ago when I asked it, but I'm in deadly earnest now. Will you work for me?"

"My God, sir!" she said, startled. "You can't be serious."

"Never more so. I know you have no formal training, but you kept alive a husband you didn't particularly care for, and probably ran his estate."

She nodded, unable to speak.

"I need a matron for Block Four to oversee laundry, victuals, cleanliness and sanitation. My chief surgeon's mate is in charge of the nursing staff, such as it is. You will circulate throughout the building, making sure all is well." He chuckled. "In your spare time, you have my permission to walk on water and turn water into wine. You will do this six days a week, from the forenoon watch to the end of the first dog watch. For this I will pay you the magnificent sum of twenty-five pounds each year."

"I spent more than that on a gown once," she commented. She wanted to appear calm, but he could probably see the pulse pounding in her neck, or maybe even her heart jumping about in her chest.

"Oh. I forgot. You will receive rations and a place to sleep in Block Four."

"Thank goodness," she said. "I was on the verge of turning you down." She stood up, too uncomfortable to remain seated. "I may have nursed an old man through apoplexy, but I know nothing!"

She looked out on the kitchen yard, with its neat rows of lettuce, carrots and beans. He joined her at the window and stared at the same view.

"You're wrong there, Lady T, with all due respect. The men didn't notice how little you knew. What they saw was how much you care. They're still talking about it this morning. And Matthew? He feels better just because he was able to help, too, by finding me. He's not as sick as he was, because he was needed and useful."

She turned to face him. "I just don't know."

"Will you think about it?"

She nodded. He smiled, yawned hugely, and left the room. Laura sat down at the table again, weighed down by the enormity of what a man she barely knew was asking of her. She had been offered a job no lady of quality would ever consider. What would people think if Lady Laura Taunton, widow of a baronet, went to work as a matron in a naval hospital?

It troubled her to no end that her few tumultuous days at Stonehouse had led her to put her mind and heart on the line for all to see. In some strange way, she felt engaged in battle. The war, so abstract before, now loomed like a monster. All she wanted to do was run away; she doubted she had the courage of Lt. Brittle or his patients.

And yet she had to admit that something about being in this terrifying place seemed to compel her to honesty, and force her to consider things previously left unmentioned. Perhaps the issue wasn't really what people would think if a baronet's widow went to work as a hospital matron.

"Maybe I am wondering if I have the kind of courage such a job requires, working with such brave men," she whispered. "I do not see how I can."

She leaned out the window and rested her elbows on the sill, regarding the carrots seriously as their feathery tops waved in the breeze. She didn't want to even consider the surgeon's offer. She snatched up her bonnet from the hook by the front door where someone had left it last night, and let herself out of the house quietly. *I will visit Matthew,* she promised herself, *hold Davey Dabney's hand during surgery, then leave for Taunton. I could no more serve as a hospital matron than forgive my father for ruining my life.*

Chapter Seven

⬯⬯⬯⬯⬯

The patients in B Ward must have been waiting for her to walk through the door. They cheered and she blushed like a maiden. She had to respond in the right tone, so she put up her hand in an imperious gesture that made the seamen settle down again.

"You're still miscreants and rascals," she scolded.

"You forgot layabouts, mum," someone said, and the others laughed.

"That, too," she agreed. "How could I ever forget?"

Laura nodded to the orderly at the desk, who looked as captivated as the men under his care. She went first to Matthew and brushed the hair back from his forehead, which made the seaman in the next bed sigh in a dramatic gust. She glared at the men.

"If there is a worse set of villains in this entire nation, I do not know who they might be," she declared.

"That's us, mum!" "On the nail," "Too right," were the replies she hoped for, because they told her much about the general state of B Ward. *It would be too easy to become attached to you mongrels,* she thought. *Thank goodness my plans do not extend beyond holding Davey Dabney's hand through a surgery.* And considering her terror of yesterday, she was having second thoughts about that.

"How are you, Matthew?" she asked.

"Better, mum."

"Did you eat your breakfast?"

He made a face. "We ate better on the *Tireless.*"

"I don't doubt that." She glanced around, noting bowls of uneaten food by bedsides. "Is there anything I can do for you?" She asked it softly, not wanting commentary on that particular query from the others.

He thought a long time, and it touched her heart, because she knew his life had no luxuries. He probably had no idea what to ask for. "There is one thing," he said finally.

"Ask away."

"Last November, I stayed at the Mulberry for a week."

"Nana told me you were very helpful in the kitchen."

He nodded. "In the evenings, she read to us from a book about a bloke stranded on a deserted island. And then I went to sea again."

For some odd reason that artless statement felt as sharp as a blow between her shoulder blades. *You have so little,* she thought, feeling her eyes well with tears, *and I so much.*

"England needs you, Matthew," she said when she could command her voice. "Are you speaking of *Robinson Crusoe?*"

His face lit up. "That was it! Please, mum, I want to know what happened. Could you finish the book for me and me mates?"

What do you do now, Laura? she asked herself. *Do you*

*lie and tell him you will be happy to keep reading where
Nana left off, and then do a runner like the poor woman
yesterday? Do you tell the truth that you are going back to
Torquay and then Taunton, where life is easy? Or do you
just tell him no?*

"I am going to return to Torquay after noon," she said.
"Matthew, I cannot do what you wish."

If he had turned away then and refused to look at her,
she would have felt better than what he did, which was to
keep smiling at her. "That's all right, mum," he told her.
His kindness made her feel as though Satan himself was
dragging burning hot fingernails down her back. *Shame on
you, Laura Taunton,* she thought. *Shame on you.*

"I will be back, though," she told him. "I promised Nana
I would look after you."

He nodded, but he seemed less certain now. He closed
his eyes.

Fiercely disappointed in herself, Laura rose and looked
around the room. The men watched her, interest in some
eyes, pain in others. *You all ask so little,* she thought, then
looked at Davey Dabney, who stared straight ahead. She
sat by his bed.

He turned his head toward her, and she knew it was an
effort, considering his wound. "I'm afraid, mum," he whispered.

"I am, too," she replied. "I would be lying if I said otherwise. I'll hold your hand."

He nodded and closed his eyes. When she was certain
he slept, she went to each bed, trying to do out of kindness what she had done for her husband out of duty. She
knew how painfully little this was, but the men didn't

seem to see that; or at least, they were too polite to mention it.

After she made her slow circuit of the ward, the orderly, red-faced, whispered to her that he needed to be excused for a few minutes. "I drunk too much tea at breakfast," he said.

"I'll be fine here," she told him, forcing down her fear of being the only able-bodied person in the room.

When the orderly returned, she sat by Davey again, awake now, and alert to every footstep on the stairs. "Dr. Brittle said he is going to explore my neck outside, where the light's better," he told her. He sighed. "I'd almost give the earth to be outside. Is it warm today?"

"Yes. Quite nice, in fact."

She could tell he was straining his voice, but he wanted to talk. "I am a foretopman," he told her. "On a sunny day, there's nothing finer than sitting in the crosstrees, a hundred feet above the deck."

"I'd be afraid."

He looked at her, surprised. "Gor, mum, I wouldn't have thought you could be afraid of anything. Not after yesterday."

It was a compliment of real weight and heft, and she knew it. "Thank you, Davey."

He only smiled and reached for her hand, which she gladly offered. He was dozing again when Lt. Brittle came into the room, in shirtsleeves and wearing his surgeon's apron. She felt her heart plummet into her stomach as she saw him. His sleeves were rolled up to his elbows and he was ready to work.

Instead of coming into the room, he leaned against the door frame, watching Davey. *What are you thinking?* she wanted to know. *How does a person go about preparing for this?* As she watched, he closed his eyes. She wondered if he was praying.

Lt. Brittle looked up, took a deep breath and came into the ward. He spoke to the orderly, who nodded and went out the door. In a moment, two men came in carrying a chair.

By now Davey was awake. The surgeon went directly into his line of sight, so he would not have to strain.

"Ready?"

"Near as ever, sir."

"I'm going to lift you into this chair, tie you to it and then tip you back so the orderlies can carry you below deck."

"I'd rather use the piss pot first."

"Wise choice. Glad to know I haven't already scared it out of you."

Everyone was awake and watching now.

"Mrs. Taunton, go below please and hold open that outside door. I left an apron for you at the bottom of the stairs."

Without a word, she did as he said, completely unnerved by the thought of what was coming. She hurried down the stairs, wanting to keep running. But there was the apron— one of Brittle's, she thought—draped over the stair rail. She put it on. Top to bottom it fit. Side to side, she ended up wrapping the ties around and knotting them in front. Her fingers felt almost numb, so it took her several tries.

She heard the men on the stairs and opened the door, holding it wide as the orderlies carried Davey Dabney carefully into the sunlight. They set him down by a table covered with a cloth, where another surgeon stood, then reclined the chair back slightly and locked it in place.

"Captain Brackett, this is Mrs. Taunton, who has agreed to hold Dabney's hand," Lt. Brittle said, speaking to the other surgeon. "He thought she would be a better distraction than Matron Willett in Block Six."

Dabney managed a smile, which quickly froze when he saw the small table. A slight wind had ruffled the cloth, revealing hardware that made Laura wince, too.

Lt. Brittle quickly stepped in front of the table, blocking the view. He gestured to Laura. "Sit there close to Davey, will you? Davey, I'm going to turn your head so you can admire her beautiful green eyes. Oh, my, she's even going to blush for us. Prettiest green eyes *I've* ever seen. That's good. Hold still. Capt. Brackett is going to lash a bandage across your cheek and under your chin just so and anchor it to the chair back so you won't move. Laura, do what you can."

He said the last in a lower voice, as Davey began to shiver. Without giving it a thought, she stood as close to the foretopman as she could get, one hand on his head and the other across his chest and holding him tight until he was breathing normally again. As Capt. Brackett expertly bound him to the chair, she rubbed Davey's chest, then pulled up a blanket that an orderly had draped across the man's legs.

He opened his eyes. "Sorry for that," he murmured.

"Nothing to be sorry for," she told him.

"Davey? Should I secure your hands?"

"No," he said, his face muffled by the bandage. "Not if mum will hold them."

"I will."

"Very well." Lt. Brittle glanced at the sun. "Captain Brackett, let us imagine a day when an operating theatre will be this light indoors."

The surgeon and orderlies chuckled.

Other men came closer now. "These are two of my surgeon's mates, Davey," Brittle said. "Everyone here does what I tell them. I'm going to widen the entrance wound a little and see what I can see, out here in God's light. You'll feel grippers on your neck. That'll be my mates pulling back the edges of the wound with tenacula so I can get a good look. Are you ready? We'll go fast. Captain, a smaller bistoury, if you please."

It couldn't be fast enough for me, Laura thought. Davey stared at her, his eyes desperate now, and she knew she had to keep her expression calm. *Focus on Davey,* she told her brain. *Don't even think about what is going on just inches from you. Don't let your expression reveal anything except the brave mum he thinks you are. When this is over you can go home to Torquay and Nana.*

Davey's eyes widened and he groaned as Capt. Brittle deftly sliced into the wound and murmured, "Sponge." Davey flinched when the tenacula went into place to hold the wound open wider. All it took was a tiny glance to convince Laura she would concentrate on the foretopman, who clung to her hands with a grip she had not expected.

She wished she could have appreciated the speed with which Lt. Brittle operated, widening the wound, then peering inside that cramped space for as good a look as he could get.

"Probe, Captain," he said, then delicately reached inside with the long instrument Brackett slapped into his open hand.

Laura's fingers ached from the strength of Davey's grip, but she returned the pressure and hoped she sounded rational as she babbled about summertime and green leaves, and how nice that it wasn't blustery and cold, and how on earth did he keep from getting seasick on the top of a swaying mast.

Lt. Brittle probed some more, then Davey closed his eyes and went slack.

"Excellent," the surgeon murmured as he stepped back and his mate dabbed at the wound. "Stay unconscious, my friend. It's a better world. Keep a hand on him, Laura."

She was only vaguely aware he had used her first name. She kept her eyes focused on the sailor, free momentarily from pain. She glanced at Lt. Brittle, who had stepped back and was talking with his colleague. She wondered why he was operating, and not the surgeon who outranked him. She focused on Philemon Brittle then, seeing him for what he was, an enormously talented surgeon brave enough to try something unorthodox to keep a man alive.

How can you do this? she thought. *How can you be so calm?* She watched the surgeons, Brackett nodding, his hands in his pockets, and Brittle now wiping the probe on his apron.

"We agree then, Captain. Find me the smallest bistoury on the table. That one will do. Brian, swab away, lively now."

The mate dabbed again at Davey's neck, and then Lt. Brittle continued, talking in a low voice to the other mates. It dawned on her that he was teaching them.

"The artery wasn't nicked after all. The biggest problem seems to be that necrotic tissue was pressing against it and wearing it down. I will trim it."

She winced as he quickly flipped a strip of black matter onto the grass, and another. He took a wad of gauze and held it against Davey's neck as the foretopman groaned and came to again. Laura tightened her grip on his hands.

He groaned only because he hadn't the strength to scream, but in another few seconds, the mates released the tenacula and the surgeon reached for short strips of adhesive as fast as Captain Brackett handed them over. Davey watched her, his eyes tortured, but his breathing slowing, as he sensed the unendurable was winding down.

"I prefer adhesive to sutures, mates," Lt. Brittle said, continuing his lecture in the sunlight of the Stonehouse quadrangle. "It's less of an insult in places like this. I would do the same around genitals. The body's full of interesting nooks and crannies."

Then he was done. The whole thing couldn't have taken more than ten minutes.

Laura let out a sigh and glanced up at Lt. Brittle. To her surprise, he was watching her. He didn't say anything, but his eyes seemed to speak his thanks. *You're welcome,* she wanted to tell him, except that her mouth wouldn't move.

With the last strip in place, Lt. Brittle wiped his hands on his apron then took it off before he walked around to the other side of his patient, still lashed to the chair. He squatted on the grass by Laura's stool. She could see the perspiration on his face, and knew it had been more of an ordeal than he had let on.

"I would like to climb again, and give Boney what for," Davey said, his eyes on the surgeon.

"No promises, Davey," Lt. Brittle said. "I've done all I can."

He did something then that Laura never in the world would have expected. He rose to his feet, leaned forward and kissed the sailor on his forehead. "Do your best now, lad," he murmured, then nodded to the orderlies to pick up the chair.

Laura sat there, dumbfounded by what she had just witnessed. She was barely aware that Lt. Brittle now leaned his hand on her shoulder, as though he was suddenly more tired than fifty bricklayers. She wanted to say something—what, she didn't know—but suddenly a bell down by the creek that flowed behind the administration building began to toll.

"God damn," Captain Brackett said, sounding as weary as Lt. Brittle looked.

"Blame Boney instead," Lt. Brittle replied. "Captain, go home. I'll take it."

The other surgeon stood where he was, and they both seemed to be listening.

"What are you listening for now?" Laura asked.

"If there is another bell in a higher pitch that means…" He chuckled and looked at Captain Brackett. "How do we delicately phrase this for a lady?"

"Lady Taunton, it means hell has broken loose and shake your asses, all surgeons," the captain supplied. "I don't hear it, Phil. Can you truly spare me?"

"I can."

"I'll come, too," Laura said, almost amazed to hear the words leave her lips.

"It's grim, Laura. They're fresh off the ships."

He wasn't telling her no. He waved a hand at his superior officer, who started across the quadrangle at a trot, then told another mate to stay with Davey upstairs.

"Come along," he said.

"Where is he going?" she asked, gesturing after the other surgeon, who by now had reached his own quarters in the same row of houses where Lt. Brittle lived. "Surely you have had less sleep than he."

"No. His wife was in confinement all last night and delivered a son. The baby is doing well, but his wife is not. I don't think she will live."

"Poor man," Laura murmured.

"Sometimes it's hard to believe that anyone dies in this world except soldiers, sailors and Marines, but it is so." He picked up his apron, turned it inside out, and put it back on. "If you were dipping your toe in the River Styx with Davey, it's time for a complete dunking now. Just do as we tell you. Remember this—there isn't anything you can't wash off your hands."

What am I doing? she thought, as she hurried to keep up with the running men. Casting dignity aside, she pulled up her skirts and lengthened her stride as a seaman in a jolly boat cast an expert line to another sailor on the pier and snugged the boat tight to the dock.

Other orderlies and mates had arrived at the dock and were helping the men in the jolly boat onto land, where some of them sagged and then collapsed on the pier, unable to move. She saw two women in black already moving among them gesturing and then kneeling beside the wounded.

"They're matrons from other blocks," Lt. Brittle said as he slowed his pace enough for her to catch up. "Good. Brian already has a bandage satchel. Here we go."

Laura stayed on the dock for three hours. It seemed strange to her that birds could still sing in such a place of carnage, but they did. At intervals between the groans and shrieks of men in more pain than she could imagine, she could hear the sound of hammering from the nearby drydocks, and in the distance, a knife grinder calling. Somewhere, at least, life was going on as usual.

She did what Lt. Brittle told her to do, asking no questions. The surgeon was scarcely recognizable, covered in blood. Once or twice, he stood away from the tree and let an orderly throw a bucket of water on him, then give him a new apron.

Then it was over. The matrons returned to their blocks, following a macabre parade of the walking wounded. The orderlies began to throw buckets of water on the bloody pier, and one gathered up Lt. Brittle's capital knives.

"Careful of those," he called. "When they're washed, sharpen them." He smiled then, for the first time in hours. "Oh, hang it. You know how to take care of them better than I do! Sorry, lad."

Another orderly helped her to her feet. She wanted to at least smile her thanks to him, but her face was stiff. She put a hand to her cheek and felt the dried blood there. She wanted to cry, but that would have taken more energy than she possessed. She just stood there and stared at the surgeon.

He came to her then and did nothing more than take her in his arms. She still could not cry or speak, until he took her chin in one hand and gave her a little shake. She gasped, and then looked at him.

"Can you manage?" he asked.

"I can," she said, only because that was the answer he needed.

He spoke to the closest orderly. "Would you walk this nice lady back to my quarters and turn her over to my housekeeper?"

"Aye, aye, sir," the orderly said with a grin. "This makes me the most fortunate bloke in the Royal Navy and the envy of me peers."

What he said struck Laura as funnier than anything she

had ever heard before. She laughed, which only made Lt. Brittle look at her closely.

"I am not given to hysterics, sir," she told him, and saw the relief in his eyes. "You must admit what he just said is funny, and indicative of the rascals this navy seems to attract. I'm a sad case and I've ruined my one remaining dress."

The surgeon's relief was almost palpable, confirming her belief that the last thing he wanted on his hands right now was a woman who could not stop laughing. He turned to the orderly. "Lad, I agree with you. She's a pretty sight, even now."

"I will never understand men," she declared, standing still and letting the surgeon wipe off her face with the damp cloth in his hand.

"Nature never intended you to," he replied. "We are an entirely different species."

When he did not come, too, she asked, "What about you?"

"I've just started my night," he replied. He followed her, wiping his hands on his apron. "Thank you, Lady Taunton," he said, "thank you a thousand times. I'll probably not be around when you leave for Torquay in the morning, but…"

"I'm not going anywhere," she interrupted. "Nana might be disappointed, but I'll write her a letter and explain everything."

"Home to Taunton, then?" he asked gently. "I'm sorry we were so hard on you."

She shook her head. "Taunton is not home. You are so dense. I'm staying here, Lieutenant. I promised Matthew I would read *Robinson Crusoe,* and someone has to hold Davey Dabney's hand." She fingered her stiff dress. "Besides, I am not even fit to ride the mail coach. Twenty-five pounds a year will hardly keep me in dresses, at this rate."

"Are you…"

"Serious? Staying? Of unsound mind? I am, indeed, sir," she told him. "All three. And know this—I intend to fight Boney in my own way, too."

Chapter Eight

Maybe it needed to happen. The jetty had pushed her beyond tears.

"I don't even know what this is in your hair, and I'm not going to look too closely," Aunt Walters said as she scrubbed Laura's hair over the large sink in the scullery. "If I thought he would listen, I would give my nephew a generous helping of my mind."

"I volunteered," Laura said, in Lt. Brittle's defense. She tipped her head forward while Aunt Walters poured warm water over it. "I wanted to," she added, when she came up for air.

"You're braver than I am," Aunt Walters said frankly, handing her a towel. "I've never screwed up enough courage to go to the landing jetty."

"It's a terrible place."

She protested, but the housekeeper insisted on delivering supper in bed. Propped up with lavender-scented pillows, she ate stew, then wrote a letter to her sister. She knew she was disappointing Nana, but Laura didn't think she could fight Napoleon in a sitting room in Torquay.

She was glad Aunt Walters sat with her as darkness came, telling her about Stonehouse, then stories about her nephew: his earlier years as surgeon's assistant on a frigate in the Mediterranean, Trafalgar, school in Edinburgh and London Hospital, and his most recent years in a fever hospital in Jamaica.

"He survived yellow fever," the woman said as she tidied the room. "Tough as an old boot, is Phil."

"I'm not so sure about that," Laura countered, and told Aunt Walters about his kiss on Davey Dabney's forehead.

Aunt Walters nodded. "He suffers agonies when they die. I wish he had a wife to talk to, for comfort."

Laura tried to compose herself. Her back still ached from bending over so many wounded men for so many hours; she wasn't sure she could lie flat.

Aunt Walters was about to close the door when Laura stopped her. "Tell me something. I looked up once at the jetty and saw Sir David Carew standing at a window. Why didn't he help?"

"And get his uniform mussed?" Aunt Walters muttered something low in her throat. "He's a physician, Lady Taunton, with a medical degree written up on parchment in Latin no one can read, a head full of theories that probably never saved a tar on the jetty, and no skill at all with capital knives. I doubt he could dismember a chicken bone at the dinner table."

That was an image Laura found vastly unappealing. "I'm not certain I care to see *anyone* carve poultry right now! Do you think…does your nephew get used to what he does?"

Aunt Walters shrugged. "How could he? Good night, Lady Taunton."

She went to sleep at once, and would have slept all night, if she hadn't been wakened by the sound of someone sobbing. *Maybe they will stop,* she thought, as she tried to burrow under her pillow and block out the sound.

It continued louder than before, irritating her, until she realized she was the one crying. Unnerved, she wiped her eyes on the sheet, just as the door opened.

"I'm all right, Mrs. Walters," she said. "It's nothing."

Lt. Brittle sat on the edge of her bed and handed her his handkerchief. She blew her nose, sobbed again, blew her nose again, then made not the slightest attempt to keep herself from leaning against his leg.

He must not have minded, because he put a gentle hand on her head. He tried to prop himself against the headboard, moving a little more onto the bed until she sat up, and without a word, pulled back the coverlets.

He was still fully dressed, but he unbuckled his shoes, took them off, then lay down next to her, gathering her close to his side as she threw her arm across his chest and cried. He held her close, saying nothing and doing nothing more than running his hand over her arm until she stopped crying and sat up again. He stayed where he was, practically asleep himself.

"Have you been in Block Four all this time?" she whispered.

He pulled her down and she found that same nice spot against his shoulder.

"Blocks Three through Six. We're stretched thin, Lady T. I came home two hours ago, changed clothes and went to Captain Brackett's quarters, where I pronounced his wife dead. He needed to talk then, as you might surmise. There are days I wish I had never left Jamaica."

She wasn't even sure of that last sentence, because his voice trailed off and he slept. She sat up, careful not to disturb him, and watched his face relax and his hands open up. Carefully, she settled him on his back, then loosened his neckcloth, sliding it slowly from his neck. As he breathed evenly and deeply, she unbuttoned his shirt, then removed his cufflinks, reaching over him to set them on the nightstand. Her breasts grazed his chest as she did that, but he did not even stir.

She hesitated a moment, then decided in for a penny, in for a pound, and unbuttoned his trousers. *You'd be an easy man to seduce,* she thought, smiling at the idea. She knew she should retreat to the downstairs sofa, but she didn't. *I'll cry again if I do,* she reasoned, as she tucked her nightgown tidily around her ankles, lay down, hesitated for only a second, then backed up against the surgeon, who responded by turning sideways, draping his arm over her and breathing steadily into her ear. She never slept better.

Laura dreamed of nothing for the remainder of the night, and woke just before dawn to the sound of seagulls this time, quarreling down by the jetty. She shivered involuntarily, trying not to think what it might be they found so attractive, then suddenly remembered she was sharing her bed with Lt. Philemon Brittle.

She turned slowly, and stared into his blue eyes. They were even sharing the same pillow. As her face grew red, his did the same. She knew the only way they could have been closer was if they were making love. As she watched his face, she felt almost as though they were.

She was relieved he didn't leap up with a horrified expression, and stammer something stupid. He stayed where he was, observing her in a way that softened her heart, peeling away layers of calculus that had formed there since her discovery, at age eighteen, that she had not one advocate in the entire world.

He spoke finally. She knew one of them had to say something.

"I should have left last night before paralysis overtook every limb."

It was a guileless apology, explaining exactly how he felt. It would have been almost clinical, if he hadn't pulled her hair back from her face.

"There is nothing to apologize for," she told him. "I could just as easily have gone downstairs, but I knew I would only be crying down there."

He turned onto his back. "I have used you abominably, these past two days."

She flopped on her back, too. Their heads touched on the pillow but neither of them moved away. "I don't recall complaining."

"You're dotty, then," he joked.

"Completely. Think how cheap you are getting my services. Come to think of it, both of my dresses, ruined now in the service of poor King George, would make a huge dent in my twenty-five-pound salary. They were made by a modiste of the first rank! See there, at this rate, I will use up my entire annual salary, just trying to replace my wounded wardrobe. Tell me. If I land in debt to the Navy Board, must I work for them forever?"

He laughed softly, and twined his fingers through her hand, holding it up. "You have better hands than I do for surgery. Look how long and narrow your fingers are."

She thumped him with her other hand. "There are limits to what I will do for the Royal Navy!"

"Very well." He released her hand. "Since I doubt I will have another opportunity today, let me tell you what I need from a matron. Every building has its own kitchen on the ground floor. All the food is uniformly bad. I said yesterday I wanted to try two things with Davey Dabney. You saw the first one."

She interrupted him. "Please tell me he is still alive."

"He is. When I left him at midnight, he told me to tell you thank'ee."

"I did so little."

"Saving his life?" Lt. Brittle took her hand again. "The second thing is this—somehow, you are to make good food come out of that kitchen. I am going to dispense with that low diet that the sickest are fed."

He turned to face her again, his expression animated. "No one can get well on that! It's folly to think that a gruel of milk and breadcrumbs will ever give men like Davey the strength they need to recuperate. Laura, for the most part, these are strong, healthy men. They've been subjected to serious bodily insult, but they are not weaklings." He made a sound of disgust. "At least, not until they spend time in a hospital. It's all backward."

She was facing him now, too. "Better food. What else?"

His face fell. "That will be hard enough. I am slave to

the almighty budget." He lay back again, staring at the ceiling. "I'm willing to use some of my own salary, but it's not exactly magnificent." He propped his knees up then, and noticed that the fall front on his trousers was unbuttoned. "No wonder I was so comfortable last night," he said as he buttoned them.

She knew she should have been embarrassed, but he was so matter-of-fact she decided not to waste her time with nonsense. This is a man with no spare time, she thought. *I doubt there has ever been a more unusual employment consultation in the history of the universe.*

"Where was I?" he asked, putting his hands behind his head.

"I believe finance had reared its ugly head," she reminded him, hugely amused by this whole experience, especially since it didn't seem to faze him at all.

"Ah, that. There is no delicate way to say this. I want Davey to have rich food. He needs meaty food, food with fresh vegetables, but nothing so rich as to make him uncomfortable."

She couldn't help herself; she was so excited she wanted to bounce on the bed. "I can do this! For three years, what do you think I was feeding my very late, my extremely late, husband? I have pages of receipts back at Taunton which are, if I may say, just what the doctor ordered. And as for the extra expense, Lieutenant, I can pay it. In fact, I insist."

He looked at her in amazement, then covered his eyes with his hands, saying nothing. He worried her, so she timidly took his hands off his eyes. "Lieutenant?" she whispered, then dabbed his eyes with a corner of the sheet. "It's a small thing."

He did not speak. Laura decided they were just two people tired of bearing heavy loads, and that was enough. Another thought struck her.

"Lieutenant, I have a cook. No, a chef."

He got to his knees then on the bed and planted a whacking kiss on both cheeks that made her laugh, and then smother her laughter in his shirt because she remembered—and reminded him, too—that he had an aunt in the house.

"She insists on sleeping downstairs in the room off the kitchen," he said, "and she's not an early riser." His face was still close to hers. "You have a cook," he repeated reverently.

"I do. Pierre Gagon is an émigré who hates Napoleon about as much as those men in Block Four, I imagine. I can have him here in a day or two, along with a scullery maid. If you want a really good housekeeper, I have one of those, as well."

He took it all in and leaned against the headboard again. "A housekeeper would free you for the other task I have in mind."

"You are a wicked hard taskmaster," she commented amiably.

"Too right. I want you to ward walk with me every day. My mates on duty accompany me, but you should, too. I want you to become acquainted with the men and their injuries."

"What do you do?"

"We walk through each ward, stopping at each bed, checking each chart. We compare notes, and I make assignments. Everyone knows what is going on."

She nodded, tucking her nightgown around her and drawing her knees up to her chin. She knew there wasn't any point in standing on ceremony with this man ever again. He would engage her in discussion during any free moment, obviously. What a relief he hadn't found her in the bathtub.

"If you can convince your cook and housekeeper to come, they can take charge of meals, and counting linen, and keeping things clean—all the scut that must be done. You might actually have time to sit with the men, write letters for them, listen to them—oh my God, *listen* to them!—and just be your cheerful self." He smiled at her then, and she could tell he was becoming conscious of where they were, even though he plunged ahead. "You have no idea how much good a pretty face can do."

"All my face got me before was trouble," she reminded him, amazed she had the courage to say that.

"Things have changed," he told her. "Maybe you've noticed?"

He got out of bed and stretched, then rotated his neck until it cracked. "I just came in here last night to check on you," he said, sounding mystified. "And now it is morning, and I have not slept better in years. Odd, that."

I haven't slept better, either, she thought, as she pulled the covers over her again and settled herself down on the pillow they had so recently shared. She already knew he could manage more frankness than most people.

"Lt. Brittle, I know this will embarrass you, but you are the only man who has ever slept in my bed all night."

He was at the door, but he turned around in surprise. "You were married all those years!" His face turned red. "I mean, he was not always an invalid."

"No. I told you of his single-minded efforts to get a son." She put her face into the pillow, shy now. She nearly stopped breathing when Lt. Brittle came back to the bed, and sat down. "Keep going," he said, his voice soft.

"He would finish, then go back to his own room," she said simply. "I was happy last night."

"I was, too."

He left the room then. A smile on her face, she listened. Sure enough, there it was. He startled whistling before she heard the door to his room close.

She completely lacked the courage to go down to breakfast. Then the matter was moot, because she had no dress, anyway. She stayed in bed until she heard the front door close, then got up and looked out the window. There he was, uniform on, running a hand through his short hair and then slinging an apron over his shoulder. His jaunty walk made her smile.

In her robe, she padded downstairs and found Mrs. Walters. She followed her into the small laundry room, where she produced yesterday's dress, stained but serviceable. "I couldn't do any better," Mrs. Walters said, as she handed it over. She took a surgeon's apron from a peg. "Phil told me to give this to you. He hopes you can come to B Ward soon, and he suggested you have some plain black dresses made."

"Not black," Laura said firmly. "I told myself, never again. Dark blue, perhaps." She held out the dress she had been wearing when Davey hemorrhaged. "Mrs. Walters, do you know of a seamstress who could use this sorry thing as a pattern, and turn it into five dresses just like it? No stains, though."

"Happen I do," the housekeeper said, fingering the fabric. "Dark blue?"

Laura nodded. "I have money upstairs. Please, Mrs. Walters, there is one more thing I need."

"A mirror to see if you have lost the top of your head and all your brains?" the housekeeper teased.

"A copy of *Robinson Crusoe*."

He knew better than anyone how much he had to do this day, but Phil took a moment to look back at the row of surgeons' quarters, his eyes going to the black wreath on the door of Captain Brackett's quarters. There would be no help from Owen for at least a week. It was a good thing he had trained his mates well.

He looked to the first-floor window of his quarters' guest room, Laura's room. "Lt. Brittle, you deserve an award for keeping your mind on business this morning," he told himself.

He looked around. It was still early and no one was in sight, so his self-congratulations were for his ears only. No need for anyone else at Stonehouse to have an inkling how besotted he was. No need for her to know how long he had been lying there that morning, watching her sleep, touched beyond measure with all the ways she had tried to make him comfortable when he so stupidly fell asleep in her bed.

Good God, Phil, only a man in a million, or one other overworked surgeon, would ever do what you did, he scolded himself as he started walking again. Thank the Lord she did not seem to mind. Why, he couldn't imagine.

It would be a memory to keep him warm. No need for anyone but him to know his keen pleasure at wakening in the middle of the night, rising up carefully on one elbow and watching Lady Taunton sleep. At first she had slept with her back to him, hunched over as though protecting herself. What had actually awakened him—and if he was to be perfectly honest, aroused him—was what happened when she must have felt cold, and moved toward his warmth.

True, she still-kept her back to him, but she moved close until he was obliged—it was a privilege, he knew—to pull her close to his own body and share his heat. Gradually, she seemed to soften and straighten out, pillowing her glorious hair on his outstretched arm with a little sigh of contentment that made him grin in the dark.

He had slept with women before. When he decided not to let yellow fever kill him, Jamaica's lovely dark women had been the perfect prescription for convalescence. What they offered him, he took, with not one single scruple.

Last night had been different on all levels, except the most basic one: he had yearned to make love to Laura Taunton. Maybe there was a more elemental level, he decided, as he walked to Ward Block Four. As much as he wanted her body, he had a feeling that any overt moves in that direction would only have played with her brain and heart in ways that would just hurt them more. This was not a woman to toy with; this was one to cherish.

And how will I ever do that? he thought as he opened the door. *Even in the best of times, it would take a brilliant lover. These are the worst of times, and I am no Don Juan; I'm just a surgeon.*

He pulled his apron over his head and tied it in back, ready to begin his day. Now it was time to concentrate on the collapsed lung in C Ward, the puzzling scrotal infection in A Ward, and the unsearchable wonders of the Almighty's hand in keeping Davey Dabney breathing. He smiled. He would rather think about Laura Taunton's legs and the length of them.

He ward walked with Edward, his night surgeon's mate, bleary-eyed and ready for the rack. They both agreed that perhaps the trocar and cannula was the next thought for the collapsed lung. The rare scurvy case was ready for discharge and return to sea, after a strongly worded reminder to take his daily lime juice without fail. The scrotal infection was still a puzzle. Could there be new infections from Plymouth's whores? Perhaps it was time to clinically examine the local doxies again. He smiled at the thought of telling that to Admiral Sir David Carew.

His smile faded. He had to face the old boy now and tell him of his decision to hire Lady Taunton as a hospital matron. As intelligent as the whole matter had seemed in Laura's comfortable bed, he had not a hope in Hades that Sir David would see it in the same light.

When he finally got to B Ward after a detour to Block Three, she was already there, sitting beside Davey, who looked more bright-eyed. What man with red blood cells wouldn't? Phil thought as he observed them from the doorway. True, her dress was stained and that apron of his was cumbersome, but there was no denying Laura Taunton was an inspirational woman for sick men to contemplate.

He could see something of Nana Worthy in her auburn hair, but there the similarity stopped. Nana was a pretty thing, with those wonderful round eyes of hers, and heaven knows Captain Worthy was a goner the moment he spotted her. From the elegant way she carried herself, to the marble of her flawless skin, to her lovely deep bosom, Laura

Taunton was beautiful. He stared at her and resisted the urge to take his own pulse.

"Lieutenant?"

His mate was looking at him.

"I'm sorry, Edward. Just thinking about…Davey, there."

They walked to his bedside, and Laura rose gracefully to move out of their way. He sat down and took the fore-topman's pulse, even though he could plainly see the man was better and breathing easier. Edward handed him the chart from the foot of the bed, and he reviewed his mate's nocturnal notes. He looked at the sailor.

"I could stare at charts all day, but Davey, how do you feel?"

"Better. When I swallow, it goes down easier."

"That dead tissue was pressing 'gainst all yer pipes," Phil replied, falling easily into the sailor's own accents. "I don't know that you'll be furling sail anytime soon, but you're not worm food, either. As you were, Lady Taunton, unless these other miscreants would like some hand holding."

She went to the powder monkey's cot. "It's Matthew's turn," she told him, which brought a chorus of groans from the boy's shipmates. Phil laughed, pleased to see the general air of alertness returning to B Ward. He looked at his mate, who was having a hard time keeping his eyes open.

"Edward, I'll stay here until the orderly comes on duty," he said.

The mate nodded, then stopped in the doorway. "Lieutenant, when were you planning to use the trocar on the lung in C?"

"Maybe by the first dog watch."

"Would you call me, sir? I'd like to see the procedure."

"That I will," Phil replied. *Of course, that's provided Sir David hasn't thrown me out of Stonehouse when I tell him I want to hire Lady Taunton,* he thought.

He made the rounds of the ward by himself, more and more unsure of what would happen when he went to the administration building. When the new orderly came on duty, he briefed him. He ended up watching Laura. *I was a fool to even suggest she serve here,* he thought. He motioned to her and left the ward.

She came quickly, to stand with him in the hall. "I can tell you're having second thoughts," she said. "I am not."

"Come with me then."

They went down the stairs quietly to the ground floor. He opened an unmarked door and led the way into the empty kitchen. Laura looked around, surprised.

"Where is everyone?"

"There hasn't been a matron or cook in years," he said. "Block Four gets its meals from Block Three's kitchen." He made a sound of disgust. "The men in here never get a hot meal. And all to economize in times of war!"

He pointed to the receipts still tacked on the wall, stained by years of smoke and cooking. "There they are—low diet and moderate diet, menus the Sick and Hurt Board has determined will speed seamen to recovery. They won't, though. Men are better off staying on their own ships than coming here."

"That can change," was all she said. "I wrote a letter this morning to Pierre Gagon, my chef, and another to my solicitor in Bath, asking for a transfer of funds to Carter and Brustein in Plymouth."

He led her into the compact servants' hall, with its dust-covered table and chairs, and walls grimy with neglect. "Lady Taunton, I…"

She put her finger up, almost to his lips. "It's Mrs. Taunton from now on."

He wanted to kiss her finger, and then her whole arm up to her elbow. He stepped back instead. "This will never work. Let me show you one reason why."

He opened a door off the servants' hall, and stepped aside so she could enter. "This would be your room, and a more cheerless place I can hardly imagine. At least there are bars on the window to keep anyone from crawling in. There's not even a bathing room. Sir David would expect the Block Four matron to stay here, and…"

"…and he—and apparently you—would be certain I would back away from such a place," she continued, looking around her and not at him. "There's no lock on that door, either."

"No. If I asked Sir David for a Marine sentry, he would laugh me out of the building."

"I would be living in a gloomy, unsafe place."

He watched, miserable, as she ran her finger over the dusty writing desk and then pushed on the bed frame, which creaked in protest. She stood looking through the barred window for a long time. Her head went forward until she was leaning against the window glass. His heart sank into his shoes. Why had this whole idea seemed so possible, lying in bed with her and talking about his plans, only a few hours ago? He knew he had a reputation for sound judgment. Where had that gone, in the short space of a day or two?

"Are you surrendering already, Lieutenant?"

He looked up, startled. She had turned around and was watching him, and there was something indomitable in her eyes that set every nerve in his body humming.

"There are so many obstacles," he said bluntly.

She clasped her hands in front of her. "You're a stingy man," she said, clipping off her words. "Maybe all men are stingy. Maybe they think no one of the female sex can be useful—truly useful. I say you are wrong, and I intend to prove how wrong you are."

She came close to him then and gripped him by his elbows, her hands firm and strong. Because they were much the same height, she looked directly into his eyes.

"I want you to tell me why it is so hard to do the right thing."

Chapter Nine

Laura didn't know she could dig down so far inside herself. Nothing in her life had ever prepared her to stare deep into a man's eyes and exert her will. She wanted to run, but he must not think her a weak woman, one who would buckle and fold in such a place as this. Even more, she could not do that to herself. She gathered him to her, so he could not see her own face if she should start to falter in her determination.

His arms came around her and she rested her cheek against his shoulder. "I listened to your plans this morning when it was still dark," she told him distinctly. "I believed them."

She held herself off from him in time to see him regarding her with an expression she could not fathom. "I sat with them this morning, I watched their faces and realized I am deep in this war now. Please don't lose your courage on my account or imagine for one second that I will falter."

She released him then, unnerved by her own vehemence. She thought of Nana in peaceful Torquay, fighting Napoleon her way by keeping the heart in her husband. *I will fight it my way, by keeping men alive to fight him again.*

"There it is," she said simply. "I will go to Sir David and tell him what's what."

She could tell that stung Lt. Brittle. He winced, perhaps thinking she was digging at him for doubting. She could reassure him, too. "I'd feel braver if you came, too." She wasn't even sure that was true, not the way she was feeling now.

Lt. Brittle nodded. "I'll happily accompany you, Lady Taunton," he told her. "In fact, I insist upon it, even though I already know you have had much worse days than the ones I seem to have inflicted on you recently. You might not even need me."

"It's true," she agreed with equanimity, "but I never really understood that, before you made it plain to me. One thing else, sir. No more Lady Taunton. I am Mrs. Taunton now. I don't mind Laura in private, because I like to hear it. We have not been precisely formal with each other, have we? Is it to be Phil or Philemon?"

How brazen. She had never been closer in mind to any man in her entire life, and she had known Lt. Philemon Brittle less than a week. She could barely comprehend what was happening to her, swept up in an avalanche of feelings mixed in with war and wounds and duty, love for her newfound sister and husband, and a sense of her own independence and all its possibilities.

"Whichever you prefer," he told her. "My colleagues call me Phil, but I like my whole name."

"Then it will be Philemon," she replied. "Do you know, before I went to sleep last night, I took my Bible and read that little letter from St. Paul again. Had a hard time finding it, I will confess."

Something in his eyes told her she had touched a chord in him, but his reply was lighthearted. "Stuck between Titus and Hebrews. Family lore says Mama was reading Philemon when her labor pains started."

"Then thank God Almighty she was not reading Colossians!"

She felt more boulders slide off her back as Philemon laughed, opened the door and became the surgeon again. On his advice, she went back upstairs while he went to Block Three. She couldn't help watching him from the landing window, as he did his quick walk to Block Three. His jaunty stride of early morning was gone. This time his head was down, as if he was already thinking hard about what waited for him there.

At noon, she helped the orderly with dinner, wondering how sick men could eat that unappetizing mess considered appropriate for wounded invalids. She asked Matthew to help one of his shipmates. Disregarding his own pain, he did as she asked, and rewarded her with a triumphant smile when his mission was accomplished. He didn't object when she helped him back to his own cot; he was asleep in minutes.

"Good go, Mrs. Taunton," the orderly whispered. "We'll give him more duties as his strength increases. I hadn't thought of that."

"Let's do that everywhere we can," she answered, gratified to see the respect in his eyes. "These men are used to much harder work. They need to feel needed." *Don't we all?* she thought, remembering how long the days had seemed after her husband's death, when a lifetime of nothing to do stretched before her.

An hour into the afternoon watch—she was beginning

to recognize the bells—Philemon came to B Ward. He had removed his apron, and wore his uniform jacket again. He smoothed down short hair that didn't need smoothing, and had tucked his hat under his arm.

"Mrs. Taunton, let us see if Sir David is in a good mood, shall we?"

She took off her apron, wishing she had a dress that wasn't stained, but happy enough that her hair was tidy under its lace cap.

"I fear I will not impress him," she fretted as they went down the stairs. She brushed at stains from yesterday's afternoon at the jetty, spent mostly on her knees.

"You already impress me," Philemon replied as he held the door open.

"You have to say that," she joked. "You want a matron. Oh, bother it!"

He stopped, mystified. "Laura, what is troubling you, above and beyond the general fright and panic that we are both feeling at this second?"

"It's this dress. So many stains, I…"

He took her arm, settling her next to him as he continued walking. "I love females," he announced to the world at large. "Females understand order in the universe far better than males, and they smell better."

"You are so clinical," she scolded. "Call me a lady, at least." When he laughed, she stopped him. "You said that to put me at ease."

"It worked, didn't it?"

They were ushered into Sir David's antechamber, where they waited at least a quarter of an hour, probably an eternity to a surgeon with more patients than time.

"He knows his game," Philemon murmured. "I'll wait him out. I'm not going to abandon you to face him alone. You've had too much of that in your lifetime, eh?"

She nodded, immensely reassured by Philemon Brittle's presence. As casually as if he sat in his office—if he even had one—the surgeon crossed his legs and opened up his case folder, prepared to review his charts.

She watched, amused, as he closed his eyes and went into one of his impromptu naps, his hands relaxing. When the folder started to slide from his lap, she rescued it and put it on her own lap.

She decided then that she loved him: common, sound asleep, completely capable and destined to never leave her mind or heart again, no matter how this interview with Sir David Carew fell out. She had never loved a man before, and the sheer blessing of it made her utter a small exclamation that woke him up.

He sat up, looked around, smiled at her lazily, then closed his eyes again. He stayed that way, giving her time to collect herself, until the door opened and Sir David himself stood there, impatience written on every line of his body and stance.

"Well?"

On contemplation of the matter later, Philemon decided that he should have pitied Admiral Sir David Carew. Once Laura Taunton swept into his office, the man didn't have a prayer. She was in charge of the interview from auspicious beginning to conclusive end.

She began with a curtsy so profoundly elegant that he could only gape like the pig farmer's grandson he was.

She followed it up immediately by thanking him for the appointment—never mind he hadn't approved it yet—and the chance to do her part to keep the Dread Corsican Monster from England's shores by tending Neptune's Brave Sons.

Good God, Philemon thought. Too bad she cannot stand for office. He moved to the window seat, the better to watch the unprecedented sight of his superior officer in the hands of a master.

Scarcely drawing a breath, Laura segued into a reminder that her father, William Stokes, Lord Ratliffe, even now languished in a Spanish prison. What that had to do with her petition to be a hospital matron, Philemon did not know, but she never gave Sir David a chance to pounce on faulty logic. The man even gave her his own handkerchief to dab at her dry eyes.

She next invoked her brother-in-law, Captain Oliver Worthy, one of the finest commanders of fighting ships, and the sinking of the *Tireless*. Philemon began to feel a little sorry for Sir David, who stood there with a stunned expression. She had never even given him the chance to seat himself behind his intimidating desk, where he liked to throw down lightning bolts from Mount Olympus.

Too bad for Sir David. She cajoled, she flirted, she begged and she insisted, and twenty minutes later accepted his signed approval of her appointment as matron of Ward Block Four. Siddons, herself, couldn't have done it better.

Only then did Sir David register his presence in the room. "You? You? I doubt the Navy Board pays your salary to malinger in my office, Lt. Brittle."

"Not at all, Sir David," he replied smoothly. "I escorted

Lady Taunton here because I have a patient management question for you."

The last thing he wanted, or needed, was medical advice from Sir David Carew, but if Laura Taunton could put on a show, he could, too. From the looks of her, that performance had worn her out.

"Very well," Sir David said, pleased, apparently, that his surgeon was stumped. He took the case folder and looked where Philemon pointed.

"Simple, my boy. Use calomel. I always do."

That is the last thing I would consider, Philemon thought, as he nodded. "Precisely, Sir David. Thank you for your help. I can escort Lady Taunton back to Block Four."

She was looking worse by the moment, but Laura rallied to give Sir David a breathtaking smile and a curtsy only slightly less deep than the first one. She held the memo from Sir David tight in her fist.

He knew all the signs, especially when Laura gave him a desperate look as they left the office. He hurried her down a hall and into a room with nothing in it, thank God, except a desk, chair and wastebasket. He grabbed the basket and held it in front of her while she vomited. She clutched the basket as he moved her toward the chair and sat her down, holding back her hair that had come loose from her cap.

When she had the matter in hand, he went into another office, where he knew there was a water cask. He came back with a glass of water, dipped his handkerchief in it and wiped her mouth, then handed her the glass. She drank gratefully.

"I'm so embarrassed," she murmured, setting down the wastebasket.

"No need," he told her, toeing it away, and already amused at what the office's inmate would think when he came back to find someone's digesting breakfast in his wastebasket. "It's not the first impromptu emesis basin I have ever held. Laura, you were magnificent."

She didn't look magnificent. She looked drained and shaken. He felt in his pockets, but knew he didn't have any smelling salts. "No hartshorn," he told her cheerfully. "If you start to see prickles of light, just put your head between your knees."

He wanted her to laugh, but she didn't. She sat still, as though unable to believe what she had just accomplished.

"In all my life, I have never stood up to anyone," she said, her voice a whisper. "Never. I have done what people wanted. Maybe what they expected. Maybe I am not as weak as I thought."

He touched her arm. "You're not weak. You never were." *And I will tell you that until you believe it,* he thought. *I don't care how long it takes.*

"The luncheon hour is about over, Laura," he said, looking at his timepiece. "Let us vacate the premises."

She glanced at the wastebasket. "Seems a trifle cavalier to leave that behind."

"That's the beauty of, er, some of the body's less appealing functions, madam matron. They're so anonymous."

She was silent until they reached the Trafalgar memorial. "Philemon, I don't have the slightest idea of what I should do," she confessed. "You know that."

"I can suggest a course of action," he told her. "I will have the kitchens and other rooms cleaned and prepared for you. It will take a few days."

She nodded. Already he could see that her fear was receding and the practical woman he already appreciated was coming to the fore again. "I will return to Taunton and retrieve Pierre Gagon. I can make financial arrangements and see what I can pirate from Taunton's kitchens and linen closets."

"By the time you return, I will have composed a list of duties in the order that I think is most important. There will also be a list of the men and their ailments, and what I think they need in the way of nourishment."

"I'm creating more work for you, aren't I?" she asked, contrite.

"I, too, am happy to offer myself on the sacred altar of service to king and country," he joked.

Her eyes grew wider. "I said that in there, didn't I?" She started to laugh.

"That and more."

"I actually do mean them."

"I know you do."

She started up the stairs, then looked back at him. "It's funny, but I didn't start to feel nauseated until I mentioned Lord Ratliffe, moldering in that prison. I hope he molders there forever."

"At least he served a useful purpose today," he reminded her.

Philemon didn't see much of her the rest of the day. The remaining burn case in Building Three occupied much of his time. By the time he made his way to Block Four, it was nearly dark and she had left the building. When he returned home, so tired he could barely drag his feet to the front stoop, his aunt informed him that Lady Taunton was already in bed.

He ate whatever it was Aunt Walters put before him, yawning and turning the pages of a text on burns he had read so often the pages were shiny. Another part of him, the part still not tired, lamented that Laura Taunton was not sitting there. Aunt Walters had told him Laura had arranged for a post chaise to leave for Taunton early tomorrow, and there was a letter for Mrs. Captain Oliver Worthy, Torquay, waiting to be franked.

He went upstairs quietly, almost wishing she were crying so he would have a reason—maybe a flimsy one—to check on her. All was still. Well, never mind. He told himself he was grateful she was sleeping peacefully.

He sat on his bed a long time, one shoe on and the other in his hand, just staring at it stupidly, fretting with himself that Laura Taunton might just change her mind and decide to stay at her estate, where life, he was certain, was much easier. *Don't leave us,* he thought, chagrined at the way he had come into B Ward earlier that evening, and looked around, hoping to see her sitting by someone's bed. What made the matter worse, all the men who were awake had looked up eagerly when he came in, as though expecting to see her, too.

"Weren't we all disappointed. What a pack of fools," he said out loud as he set his shoe on the floor and took off the other one. He arranged them carefully as he arranged all his clothing, making sure everything was ready to leap into, if someone should call him in the middle of the night. It happened often enough, and he was used to it.

At twelve he had gone to sea, and soon found that his place in the world was the orlop deck, where the wounded were. *And here I am,* he thought, as his eyes closed. *It's the devil of a life.*

Brittle woke in time to escort Laura to the gate of Stonehouse, where the post chaise waited. It was raining, thank goodness, so he had every excuse to pull her close under his umbrella.

"I shouldn't be delighted that it's raining, but I am," she told him. "My dress is so ruined the coachman will think I have murdered an old widow named Lady Taunton and am running away in her post chaise. A cloak will cover a multitude of stains."

Ah, the females, he thought. "What will happen when your dresser at Taunton sees it?"

"It doesn't bear thinking on," she replied, moving closer to him. "I believe I am more afraid of her than I am of Sir David Carew."

"She's a dragon?"

"Most decidedly."

"Well organized?"

"Beyond belief."

"Stonehouse's head matron needs an assistant."

"You might be onto something," she said. "Peters—her name is Amanda Peters—would amaze your head matron."

The coachman got down off his box, directing the postboy to open the door.

"I'll deliver your wife safe and sound by noon."

My wife, he thought, and made no effort to correct the man. Neither did Laura, which gratified him. *One of us has to move,* he thought, as they both stood there in the shelter of his umbrella.

The coachman acted, taking the umbrella from him, but still holding it over them both. "Give her a kiss, so we can get your lady on the way. Time's money."

She'll either slap my chops or kiss me back, Philemon thought as he took Laura in his arms and did what he had wanted to do since Torquay.

She certainly didn't slap him. After the smallest hesitation, she stepped into his embrace and held him firmly across the back, looked him in the eyes, then closed them and let him kiss her.

It was a kiss that lingered. After a deep breath, he kissed her again, and then one more time for good measure. Even then, there didn't seem to be a good reason to let go of her, even if time was money, and horses—what little a seaman knew of horses—didn't much like to stand.

Neither did coachmen, apparently. "Jaysus, Mary and Joseph, I promise to bring her back," the man said, amused, as he tried to hand over the umbrella again.

The bell at the jetty began to clang then, and they both stepped away from each other.

"I can stay and help," she said.

"No. You'll help more by getting me a chef," he replied as he grabbed his umbrella. With a wave of his hand, Philemon ran for the landing. There was so much more he wanted to say, but the bell was ringing.

Laura arrived in Taunton before noon. When she wasn't thinking about kissing the surgeon, she found herself fretting about what horrors Philemon had found at the landing jetty. She thought about Davey Dabney, too pale and not thriving on that low diet, and Matthew with his questions about the future, and all the other inmates of Ward B—the scoundrels mixed in with the saints—who occupied her mind and heart now.

Philemon would probably never believe her if she told him she had never been kissed before, but it was true. Her husband had made her role amply clear, and it did not involve kissing. She was to spread her legs dutifully and give him every opportunity to get a child. The shame of it made her close her eyes, as she remembered his efforts that went on until she was sore and in tears.

She knew he derived some pleasure from his futile exercise, because he would cry out sometimes, and gasp and breathe heavier and heavier. There were a few—a precious few—occasions when she felt some deep spark and wanted him to continue. She never asked for such a favor, partly because by then he had rolled off her and was on his way out the door without a backward glance, and partly because she didn't know if those tantalizing glimpses of pleasure meant she was a woman no better than her mother.

There was no one to ask. She had kept her thoughts to herself and did her best to provide Sir James with what he wanted. And yet, her glimpse of Oliver Worthy kneeling in front of Nana and resting his good ear against her belly while Nana kissed his head, made Laura think there was much she was missing.

"You can ask Nana," she told herself, as she watched the rain. "Nana will tell you."

She found she did not dread the drive to Taunton. There

was nothing in the estate now to cause her pain. Because they had been informed by her earlier letter to Pierre Gagon, the servants were ready for her, opening the door as soon as the postboy helped her from the chaise, clucking over her, taking the bandbox, practically lifting her up the broad steps to the entrance. Even Pierre came up from the kitchen, wiping his hands on a towel and assuring her luncheon would be served directly.

Peters, her dresser, took her in hand. Frowning as usual, she unhooked the frog closing Laura's cloak. Before she could warn the woman, Peters was staring at the ruin of her dress, the wreck of several long hours at the landing jetty, surrounded by dirty, wounded seamen and Marines.

She surprised herself again by feeling no fear of her dresser. "Peters, they bring the wounded to the jetty from the ships in the harbors. I…I held one burned man until he died. Human carbon is hard to remove from fabric, I have discovered."

Peters burst into tears. Laura stared at her, openmouthed. She touched her dresser's arm, something she had never dared to do. "Peters, I didn't mean to disturb you. Any of you," she said, looking around at the other shocked servants.

True to her nature, Peters recovered quickly. "My nephew died in the retreat from Corunna," she said quietly.

"I had no idea," Laura said. "No idea."

That seemed to put the starch back into the dresser. "Why would you? Sir James was on his deathbed."

Would you have told me even if that hadn't been the case? Laura asked herself. *Of course you would not, because you are here to serve.* She looked around at her servants. *I never knew you,* she thought.

She had no time to waste, and summoned them to the sitting room when luncheon was over. The room was utterly silent as she told them of Torquay, her sister, Stonehouse, Davey Dabney, the men of Block Four and the jetty. She minced no words.

"I have decided to work as a hospital matron," she said. "I wrote to Pierre and asked him to accompany me. His receipts for Sir James are precisely what the men in hospital need to restore them to health." She smiled at her chef. "He has agreed."

She let that news sink in. "That is all, really. I wanted you to know. Life will go on here at Taunton as usual. You may go now."

No one moved. Her servants looked at each other, but they remained in place. Her housekeeper, a doughty woman almost as implacable as Peters, spoke first, as was her right, in household order.

"Begging your pardon, mum, but I'm coming, too," Mrs. Ormes said. She looked around, defying anyone to contradict her. "I'd be the last person to say you don't know much about the state of linens and how to make servants mind, but I could do that while you spend time with the sailors."

"Provided they are not smelly and disorderly," Peters said. "We can't have that."

Laura laughed. "Peters, you will always protect me, won't you?" She leaned forward, not disguising the intensity she felt. "These men are giving their all in the service of our country. I doubt we can ever repay the debt."

"I'm in," Mrs. Ormes said, holding her head high.

"I'm coming, too," Peters said, militant again.

"As it turns out, Peters, Lt. Brittle did mention there was

an opening for assistant head matron. Of course, you won't make as much salary as I pay you now."

Peters looked down her long nose at Laura. "I could do this for Corporal William Peters, couldn't I? Something useful in his memory." Her voice trembled, but she regained her composure without losing a beat.

"Very useful. Can you leave tomorrow with Pierre?" She looked at her housekeeper. "Mrs. Ormes, I welcome your help, too, and will continue paying your salary at Stonehouse, because you would still be working for me."

Philemon returned home late that night, bone weary and desolate because Laura would not be there, awake or asleep. He ate the meal Aunt Walters had left for him on the table, then went upstairs to the room Laura had lately occupied. He took off his shoes and lay down, hopeful that his aunt had not taken the time to launder the sheets or pillowcase, because her fragrance might linger.

It wasn't any particular scent, just a pleasant, womanly odor that his keen nose had no trouble identifying, especially not in the world of men he inhabited. Drat it, anyway. Aunt Walters had already changed the bedding. He trudged to his own room.

He lay there wanting Laura Taunton with a longing almost painful. He was professional enough and good enough to know that he would never abandon his patients to run after her. For the first time, though, he wanted to.

He had called time of death on three patients this night alone, and it bothered him because he had no one to talk to. Captain Brackett was useful, but Owen had buried his wife today. Owen was the one needing to talk.

The worst death was the amputee in the bed next to Davey Dabney. He had seemed well enough earlier, but there was no mistaking the angry streaks around his stump, and the lethargic, sunken look in his eyes.

He was under no illusion that Laura's presence could have kept Tom Severn's gangrene away, but it would have made it more bearable. As it was, he had sat by Tom's bed and told him he could take off the rest of his leg up to the hip joint, but he could not guarantee success. "I can do it," he told the seaman bluntly, "but would you survive it?" In the end, Tom decided to let go of life. He didn't complain, except to tell Philemon, "Wish that pretty lady was here to hold me hand."

He let Philemon hold his hand instead—a poor substitute—and had the kindness to die just before the orderly pounded upstairs with another crisis. A quick look at his watch, a scribble on the chart, a hand to close Tom's eyes, a flick to the sheet, then on to another crisis.

He knew he had to sleep, even as he wanted to think about Laura, and what she was doing to him. *Ask me anything about anatomy,* he thought. *I could probably educate the average female about her own body. Do you need a potion? I can formulate one. How do I court you? That involves time, and I have none.*

Chapter Ten

One day after seeing off her chef, housekeeper, dresser and several maids, Laura found herself in the sitting room of Miss Pym's Female Academy in Bath, a place she liked even less than the jetty. She wanted to pace the floor, but her pride wouldn't risk the chance of Pym catching her at it.

It wasn't too late to leave the building. Her post chaise waited, ready to return her to Stonehouse. Although she had received the letter in March that set off this whole adventure, she had not seen Miss Pym since her marriage to Sir James.

She heard footsteps and tensed herself. For a moment, she wished Philemon Brittle were sitting beside her. She craved the sight of his comforting bulk and the unalterable fact that he would never fail her. How she knew that, she could not tell. It was enough that she knew it.

Here was Miss Pym, looking older and more gray. Laura didn't want to look into the woman's eyes, but she did, and was shaken by something she had never seen there before: uncertainty.

They curtsied and went through the preliminaries that

civilized ladies must perform, down to the tea and cakes brought into the room, even though it was too early for cake and Laura had no desire to drink tea with this vile woman. "Miss Pym, I am here for one reason. I want to know who my mother was. That is all."

She could have felt some triumph at the way Pym's mouth dropped open and her eyes widened in total surprise. For luscious seconds, Pym looked like the least-mannered girl in her school, and not the unflappable headmistress she claimed to be.

"My God, why?" Pym exclaimed, apparently without a moment's thought to how cruel it sounded. But that was Pym.

Laura fixed her with a gaze that she hoped was repellent enough to peel paint. "I want to know," she repeated, giving each word weight and heft.

Pym took a moment to recover. If Laura had been a vindictive woman, she would have rejoiced. As it was, she began to feel sorry for her. That feeling lasted until Pym spoke.

"It was Sophie Something. No one to be proud of, Lady Taunton," Pym said, trying to regain her toplofty manner.

"She was my mother!"

Laura hadn't meant it to sound so anguished. Again, she wished Philemon were there. She took a deep breath and calmed herself with the knowledge that, in a sense, he was. So were Nana and Oliver. She may have been sitting in that room by herself with no visible allies, but this time she knew there were people who cared about her. She wasn't alone, and the knowledge gave her power.

"Tell me more, Pym, or I will write a letter to every parent whose daughter is in this place and have you shut down so fast you will feel the breeze." Laura was trembling inside, but one look at the headmistress's face told her Pym believed her.

It was Pym's turn to pace the carpet. "She was an actress, or claimed to be. Thought she was the next Sarah Siddons. Fool." Pym stopped. "I'll grant you she was beautiful. You look so much like her, right down to that little mole by your eye."

"What happened to her?" Laura asked, thinking about an ambitious girl tangled in her father's web. *He probably made her all sorts of promises,* she thought. *Men do that.*

"I think she would have found an alley abortionist, except she was too poor even for that. Your grandfather was still alive. When he got wind of his son's indiscretion, he took charge and made her promise to bear you, and provided her a sanctuary until she did. If it helps, I remember the scolding he gave my dear brother," Pym said drily.

Nana had told her of the previous Lord Ratliffe's reformation to Methodism, and his years spending the family fortune in establishing an orphanage for by-blows, and a school for Pym, his own illegitimate daughter, to manage.

"She left me in an orphanage?"

"She wanted nothing to do with you or my brother again." Pym shrugged. "I can understand why she would want nothing more to do with William, but you were such a pretty infant. Ah, well. She returned to London. Your father had the prudence to avoid her, but he did say she managed a shabby career on the fringes of theatre. You came here when you were six years old, and you know the rest."

She did. "Where is my mother today?" She clutched the arm of the chair so tight that she heard the wood protest, but Pym was pacing again, and didn't seem to notice.

"She died two years ago. Someone found her in a rented room in Spitalfields. William saw to her burial."

"How kind of him."

"Yes, I thought…"

Pym stopped when she realized Laura's tone was sarcastic. She stood directly in front of Laura. "He could have done nothing, and she would have been dumped into a pit and covered with lime."

"I want to see my sister, Polly Brandon, before I leave. I'll be outside."

Pym was all solicitousness. "You may wait in here, Lady Taunton."

"I would rather die than stay in this building one more second."

The air was much nicer outside. She took a deep breath, enjoying the fragrance of roses in the garden in front of the school. She thought of the hours she and the other girls had tended roses as part of their duties. In fact, she had first met Nana Massie there, newly come from Plymouth and so homesick that she looked up with tears in her eyes at every seagull that flew around Queen Charlotte Square. As one of the older scholars, she had shown Nana how to strip the dead leaves and avoid the thorns. *If only I had known she was my sister,* Laura thought. *What a waste.*

"Lady Taunton?"

She looked up from her contemplation of the roses. There was Polly Brandon, her other half sister, standing at the top of the steps. She smiled at her, returning her curtsy.

"Would you walk with me to the square?"

In another moment they were seated on one of the stone benches. "I believe you know who I am. Nana told you."

Polly nodded. "She did, Lady Taunton."

Laura put her hand on the girl's arm, and was gratified when Polly took her hand and held it. "It's just Laura. Polly, I know Oliver is paying your tuition now and making things comfortable for you, but you don't have to stay here."

"He and Nana told me that, too." She hesitated. "Sister, I like it here well enough, and you can tell by looking that our father never troubled to have a miniature made of me. I was quite safe."

All Laura saw was a pretty girl, one wearing spectacles, to be sure, but still a pretty girl with auburn hair like her own and Nana's, and an air of real intelligence. She was taller than Nana, and plump in the way of young girls about to turn into young ladies. She could see no reason why Polly Brandon wouldn't break hearts someday. She also had an idea.

"Polly, *I* would like to send a miniaturist to you," she said. "I can think of nothing nicer than to have your likeness to sit on my desk, and I know Nana would think it a wonderful Christmas gift, too. Would you mind?"

Then their arms were around each other, Laura not holding back her tears, and Polly patting her on the back, soothing her with that same generosity of heart Nana possessed. *Maybe we are more alike than anyone could have imagined, and from such a father,* Laura thought.

"I'd like that above anything," Polly assured her, when she could speak. "I will also petition such a present from my sisters." She had mischief in her eyes. "In Nana's case, I think I will have her defer until our niece or nephew is in the picture, too. Maybe even Oliver, if he will stay in port long enough. Theirs will be more than a miniature!" Her face turned serious again and she tightened her grip on Laura. "We came so close to never knowing."

"Don't think about that," Laura murmured. "Nana is my heroine."

"Mine, too. Will you write me?"

"Once a week, without fail."

Arm in arm, they walked back across the street, hugged each other again, then Polly went up the steps to the Female Academy. "Time for Latin," she said, with a wave of her hand, and then a kiss into the air with it.

Laura took another deep breath as more of the weight of the years fell off her shoulders.

Laura arrived at Stonehouse after dark, debated briefly whether to go to Block Four or Philemon's house first. The surgeon's house won with surprising ease, but she justified her choice by reminding herself that Aunt Walters had promised to have those dresses ready for her. Besides, it was only eight o'clock; Philemon was probably just getting his second wind. She wouldn't know where to find him.

To her surprise, he opened the door just as she raised her hand to knock. From the looks of him, he had been on a rapid walk from the back of the house and was ready to hurtle himself down the steps. Instead of knocking her down, he grabbed her around the waist and pulled her inside.

She gasped, then laughed as he picked her up, whirled her around, then set her down, as if suddenly reminding himself that sometimes an ordinary "how de do" would suffice.

Somehow, her bonnet had been tipped sideways by his

exuberance, so she set it straight on her head. "I was only gone four days, and not two weeks."

She must not have had her bonnet set precisely, because he adjusted it, standing close enough for her to notice the stains on his shirtsleeves.

"You need to wash that shirt," she scolded.

"You sound like Aunt Walters," he replied cheerfully. "No time. Two amputations this afternoon, and then I had to deliver a baby in the laundry."

"The laundry?" she asked. He still stood so close, which bothered her not at all.

He wrapped his finger around one of the ribbons that tied her bonnet. "Those poor women work up to the last moment. Still, it was a welcome change from the usual butcher's bill."

"Is there anything you *don't* do?"

"I leave pulling teeth to my mates. I hate using that dental key." He shuddered elaborately, then pulled her close into his arms, as if he wanted to put an end to a silly conversation as much as she did.

He didn't try to kiss her. He just held her, and it was precisely what she craved. It made her brave enough to say into his questionable shirt, "I went to Bath to ask Miss Pym who my mother was."

"What did you find out?"

Safe in his arms, she told him. "She was just a foolish girl and a willing mark to be preyed upon by someone like my father."

Since they were much the same height, it was so easy to put her arms under his and hold him tight across his back. She knew he was a muscular man because she had seen him lift patients with comparative ease, but he was holding her so gently. "How is it you know what I need?" she asked quietly, not meaning to say that out loud, but suddenly wanting to know.

"Call it practice," he said. "Only loobies think doctors just tend the body."

He was taking prodigious good care of her body, one hand rubbing the back of her neck and the other slightly south of her waist. He pushed her closer to him and she didn't mind.

She turned her face toward him then, looking him right in the eyes. She knew he would have kissed her, but the clock in the sitting room started to chime and he stepped back, his face red now and his hands on her shoulders.

"I'm late," he said, and it sounded like an apology. As if to make up for it, he kissed her cheek. "Come with me. You have to see what's happening on Block Four."

She let him take her by the hand and hurry her across the quadrangle and up the front steps. "I have to take a quick look on C Ward, then we'll check out the miracle downstairs. Laura, you are a nonpareil. Will you take notes?"

"What, on my nonpareilness?" she teased, taking the pad and pencil he handed her.

He introduced her as Mrs. Taunton, the new matron of Block Four. His statement elicited a hooray from two of the men who appeared to be rapidly on the mend. Philemon gave them a long stare and the noise stopped.

True to his nature, he softened his discipline quickly. "If ye salty dogs will treat her kinder than your own mums, she might find the time to read to you and overlook your general nastiness."

The men in the beds laughed.

"She's going to ward walk with me mornings," he told them. "Mrs. Taunton has already seen it all, so none of you can possibly surprise her. She's also only slightly less brave than Lord Nelson himself, so ye need have no fears."

Laura felt her eyes begin to well up, but she willed the tears away. She marveled again at Philemon Brittle's innate ability to gently nudge out the best in her. *I am not that brave,* she thought, *but now I want to be.*

They went from bed to bed, Philemon observing patients, chatting with those who were up to it, taking his time with pulses, putting his ear to chests to listen to the message inside, checking bandages, and sitting silently with one sailor with bandaged eyes, holding his hands for a long time.

"He was too close to an exploding cannon and he can't hear, either," he told her when he stood up, still holding the man's hand. "I want you to do this as often as you can." He looked down at his patient. "They don't teach this in medical school. More's the pity."

Still he stood there, then gestured her closer, and handed his patient off to her. She held his hand gently; as she watched him, he smiled.

"Trust the Navy to know a good thing," Philemon said, his voice low. "Laura, when you came to Nana's house and she hugged you, I had the feeling that was the first friendly touch in a long time."

His lips were close to her ear because she knew he didn't want the other patients to hear him. She leaned closer. "Is twenty-six years long enough? No one had ever hugged me before. I supposed it's not recommended in orphanages, and heaven knows Miss Pym would never consider it."

He winced as though she had sworn at him. "Dear God, what a waste," he murmured. "You have some catching up to do."

At the foot of each bed, he wrote on the chart hanging there, then gave her whispered instructions. They both quickly realized another advantage to her height. It was an easy matter to speak right into her ear, without seeming obvious in a roomful of patients.

They walked the ward, then continued to B, where she looked immediately for Matthew. He was sitting on a seaman's bed, playing backgammon. He must have sensed her presence, because he turned around before she spoke, his face all smiles, and held up his bandaged arm. "Getting better, mum."

Thinking of what Philemon had just said, she put her hands on his shoulders and kissed the top of his head. "That's from Nana," she said. "You know she would do that if she were here."

Delighted at Matthew's appearance, she looked at Philemon.

"He's fast becoming my star patient. He's also discovering how much he can do with one hand."

"The doctor's going to have a hook made for me," Matthew said.

"Only if you promise to be a force for good," Philemon warned. He looked over his shoulder. "Here's my other star pupil."

She turned around to see Davey Dabney smiling at her. He was still propped halfway into a sitting position, but the wan look had been replaced by what she could only describe as a hopeful expression. Startled, she looked at the other men. That was what was different about the ward. She looked back at Philemon, a question in her eyes.

"Pierre Gagon has only been here two days, but, gentlemen, can we safely say that he has already raised the dead? Who would have thought a soufflé could have come out of that kitchen?"

Laura clapped her hands in delight. "He has wasted not a moment!"

"I wouldn't have believed it myself, if I hadn't seen it. You're right, Mrs. Taunton. He's a treasure."

He said something else, but Laura wasn't listening. She was looking at the cot beyond Davey, where the man with the amputated leg used to lie. Someone else was there now. She turned back to Philemon and saw the sadness in his eyes. She waited by Matthew until the surgeon finished talking to the orderly at the desk, leaving his instructions for the night.

He went to the door then. She said good-night to Matthew, promised them all she would return in the morning, and left the room. Philemon stood on the landing, looking at his notes, almost as if he was ashamed to see her.

"What happened?" she asked, as gently as she could.

"His leg was septic, with great red welts shooting into his groin. I…I just couldn't help him enough."

She could almost reach out and take hold of his sorrow. Instead, she applied his own remedy and put her arm around his waist. He put his arm across her shoulder and they walked slowly down the stairs together.

By the time they reached the ground floor, he was in control again. "Now you need to see the miracles in that dungeon of a kitchen I tried to foist on you."

She smelled what was going on even before he opened the door. "Pierre is making profiteroles," she said with a sigh.

"We call it manna. I've been prescribing it for everything from glaucoma to hemorrhoids."

She laughed out loud and walked into the kitchen. All was neat, scrubbed, swept and tidy, with food on the shelves. There were even curtains at the windows. She looked closer. They were remarkably like the curtains from the kitchen at Taunton.

Pierre bowed and whisked out a platter of the delicacies in question. Philemon took two.

"I feel a slight tickle in the back of my throat," the surgeon said. "Here, Laura, you look a little jaundiced. Oh, wait, no. That is the lantern reflecting off your cheekbones."

"Wretch."

She took a profiterole as Mrs. Ormes came out of the scullery. "It appears that you have all been making yourselves completely indispensable," Laura said.

"I believe we have, Lady Taunton," the housekeeper replied. "Lt. Brittle has already said that he will throw himself under a brewer's wagon if we ever leave."

"I will, too," Philemon said cheerfully. "Laura, I even offered to marry her, but she said her tastes don't run to youngsters, and she prefers to remember Mr. Ormes."

The housekeeper pinked up nicely at his teasing. "Lady Taunton, I should warn you about the navy."

"My sister already did, I assure you."

Her eyes practically twinkling, Mrs. Ormes leaned closer. "Is she the one in the family way?"

"Yes, alas, she did not take her own advice."

While Philemon talked to the chef and made some notations on a chart listing all the patients, Laura followed her housekeeper into the rooms, exclaiming over the brimming pantry, inspecting the pots and pans in the scullery, and admiring the table and chairs in the small servants' hall. She smiled to herself; the rug in there looked familiar, too. She could have sworn it was last seen in her butler's parlor. Poor Taylor; how he had wanted to come along, too.

"Here is Monsieur Gagon's room, then mine. The pots and pans girl had a little alcove off the scullery." Mrs. Ormes lowered her voice. "After the maids finished cleaning, I sent them back to Taunton. Too tempting for the patients, I vow."

"Mrs. Ormes, these are sick or wounded men."

The housekeeper just clucked her tongue. "They're still the navy, Lady Taunton, begging your pardon."

They stopped before the last door. "Is this my room?" Laura asked.

Mrs. Ormes opened the door. Laura saw scrubbed walls, her desk from her personal sitting room, a rug from her bedchamber, and her favorite chair and ottoman. The bed had no mattress.

"Lt. Brittle said he has a feather bed in his quarters he will have sent over tomorrow for you," she said.

"I'm sure that isn't…"

"He insisted, and I don't really think he likes to be contradicted, Lady Taunton."

"We will humor him, then," Laura replied, amused. "And Mrs. Ormes, I am to be addressed as Mrs. Taunton here. I don't want to give even the appearance of putting on airs, because believe me, I am here on sufferance. The administrator is not looking on this venture with a kindly eye."

"Perhaps that is best," Mrs. Ormes said doubtfully.

"It is," Laura assured her. "I will move in tomorrow." She thought a moment. "Did Peters return to Taunton with the housemaids?"

Mrs. Ormes shook her head, her eyes lively again. "Not her, Lady…Mrs. Taunton. True as Lt. Brittle said, she's assisting the head matron now, and had slapped even more fear into the orderlies than the surgeons!"

"Amazing," Laura murmured. "She always frightened me. Now it's for a useful purpose." *Good for you, Amanda Peters,* she thought. *Your nephew, dead in the snow on the retreat to Corunna, is not the family's only patriot.*

She protested when Lt. Brittle insisted on walking her back to his quarters before continuing with his rounds. "It's only across the quadrangle, and I know how busy you are."

He made no reply, but offered her his arm, which she took, after making a face at him that made him smile. He seemed to read her mind then. "I can spare a feather bed for you, make no mistake. There'll be nights when you'll be so tired you won't even bother to remove your shoes, but at least you can sprawl in comfort. It's one concession I make for myself, too."

"You're such a sybarite."

"Indeed I am. Three years' duty in Jamaica ruined me from ever wanting to be a cold bath, porridge kind of Englishman again. Ah, Jamaica."

"I believe it was a fever hospital," she reminded him. "Lots of death and drudgery and probably an administrator as obstructive as Sir David."

He opened the door and ushered her in. "Wrong there. He died while I was recuperating. You would like Jamaica.

If we can ever eliminate yellow fever from the island, I'll book you passage on the next ship out. Until then, never. As for now, all I can offer is my bed."

He must have realized what he said, because he chuckled. "You know what I mean! Good night, Mrs. Taunton."

He left, hurrying back across the quadrangle. She knew she was tired, and she tried to sleep, but her eyes didn't close until he was home again, three hours later, and in his own room. *Dear man*, she thought, *dear man*.

Chapter Eleven

Laura slept long and well, aghast with the lateness of the hour when she woke. She dressed quickly in one of the new dresses Mrs. Walters had left in her room, then noticed the surgeon's apron hanging on the doorknob. There was a note in the front pocket.

Laura, have some of these made, too. We may be the same height, but your patients, bless their navy hearts, must yearn to see you in something conforming more to your figure than mine. Aunt Walters can measure you and one of my aprons as a pattern. Good tidings to you from the man who has turned you into a working woman. Shame on him. P.

P.S. Don't you rush off without breakfast. You never know when you'll get to eat again. P2.

She had obviously missed ward walking, so Laura went to the kitchen first, amused to see all the surgeon's mates eating porridge and drinking the fragrant orange-flavored

tea she remembered from her own breakfast room at
Taunton. She smiled inwardly at their guilty looks in her
direction, but no one abandoned breakfast.

She went from ward to ward. Philemon had left notes
for her, asking her to check on one patient or another, detailing what to look for. Remembering yesterday's lesson,
she sat with another powder monkey in far worse shape
than Matthew, digging into her reserve of nonsensical
chatter to distract him from pain. She doubted her success,
but made a mental note to send Matthew to sit with him.

She spent more time with the blind and deaf man,
holding his hand, stroking it and talking to him.

"Tar can't hear ye, mum," said the man in the next bed.

"I know. It just makes me feel better," Laura told him,
not taking her eyes off her patient.

"Ye can come hold my hand."

She frowned and looked at the man. He licked his
lips, and she turned away. She still felt his eyes boring
into her back.

"As you were, gunner."

Philemon stood in the doorway, glaring at her heckler.
The man turned away, unwilling to face quiet authority
with a world of hurt in it.

"Address her as Mrs. Taunton, gunner, and give me no
cause to mention it again."

Philemon pulled up another stool and sat beside the
patient, putting his hand on his chest and then his forehead.
The patient smiled. "Sir, her hands is softer."

Philemon took Laura's other hand and put it on the
man's chest.

"After a few minutes, give him a pat, then come upstairs

to B Ward," he said. "Someone wants to see you." He stood up, his eyes shifting to the other bed. "Let me know if anyone—*anyone*—is smart with you."

She sat a few more minutes, wishing she could communicate with her patient. She glanced at the other bed, where the impudent gunner still stared at her. She said nothing to him, but forced herself not to hurry from the ward.

"I'll keep an eye on him, Mrs. Taunton," the orderly said, as she passed his desk.

She nodded and hurried up the stairs to B Ward, where her brother-in-law was chatting with one of his men. "Oliver!" she exclaimed.

In a moment, she was in his arms for a hug and a kiss on her forehead. "Has Nana given up on me?" she asked. "I took a detour in Plymouth, where…"

"…where you have been pressed into His Majesty's service," Oliver concluded. "That hug and kiss were from her. I am under orders, too." He turned to Philemon. "Now, Lieutenant, I am yours," he said, as he seated himself.

Laura sat by Matthew as the surgeon removed Oliver's bandage.

"Nana's been taking good care of you," Philemon said at last. He touched Oliver's ear. "Let's leave the bandage off now and let the air get to it." He took a jar from his apron pocket. "I compounded this for you. Apply it twice daily, and give Boney hell."

Oliver nodded as his men cheered. "First things first! Lads, the court martial went our way, and we have been given a new ship, the *Tangier,* a 46-gun frigate."

"Moving up in the world," Philemon said, pleased.

"Aye, but not to the Channel." There was no mistaking the admiration on his face as he looked around the ward at his men. "Not with some of my best gunners here! We have orders to take the *Tangier* on a shakedown cruise to Washington, D.C., United States. We're to drop off a diplomat. When I come back, I expect to find all ready to serve."

"We can see to that," Philemon said. "They'll be fit for duty."

"Except me," Matthew said to Laura in a whisper.

"I heard that, Matthew," Oliver said, coming now to sit beside his powder monkey. "My ugly ear still works." His voice was kind. "You're afraid there is no berth for you on the *Tangier?*"

Too miserable to speak, Matthew nodded.

Oliver pulled no punches, speaking to the boy as though he were an equal. *Maybe this is how leaders lead,* Laura thought. She glanced at Philemon, who was watching her. *That is how you lead, too.*

"Your gun deck days are over, Matthew, but I have a proposal. I can either discharge you from the navy and you can go to Torquay and work for Nana. Or you can join me on the *Tangier* as my steward. Nana says I need someone to watch after my clothes and see that my sleeping cot is made. You'd serve my meals, too."

"I can do that, sir?"

"That and more." Oliver patted his shoulder. "Not this trip, though. I expect you to mind the surgeon and heal as fast as you can. I don't know why you can't continue in my service, especially since I need you."

We are in the hands of a master, Laura thought. *The beauty of it is he means every word.* She looked at the men, all of whom were absorbing just what that message was, and for all she knew, resolving to get better sooner than any wounded crew that protected England.

"It's your choice, Matthew."

"Aye, aye, sir. I'll sail with you."

"Excellent. I require one more thing of my steward. He must read and write."

"I dunno how, Captain."

"You have about three months to learn."

"I can teach him."

Oliver turned to look at Davey Dabney, who, like the others, had been listening to the exchange. "You're not from the *Tireless*. What's your ship?" he asked.

"I'm foretopman Dabney of the *Excelsior,* which sunk off Basque Roads."

"After a stiff fight, according to the *Chronicle,*" Oliver replied. "I knew your late captain well. You can read and write? Of course you can. Everyone knows foretopmen are the brightest men in the service."

"Aye, sir." Davey smiled at the praise, and turned his head slowly to look at Philemon. "Lieutenant, if I'm teaching one, I can teach more."

"That can be arranged." Philemon nodded to Laura. "Mrs. Taunton, I'll provide the storeroom on this floor, and requisition tables and chairs, if you can unearth books and paper."

"Aye, sir," she said. "When we're ready, I can make the announcement throughout Block Four."

"It appears then that we will have a school, thanks to foretopman Dabney," Philemon said. "Matthew, I know you will become proficient in three months."

The boy grinned, then glanced shyly at his captain. "Sir, maybe I can learn to cipher."

"I will insist upon that, too, then," Oliver replied. "But the reading and writing come first. Lads, good day to you all. I expect nothing but good conduct and fast healing from all of you before I return from the United States. Mrs. Taunton, walk with me. As you were, men."

She took him to the kitchen. Oliver was a different man over a bowl of soup, telling her about her sister's precarious days at the Mulberry Inn, when Gran would send Nana on made-up errands to the other inns so they would feed her. Laura was again reminded how much she could have done for Nana, if only she had known of her existence sooner. She said as much to her brother-in-law, who listened with great sympathy, but shook his head.

"Laura, I must be selfish. If you had swept my beloved away to Taunton, I would never have met her. Sometimes, the best things come from the worst things."

"Perhaps you are right, but I remain skeptical," Laura admitted. "I fear I can never see our father as anyone but a dreadful man."

"He's incarcerated in Spain. It cannot be pleasant." Oliver put down his napkin. "I am back to the docks. There is much to do before we sail." He kissed the top of her head. "Laura, forgiveness is a virtue."

"Has Nana forgiven him?" Laura asked bluntly.

"Not yet. I am convinced that if you do, she will." He took another slice of bread from the plate. "Go see her if you can. She gets lonely."

She nodded, struck by the longing in his voice. "I'll visit, Oliver. As for the other, I cannot promise a miracle."

* * *

I think I can escape to see my father, Philemon thought, as he hurried downstairs. If Oliver was in Plymouth, then Dan Brittle was, too. Oliver waited outside, looking like a man with questions.

"Are we going the same way?" the captain asked.

"Only if my da is already on the *Tangier*. Rigging sail, is he?"

"You know he is."

Oliver didn't speak for a few minutes, once they left Stonehouse. Philemon glanced at him, amused to see embarrassment on Captain Worthy's face. *Let me guess,* he thought. *It must involve Nana.*

"Hemorrhoids troubling you, Captain?" he joked.

Oliver laughed out loud. "No! I have a question. Don't know how to ask it."

"Just come straight out. I doubt you'll surprise me."

"I doubt I will. Nana tells me we can…well…"

"Enjoy sexual union, even with a baby on the way?"

Oliver nodded, his face red. "I was more than happy to oblige a time or two in the past week—oh, more than that—but I don't for the world want to hurt Nana."

"You won't. Babies are well-cushioned, Captain."

"God Almighty, Phil. After a question like that, at least call me Oliver!"

"Aye, aye! Let me add this caveat." He waited until they passed a group of women carrying baskets of fish. "When you come back, I would advise against it. She'll be about one month away from her confinement by then, and you can rely on fond memories to get you through."

Oliver nodded, even as his face turned redder. "After the baby comes?"

"Give her six weeks, but I insist on a month."

They walked in silence, Philemon enjoying the sun on his face. He felt his shoulders relax; he knew that for a couple of hours, no one would come running to him for help, no one would have a complaint, and he wouldn't hear any cries of pain. He could walk with a man he considered a friend and let *him* feel the tension for a change, with his questions about love and birth. Maybe he could even ask some questions of his own. *I could do that,* he thought, *except Oliver has more to say, I think.*

"Phil, it's hard to go to sea this time. I never thought I'd say that." Oliver sat on a low stone fence and Philemon joined him. "When it's time for me to leave, she loves me even more fiercely, but she never says or does anything to stop me."

"The perfect captain's wife."

"Aye. It's harder and harder to leave, all the same."

"Oliver, you know you belong on a quarterdeck."

"I thought I did. That's what the right woman can do, I suppose."

I can understand that, Philemon thought, as they sat there. *I'd be useless now if Laura Taunton decided to return to her estate. I doubt I could roll a pill.* He shook his head at that absurd notion. *No, I could roll pills, but not happily.*

He decided to throw caution to the winds. "I think I'm in love with Lady Taunton."

"Think? Think?" Oliver chided mildly. "Are you aware how your eyes follow her? You're beyond the thinking stage. You're a gone man."

"It's wrong, isn't it? She's the widow of a baronet, and you know who my parents are as well as I do."

"This is going to sound cruel, but it's what Nana lives with, too. Laura Taunton is the illegitimate daughter of a spendthrift. She's a bastard."

"Oh, now, wait…"

"I mean it. Only in the last month or so has my darling started to think of herself first as the wife of a captain in the Channel Fleet, instead of as some care-for-nobody's by-blow. Lord Ratliffe scoured his daughters more than we know, or at least, as I have come to realize, living so intimately with one of them."

They were both silent as two ranks of schoolchildren passed them, led by a clergyman.

"I didn't know I was so obvious," Philemon said at last.

"You are to me, because I'm in love, too. A year ago, when the *Tireless* was my mistress, I probably would have just wondered why you seemed a little distracted, and put it down to bad beef."

"How do I actually *love* this woman?" Philemon asked, marveling at the absurdity of the situation. He never asked advice of anyone.

"She needs to feel useful and worthwhile. Needed. Just love her, Phil."

"She might not want to be touched by any man, after her experience with Sir James."

"Are you sure? Ever tried to be a lover?"

Philemon thought about that exquisite night with Laura, comforting her and feeling completely at ease. He looked at Oliver Worthy and saw every inch of what he was: sea captain of a fighting ship, an iron man commanding the wooden wall that protected England. Also, under the well-worn uniform was a loving husband and a man eager to be a father. *If he can, I can,* Philemon thought.

"You do know what goes where?" Oliver asked, amused.

"Better than you, Captain. I've studied females in medical school and you haven't."

Oliver threw back his head and laughed. "Those were cadavers!"

In the weeks after her brother-in-law sailed, Laura knew Philemon had told the truth. He promised her there would be nights when she was too tired to remove her shoes before collapsing on her bed and he was right.

She did manage a quick trip to Torquay with Matthew after the *Tangier* sailed. Nana's resolve had failed her completely, and she sobbed her heart out in Laura's arms. Laura held her sister gladly, coming to see that value lay in their sisterhood. The realization was a salve to her spirits, probably greater than the ones her dear Philemon compounded in his workroom.

When Nana was on an even keel again, Laura and Matthew returned to Plymouth to scour the shops for paper, pencils and primers. That day ended successfully, and not a moment too soon, because Matthew was looking the worse for wear, although he would never have admitted it.

"I'm afraid I wore him out," she told Philemon that evening, after supper was over and he was in his workroom, making plasters. He had assigned her to scraping lint and gathering the soft fabric into bags.

"He's young. He'll recover. I think the others on B were envious he escaped." Philemon mixed lead monoxide with pork lard. "Hand me the olive oil behind you. Ta." He added it slowly.

"What are you making?"

"Plasters. I'll add water and stir until it's white, then store it until I add medicine." He shook his head. "Maybe it even does some good when I warm it and spread it on a wound."

There was something in his voice. Laura touched his arm. "Who died?"

"Our blind and deaf friend." His expression hardened. "He told me to tell you 'thank'ee.'"

She swallowed, blinking back her tears. "How do you do this?" she asked, when she could speak.

"I must admit it's not easy." Without a word, he picked up her hand resting on his arm, kissing her palm and then her wrist.

She felt her breath coming faster. Tentative, she leaned forward and kissed his cheek right next to his ear, not sure she should, but knowing she must. Somehow, this was different from the peaceful night they had spent together, the one she seemed unable to erase from her mind. That kiss before she left for Taunton hadn't been her imagination, either, but still, this was different.

"Laura," he said. "Laura, help me," and kissed her lips this time.

She was as little skilled in kissing as he was, but it didn't matter. All she wanted to do was remove some of his burden of constant worry and decisions a lesser man would never make. If a kiss would help, she would do her best.

His arms went around her then, pulling her close as he continued to kiss her. His canvas apron was stiff against her, but she could feel his body stirring underneath it, even as she knew hers stirred in ways that Sir James had never touched.

They both heard running steps on the stairs at the same time. "Lt. Brittle!" someone yelled. Philemon pulled away from her, quickly removed the pot from its small flame and left her without a backward glance, running up the stairs.

Her arms were empty. He might never have been there at all.

Chapter Twelve

Laura wanted more from Philemon Brittle, but events conspired to fill every hour the surgeon possessed. After a restless night, she woke to the clang of the jetty bell. Instantly alert, she hurried into her clothes, calling to Pierre to prepare more porridge than usual.

She ran to the jetty, almost dreading the sight of so many jolly boats. So many mother's sons, she thought, as she plunged into the dockside chaos.

Philemon gestured to her with a bloody hand and she ran to his side, kneeling there. He nodded toward a canvas bag.

"It's full of compresses. Sling that over your shoulder and follow Brian. He'll tell you what to do."

She grabbed the bag even as she asked, "Am I ready for this?"

"Beyond it, Laura. You're one of my mates now."

He had no idea how that terrified her, but he had already turned away. She found Brian Aitken, Philemon's chief mate, by the water's edge. Before today, she had only been able to understand one word in ten of his thick Scots brogue. She discovered how quickly spurting blood could clear the intellect.

His face speckled with blood, Aitken hummed as he worked, probably to take his mind off what lay before him. He worked as efficiently as Philemon—probably had been trained by him—and she had no trouble keeping up. After an hour, she found some clean water and mopped the blood from his face. He surprised her by returning the favor. She had no idea she looked as ghoulish as he did.

At midmorning, when she had a second to look around, she noticed Amanda Peters, her former dresser, kneeling beside Captain Brackett. She waved to her, and Peters nodded, her hands too occupied to wave. *We've changed in a few weeks,* Laura thought. *I used to be terrified of her, and she used to fuss if my cap was set slightly askew. Imagine.*

She imitated the more experienced matrons as they turned their bloody aprons around and tied them again, then hurried back to their own blocks as the work continued indoors: shaving heads to prevent spread of lice, washing the men, finding nightshirts and beds for them, then porridge for those who could eat. Mrs. Ormes and even the scullery maid—shy at first, then useful—came upstairs to feed the wounded.

By midnight, the butcher's bill was tallied and Philemon, his eyes burning like coals in his head, gave her permission to go below. She collapsed on her bed without even removing her shoes or her bloody apron, then leaped up at dawn when the jetty bells clanged again.

So it went for a solid week, as battered ships of the Channel Fleet put in to Plymouth, discharged their wounded, revictualed, roamed the streets for unwary merchant marine seamen to snag into service, and sailed again. She was relieved that Oliver Worthy and the *Tangier* had sailed to the United States, instead of to a weary continent in flames.

Her only respite came when she stole a moment to visit Davey Dabney's classroom. He still wasn't allowed to sit upright yet, but some enterprising orderly had padded a wheeled chair and reclined the back, so he could supervise the seamen able to sit at desks and write their alphabet.

Matthew sat in front, ready to leap up and help, handing out paper and primers, and using his hand and elbow to maneuver Davey back to the ward when the hour-long lesson was done. By the end of the first week of class, the foretopman could manage an hour in the morning and another in the evening without exhausting himself. She knew Matthew was tired, too, but she saw the determination on his face.

She was standing in the doorway watching, one late afternoon, when Philemon came to stand beside her.

"Do you think Matthew will be fit to sail when Oliver returns?" she asked, not even looking over her shoulder. She knew who stood so close.

"I reckon he will. D'ye think he'll be reading and writing by then?"

She nodded. "I wish he would go to Torquay."

"I know you do. So does Nana. He's still in the navy, Laura."

"He's not even twelve!"

"So was Oliver. So was I."

"What has it got you but no sleep?" she fretted.

He put his hand on her head and gave it a little shake, then walked away. Stay with me, she wanted to ask, but knew she would only be demanding what everyone in the block wanted: more of his time.

He turned back; maybe he could read her thoughts. "I never thanked you for all your help this week."

"I'm only earning my twenty-five pounds a year."

"Do you want to help some more?"

"You know I do."

"After tomorrow's ward walk, follow me to the second floor. I'll teach you and my new orderlies how to change dressings. It's not appealing, so we'll do it before breakfast."

Philemon could have flogged himself with such talk, especially when he yearned to tell her how much he loved her. He came so close yesterday, when she was leaning against the wall outside the washroom, chamber pot in hand and too tired to move. The absurdity of declaring himself over a piss pot was not lost on him and he laughed to think about it. He sobered soon enough. There was never going to be any better time, and he'd better come to an understanding about that.

Every second of his life belonged to the Royal Navy and the men in his care. He was not a physician; there had been no reciting of the Hippocratic Oath or gowning ceremony. A mere surgeon, he had bound himself to the same rigid code of ethics that demanded he be present when required, that he do no harm, and that he surrender everything he possessed for the care of the sick and wounded; even his life, if necessary.

Where did a wife fit in? He thought of poor Owen Brackett, back at work too soon with no time to grieve, and barely time to make arrangements for his sister to take his son to her home in Gloucester. Like as not, this war would drag into another decade, and Brackett would never know his only child. They would meet awkwardly, if at all, and the tally of war would have a son and father on its list, as well as those dead in battle.

Philemon knew he didn't want a life like that, one with no time to love his wife; to lie in bed with her on chilly mornings doing nothing but talking; to spend time with their children, teaching his sons to sail in Torbay and his daughters how to weave marsh grass into mats. Still, if Laura could love him, maybe even the smallest comforts would be worth all the deprivation.

He knew she liked him. She had raised no objection that wonderful evening he fell asleep in her bed or when he kissed her as she departed for Taunton. He had been so ready to kiss her more thoroughly in his workroom that night he was making plasters and she was scraping lint. Duty had called and he had dropped everything. Since then, they had barely seen each other.

I cannot court a woman in such circumstances, he told himself that night as he dragged himself to his bedchamber. He was happy to be in his own bed, and not snatching sleep on an operating table, but dismayed that he shared it with no one. All he wanted to do was make love with Laura Taunton; to enjoy the pleasure of sweet release from all his care—he had more than most men—with her arms tight around him.

There was the matter of her unhappy marriage to aggravate the issue. True, she seemed willing enough for his hugs and touch, but what would happen if she were naked and lying under him? Would her courage fail her? Would she assume that all men were the same, or would she understand that Sir James was only a violator?

Oliver Worthy had urged him to forge ahead, but his wife hadn't been sold to pay creditors. Nana had never been alone, without any help from any source. Circumstance may have trod on Nana's dignity, but it had not shredded her to the bone.

I need to talk to Laura, he decided. He already knew he could talk to her about caring for wounded men's bodily needs. He had seen her wiping men clean from defecation who were too weak or wounded to help themselves. Aitken had showed her how to administer enemas, and she had barely flinched when a poor gunny vomited on her when he saw his own wound for the first time.

That was different. *How can I tell her that I want to love her as a true husband loves his wife, and not remind her of misery with a husband who had used her meanly in his obsession for a child, and then used her harder as he died by degrees?* To put it simply, would such a woman want anything he, an always-exhausted surgeon in the Royal Navy, had to offer? He doubted it supremely.

She was at his clbow in the morning for the ward walk. Both he and his mates had come to rely on her excellent notes and her no-nonsense questions. When she didn't understand something, Laura always asked, which often served to simplify things in his own mind.

"You're looking cheerful, Mrs. T," he commented. "I'm counting my blessings. Most ladies would want to thrash me after I had worked them like galley slaves."

"I never was too wise, Lieutenant," she said. "May you never be cursed to know the total boredom of nothing to do."

It sounded almost heavenly to him, or would, if he

could spend such a year with Laura Taunton. Still, there she was, looking beautiful, even with her hair tucked under a cap.

"You're wearing a new apron. One that fits," he said.

"It does," she agreed. "Captain Brackett told me yesterday that all the lads will feign illness to stay longer on my wards. I told him he was cheeky and he laughed. I don't think he has done that in a while."

"I doubt he has." *Go ahead,* he told himself, *flirt a little.* "You're a tonic for all of us."

My, that was tame, he thought, disgusted with himself. *Even my flirting is medical. I speak of tonic when I want to tell her like a schoolboy that I worship the ward she walks on. There I go again; I am hopeless.*

His new orderlies were waiting in A Ward, looking appropriately anxious. He decided the Marine corporal in bed four seemed the best candidate to introduce his neophytes to the world of bandage changing. He had a nice soft tissue wound in his thigh, with a simple entry and exit and nothing hanging out. The man, half dozing in that way of the wounded, looked up in alarm to see such a delegation around his bed. "Hey, now," he began, and tried to sit up.

"Corporal, as you were," Philemon ordered. "You have sufficient rank to make me think you're the best candidate to be my teaching tool. I wouldn't ask just any patient."

He glanced next at the other men in the ward. Those who were aware, were beginning to enjoy themselves. He glanced next at the ward's orderly, who wheeled a small table to the bedside. The corporal's wariness changed to something near panic.

"Corporal, I want to show these three how to change a bandage. Lie down and…"

The Marine looked from Laura to Philemon. "Beg pardon, sir, but she'll see my…my…you know."

"She might. Mrs. Taunton has been tending the wounded long enough not to be surprised, provided your…you know…isn't anything amazing."

One of the orderlies turned his bark of laughter into a cough sounding almost consumptive. "You'd best get that cough seen to, if you can find medical assistance," Philemon joked, as he pulled back the sheet. He tucked it against the man's other leg, shielding his privates. "There now. She doesn't have to be amazed, after all, Corporal." He looked at his students. "Do that whenever you can. We all like a little dignity, even those of us in George's navy."

Speaking quietly and working quickly, he took his students through the process of removing the bandage and compresses, cleaning the entry and exit wounds, and showing them how to use a syringe. "I don't mind a little pus, but too much can be painful. This is healing well. It appears that nothing of importance was hit."

"Course not, Doc. He's a Marine. There's nothing there," someone from another bed observed. "Like 'is 'ead," someone else contributed.

The patients all laughed, including the orderlies. Philemon looked at Laura out of the corner of his eye, as she struggled to maintain her composure. Even the Marine was smiling, relieved, perhaps, that nothing could be too bad if someone could joke about it.

He had them each clean the wounds and dress them as the Marine gritted his teeth and pretended he didn't mind.

When it was Laura's turn, she took a moment to wipe the perspiration from her patient's face and thank him. He melted like butter, which made Philemon smile inside.

"That is how you teach?" Laura asked, when they moved on to another ward.

"What passes for it in the navy, I think. Are you disappointed?"

She surprised him. "Quite the contrary. I'm certain the navy doesn't pay you enough."

Gratified by her flattery, he progressed through two other cases, each more difficult, teaching and coaxing courage out of his patients. One man was unconscious and behind a screen, so he could tell them how important it was not to register any emotion when they removed the bandage.

"If he were conscious, he'd be watching your face, and not his wound. No one likes to look at a wound," he assured them. "It's your turn, Mrs. Taunton."

She did as he gently directed, her concentration fierce, a frown between her fine eyebrows. She sniffed the used bandage, then set it aside. Her hands shook a bit as she pressed the syringe into the abdominal wound to draw out exudations, flinching when the unconscious man flinched. He wanted to finish for her, but that was no way to learn. After she bound the wound, she sat back, drained. It was all he could do not to touch her.

"He isn't going to live long, is he?" she whispered.

He was squatting beside her, so she didn't have to raise her voice. "No. He will probably be dead by the first watch."

She rested her hand on the man's neck. "Poor lad. He can't be over eighteen."

"Seventeen." He looked at the little group around the

bed. "When he is gone, I will do a post mortem, which you may attend. I think there is something in the wound that his surgeon aboard ship was unable to retrieve, and I want to know what it was." He stood up. "That is all we have time for today. Report to your usual stations."

Laura stayed where she was. "May I sit here with him?"

"As you wish."

He scanned the room before he left, because he did not feel easy about this ward. The orderly had told him a few days ago how cheeky one of the seamen was to Laura. He wanted to certify that tar for duty immediately, but he had a nagging wound on his upper arm that would not heal. Philemon toyed with the idea again. As usual, his head trumped his heart; the sailor wasn't ready for sea.

She sent him a note at three bells into the afternoon watch. He wanted it to contain some words of love, but it was the bald announcement that the patient had not survived the first bell. His heart went out to her as he read:

He did not die in pain, but I confess to enough of that, on his behalf. This is onerous work. LT.

Why am I doing this to such an excellent female? he asked himself later that evening as he walked to the room off the dead house, where he and Brackett performed autopsies. There lay his naked patient, dead of his wound or his surgeon. He nodded to the one orderly who cowered in a corner of the room, and sat on a stool beside the corpse, trying to understand why he drove Laura so hard, and why she let him.

I want her with me. I am so busy with duty that there is

no other way right now to accomplish my selfish desire to be with her, he decided. He allowed himself to think that maybe, just maybe, she did what he wanted because she wanted to be with him, too. It was absurd, but made him almost cheerful as he contemplated the mortal remains of a young man dead too soon.

He looked at the toe tag. "Junius Craighead," he murmured, dignifying the naked body with its grievous wound. "Able seaman. H.M.S. *Dauntless.*" He knew nothing more—not where Junius was born or raised, who his parents were, what his plans might have been, had Napoleon not decided to dominate the world.

He proceeded with the post mortem, teaching the orderly, who finally fled the scene, muttering something. Philemon wondered if he would be back in the morning.

That was when he turned around to see Laura Taunton standing there, her eyes wide and staring at Junius Craighead spread open wide. Philemon looked into her eyes and got off his stool, fearful she would faint. He noticed, instead, that she was chewing on the inside of her cheek, which she did often enough at the jetty.

He wanted to cover her eyes with his hands, but they were bloody, as usual. "Laura, you don't need to see this. I was a fool to ask."

She didn't leave, but came closer gradually, until she was standing behind him, partly hidden and clutching the back of his trousers. Her fingers were warm against the fabric at his waist and he had no objection.

"Did…did…did you find what you were looking for?"

Her voice was so low he had to lean closer to hear her. "Aye. Take a look."

She shook her head, then leaned her forehead against his back, which somehow touched him more than it aroused him. What happened then was one of the many things he appreciated about Laura Taunton. She slowly leaned around his arm and looked at the slimy scrap of cloth on the edge of the table.

"It's part of his shirt, isn't it?"

"Aye. His or someone else's. The surgeon on the *Dauntless* was able to remove the ball, but probably hadn't the time to probe a little deeper."

She made a small sound of irritation.

"Laura, be easy on my colleagues. I know this scene, because I have been in battle, when the wounded are piling up in the companionway, and everyone needs help at once. That wasn't his only problem and was likely not the fatal one. Come look."

She could not bring herself to come closer, so he gestured with a bistoury. "See there? The ball nicked his large intestine. Even God Almighty cannot help a man whose body wastes pour into his abdominal cavity. Better go into battle on an empty stomach."

Her face was close to his, so he rubbed his cheek against hers, which made her turn her face into his shirt with a sob. "How can you do this?" she asked.

"I do this because I love the human body."

"It doesn't scare you?"

He could barely hear her, but he knew what she was asking. He handed her his bistoury. "Go ahead. Have a care—it's sharp. Just lift that portion of skin. This is how you learn."

"Don't touch that corpse, Lady Taunton!"

Laura gasped and dropped the bistoury. Philemon felt the hairs on his neck rise. He turned around to see Sir David Carew, his face mottled with anger. His administrator glared at them from the doorway, but did not come closer.

"I saw the orderly run out," Sir David said, barely moving his lips. He pointed his finger. "Brittle, have you no sense? What is *she* doing in here?"

"Learning," Philemon said. He gestured toward the corpse. "You can, too, but you must come closer."

Sir David looked with utter distaste on Junius Craighead. "Never."

"So this is your first post mortem, Sir David?" Philemon asked, before he thought.

He should never have said that, even if it was true. If ever a short man towered in anger, it was the admiral. Cursing his own arrogance, Philemon could hardly blame him.

"How dare you address me that way! I will have your license pulled if I ever see anyone besides a surgeon or a mate in this room! Lady Taunton, you have gone too far," he concluded, taking Laura by the arm.

"Don't touch me!" she said, and there was nothing timid in her voice. "I am not very brave yet, but you have no idea what I have learned in here."

"And you can forget it all!" Sir David roared. He released her, only to shake his finger in her face, practically beside himself with fury. "I knew no good would come of this." He looked at Philemon then, who was wiping his hands. "She is on notice as of right now, Lieutenant. If there is one more… one more!…untoward incident, she is sacked, and you will do it! And you, Lieutenant, you… By God, if we were not shorthanded, you would be back in a fever hospital!"

He slammed the door behind him. The room was deathly quiet. Philemon shook his head. "I'm sorry, Laura. So sorry. God, why did I *say* that?"

He was so embarrassed he didn't even want to look at her, even though she stood so still, her arms around herself, shivering. He made himself look at her, and was startled by what he saw, even more than by Sir David's sudden appearance. He had thought she was afraid, but he was wrong. She was ferociously angry.

Chapter Thirteen

Stunned by her expression, Philemon washed his hands as fast as he could. Before they were even dry, he reached for her, not knowing what she would do. His heart fell when she stepped back, but she stopped with a visible effort, and willed herself calm before his eyes.

"I'll be on the landing pier," she said, and turned on her heel, closing the door more quietly than Sir David.

Unnerved, he sewed up Junius Craighead, carefully covering him with a sheet. In the morning, the dead house attendants would prepare him for burial. For one small moment, Philemon wanted to crawl under the sheet, too.

He didn't think she would be at the jetty, but she was, dangling her feet off the pier and leaning against the piling, looking so alone. He sat down beside her, still numb.

It was a long time before she spoke. "I wanted to kill him," she whispered finally. "I told myself when James died that no one would ever grab me like that again, or shake a finger in my face. It's a good thing I dropped the bistoury." She turned to look at him. "What are you going to do with me?"

He didn't hesitate. "Just this," he said, putting his arm around her waist.

She sighed with relief, which soothed him as nothing else could have.

"I don't get angry often," she said, and it sounded apologetic. "Never, in fact. He should not have grabbed me." She sobbed out loud. "No one should do that to a woman!"

The night was warm, but he felt himself go cold. She wasn't speaking of Sir David. He kept his arm around her. "It's almost pleasant here," he said, after a long pause for both of them to collect themselves. "I'm surprised."

She seemed to welcome the change of subject. "I thought if I came here tonight, I might not dread it so much when the jetty bell rings."

She shivered, and he tightened his arm around her. At the same time, he realized it was all too much for her. She had enough to bear without tackling ward blocks full of wounded men, constant demands, no sleep, the dead and dying, endless war, and now an administrator who would be watching her every move. *You cannot possibly want a man who would further complicate your life,* he thought miserably.

"Laura, I think you should go to Torquay." The words felt as if they were wrenched out of his stomach.

She shook her head vehemently, then turned to watch him. "Only if you do not want me around here anymore," she said. "Only if you don't really…"

She couldn't say it. He could, though. "If I don't really love you? Laura, that day will never come. I believe I've loved you since I saw you in Nana's sitting room."

"Even when I have more defects than any sane man would willingly shoulder?"

"Would a sane man live the life I'm living?" he asked, in turn. "Laura, you have every right to be furious with Sir David, with Sir James, with your father. It's no crime to want to protect yourself."

"Then why couldn't I?"

It was the cry of the ages, and it clanged in his brain like a gong. What could he say? He had to try. "Women aren't taught to fight back, not when people they know they should trust betray them. Or so I think." He kissed her hair. "As for your defects, have you ever considered that maybe no one sees them but you?"

She looked at him in utter disbelief, and he could think of nothing to say. Gradually she relaxed against him. "I should trust you, shouldn't I?" she asked at last. "I wish I did."

Be light about this, he told himself. "No woman wants to marry an idiot," he said. "Did you *hear* what I said to Sir David? I...I asked him if he had ever seen a post mortem before! What an arrogant ass I am."

She looked at him seriously. "You're talking about marriage, after I have told you what a bad bargain I am?"

"I love you! And I've just told you what a jackass I am. I'm not exactly an answer to a woman's prayers."

She couldn't help but smile, which pleased him more than if she had flung her arms around his neck and knocked him backward in the grass—which sounded good, too.

"Do you think he has seen a post mortem before?"

"I have no idea," he replied, laughing. "Do you love me?"

"I would like to."

He helped her to her feet. "Here we are, two sillies, sitting on the landing pier at two in the morning while that Marine guard over there probably wonders if we are spies! Give me a kiss, Laura."

He didn't know if she would, but she did, holding his face in her hands and touching his lips lightly with hers. She did it again. He was in heaven. He walked her back to Block Four, ready to see her to the kitchen, when he heard someone calling him.

"Sounds like duty," he told her, slipping his hand from around her waist. "It's just twenty steps to the kitchen."

"I can get there by myself."

He could see her hesitate, too shy to say anything. He kissed her cheek and ran to the orderly.

Except for the lights kept burning on each floor, Building Four was dark. Her mind on Philemon, she hurried to the kitchen and stepped back with a gasp when a man rose up from a crouch by the door.

She had nothing in her hands for self-defense, but stood her ground, drawing herself up as tall as she could. "Who are you?" she demanded, in her frostiest voice, even as her knees practically knocked together.

"Billy from C Ward. I'm hungry," he said, coming closer.

Her lips tight together, Laura looked closer, disturbed to see the man who had been so rude to her, and whom Philemon had chided, as well.

"Breakfast is at six bells, Billy. You can wait."

"Aw, mum!"

"Go on."

He came closer, but she refused to budge. The seaman

smiled, showing a jagged row of teeth. His breath was foul and she wondered why she had flinched at the sight of Junius Craighead. This living man was worse.

"Go back to bed, Billy, and I'll overlook this." She kept her voice low because she knew it would betray her in an undignified squeak if she talked louder. What she hadn't expected was the intensity of it.

Apparently it impressed Billy. "I can't make it up those stairs by meself," he whined, defeated.

"Yes, you can," she snapped. "You got here, didn't you?"

They stared at each other; Billy blinked first. Clutching his scrofulous arm as though begging for sympathy, he mounted the steps easily enough, stopping once to give her a look that would have toppled her if she hadn't been leaning on the doorknob.

Inside the kitchen, she went to the knife drawer and stood there a long moment, just looking at the blades before she closed the drawer.

She went to her room, where she tugged her armchair in front of the door and huddled on her bed, knees close to her chin, until she heard four bells, and Pierre and the scullery maid moving around in the kitchen. She allowed herself to close her eyes, even if it was only for thirty minutes. She wanted to think about what Philemon had said to her, but all she saw when her eyes closed was that man rising up from the dark, coming toward her.

She knew it was insane, but she felt that same bath of fear that covered her when Sir James opened her door and came to her bed, terrifying her with his demands, reminding her all over again how friendless she was. It was as if nothing had changed.

* * *

She's as tired as I am, Philemon told himself as he, Aitken and Laura finished their morning ward walk. *I hope my declaration of love is not the cause of her discomfort. No, she is just tired.*

He decided he would tell himself that, even as she gave him a wan smile and shook her head when he suggested they adjourn to the kitchen for tea, a ritual that was fast becoming his favorite luxury of the day—he had so few.

"It will only take a moment," he said, trying to cajole her. He moved closer and she backed away, sending a chill down his spine.

"No! I have said I do not want any tea now," she declared. She put her hand to her head in a gesture of distraction. "It is nothing, Lieutenant. I think I will check on Davey's classroom."

He looked around. No one else stood in the corridor, but she had called him Lieutenant anyway. Something had changed in the three hours since he had kissed her and said good-night; what, he didn't know. He hadn't time to delve into the matter, but he knew enough about human nature to know when someone preferred to be left alone.

"Very well, Mrs. Taunton," he said formally. "Let me know if you need anything."

To his further unease, her eyes immediately filled with tears. She said nothing, but fled up the stairs, her face stark. *How do I read you?* he thought miserably. *I know how your body works, maybe better than you do, but I do not know how to reach your heart.*

It was a disquieting thought, and he tried to drown it in work, which had never failed him before. It failed him now. How many times had he asked Aitken to repeat himself that afternoon, when his mate was explaining a simple procedure? And when Aitken finally asked him what the matter was, he had no answer.

The month passed in an odd way. He seldom bothered to glance at a calendar, but the air was crisper now, and he knew autumn was here. He was busy every minute and Laura Taunton was right there to help, not flinching from any misery he threw her way. He didn't work her harder because he wished to increase her obvious turmoil, but simply because he needed her skills.

There was Napoleon, always Napoleon. Wellington's steady march through Portugal and back into Spain meant more work for everyone, as simple as that. The sound of the jetty bell—a demand that could not be ignored—was becoming almost a daily occurrence. The sound reminded him how puny he was, how swept along he was by the fortunes of war. Whatever pride that had made him speak so arrogantly to Sir David was gone now.

Sir David Carew harassed him now with daily memos, urging more economy in his expenses on Block Four, even as he sent his loblolly boy around for free meals from Pierre's kitchen. Philemon memoed back, reminding him that Lady Taunton was making up whatever difference there was to the budget, but the memos continued.

The administrator watched Laura all the time now, standing at his window overlooking the jetty as they worked to save lives. Philemon was forced to return her to mere hand-holding with the wounded at the wharf, to keep Sir David at bay. The ward block was a different matter;

the administrator stayed away, and he could use Laura to the extent of her growing skill. She never complained.

Between Laura Taunton's distance, overwork and administrative tomfoolery, Philemon Brittle was an unhappy man. His mood only worsened with the disturbing case of Gunner Alex Small in D Ward.

"There's something else in his abdomen," Philemon said one morning, announcing the obvious to his staff, who had already reached the same conclusion days ago, he was sure. "I've probed until I fear to do harm."

Aitken rewarded him with a wry smile of understanding. Laura continued sitting beside the gunner, who was conscious and watching her for any sign of anxiety. Philemon was pleased with the way she revealed nothing about her own feelings. He had trained her well; more likely, hard duty as Lady Taunton had trained her even better.

As he watched, she touched the gunner's inflamed skin, feeling his swollen abdomen gently, watching his face for distress as she pressed and released as he had taught her, trying to divine the place of trouble.

"If we could see into your body, Gunner," she said, addressing her patient as though he was the only man in existence.

"Aye, mum, you'd see lots of grog, hardtack and old machine parts, for all we know," he joked.

Philemon found her in D Ward several times a day for the next week, as Gunner Small began to drift in and out of consciousness. Late one evening, when the ward was quiet in sleep, he risked a casual hand on her shoulder. She did not lean against him as he craved, but she did incline her head in his direction.

"You cannot probe again?" she whispered.

"I dare not. I cannot do him harm." He crouched by her stool. "If he is even slightly conscious, his abdominal muscles tense up when I insert a probe. I might as well drill through a brick wall."

"If he is unconscious?"

"It is too brief." He held up his hand. "I could wish for longer fingers, because I can't *feel* anything with the probes."

"And you're the best there is," she said softly.

He shook his head, but would never have denied what her praise meant to his starving heart. "Ask any physician. I'm just a surgeon."

"You're far more," she said, touched his knee and left the ward.

He sat by the gunner until he had collected himself, then left his list of instructions with the orderly, and trudged to his quarters. He stared at his bed a long time, debating whether to strip or take off his shoes; he decided to strip. He put himself between the sheets with a sigh, too tired to extinguish his lamp.

He woke to footsteps on the stairs, which didn't surprise him overmuch. During these days of emergency, he left his front door unlocked, so his mates and orderlies could pound upstairs and shake him awake. He lay there listening, and realized it was Laura Taunton.

She came up the stairs quietly, but with no speed, almost as though she didn't want to be doing what she was doing. *And what is that?* he asked himself, wishing he had at least put on his nightshirt.

His door was open, but she knocked on it.

"Come in, Laura," he said, hoping his voice wouldn't squeak like an adolescent.

She stood in the middle of his room, carefully clothed in her dark dress and neat apron, with her hair in its cap.

"Hold up your hand."

Mystified, he did as she asked, sitting up and tucking his sheet carefully around his bare body. She came closer and put her hand against his.

"My fingers are longer than yours."

"I've told you that," he said, not moving his palm from hers. "I don't have surgeon's hands." He chuckled, trying to break the tension building inside him. "Would you be disappointed in me if I said that your hands were the first thing I noticed about you?"

"I would say you don't know much about impressing ladies."

He was relieved with her lighthearted answer. She kept her palm against his, and he felt her hand begin to tremble slightly.

"I want to probe Gunner Small. I have to try, because he is dying and I cannot bear it."

He lowered his hand, looking at the tears sliding down her cheeks.

"Perhaps I can feel something in there you cannot. And if I can, perhaps I can reach just a half inch farther with a probe and retrieve it."

"And if you cannot?" It seemed heartless to say, but she had to know what defeat might feel like. Heaven knew, he had experience with that.

"I will at least know we have tried everything we know to do."

"You'll have to work as fast as you can."

He was all business now, even as he sat naked by the person he loved most in the world. "Wait for me downstairs."

"No. Let us not give Sir David anything to look for if he's watching out of some window! Dreadful man. I will meet you on D Ward."

By the time he got to the ward, the orderly had already placed a screen around Small's bed. Laura had put his instruments in hot water. She stood there, looking down at the gunner in what was an imitation of his own stance before beginning surgery, whether she realized it or not.

"Give us all the light you can," Philemon told the orderly.

"Might you wait until morning?" the orderly asked, as he took the lamp from his own desk.

"We cannot." He took the orderly by the arm. "If word gets out that Mrs. Taunton has been assisting me, we will be in trouble." He glanced down at the gunner and listened for a moment to his labored breathing. "As it is, we may already be too late."

"Aye, sir, I understand."

While the orderly went in search of more light, Philemon took his longest probe from the water, dried it, and set it on a clean cloth. He took her hand.

"What am I feeling for?"

"I have no idea," he replied honestly. "Could be a piece of bone from someone else's body—he was standing next to the second lieutenant. More than likely it's cloth from his own shirt."

"Like Junius Craighead?"

He nodded. "The ball's trajectory goes down. I've been thinking about this. You might want to stand on the other side of him and lean over him. I never did that, but it might be a better angle."

She put her lips next to the gunner's ear. "Alex, we're going to try one more time. I'll do my best not to hurt you."

"I don't think he can hear you," Philemon said, touched by her concern.

The gunner muttered something and his eyelids flickered. "Well, I'm proved wrong," Philemon said. "Laura, you'd wake the dead."

Her eyes were troubled. "I never want to do that."

While the orderly was setting up the lights, Philemon removed the bandage and pad, sniffing it. "No putrefaction yet, that I can tell," he murmured. "I'll take off the adhesive and widen the entry as much as I dare. Let me syringe out what I can of the exudations."

He worked quickly as Laura watched, her lips tight. He could tell she was nerving herself. When he finished—the gunner barely groaned—and the area behind the screen was as light as possible, Laura walked to the other side of the bed.

"Roll him on his side," she requested, and he obeyed, steadying the gunner.

"Just ease your finger down."

"He's resisting," she muttered. Perspiration was already springing up on her forehead; he wiped it with his apron. She leaned farther over and pressed harder. Gunner Small groaned out loud and Philemon saw her tears. Then he noticed the gunner's shoulders relaxing.

"Blessed syncope, my dearest," Philemon said. "He's unconscious. Work fast. Wiggle your finger around. Press in harder."

"Nothing," she gasped. "It's such a jumble in there."

"Try your middle one," he ordered.

"Roll him back."

She wiped her hand on her apron and eased in the other finger, bearing down as hard as she dared, leaning over the gunner. He watched her face, noting her frustration, then held his breath as her expression changed.

"I feel something."

"Can you tell what it is?"

"I don't…little strands of metal and more fabric."

He knew what it was. "It's part of that lieutenant's epaulet. Can you snag any of it?"

She took her finger out and held out her hand. He slapped a probe in it. Slowly she drew out the probe, then swore in exasperation.

"I had it, but I dropped it."

He took the probe from her, retrieving the metal where she had dropped it, farther along the bullet's abdominal path. Without even a word necessary between them, they worked for several minutes, Laura angling out the scraps as far as she could, then letting him take them out the rest of the way, because of his experience in retrieval. In less than five minutes, they had a small pile of metal shards and slimy cloth.

Then she was through. "I can't feel anything else except—oh my goodness—his intestines?"

When she removed her bloody hand, he put his nose right at the wound's opening. "No bowel smell. It could be our gunner is luckier than Junius Craighead."

Laura eyed the miniscule pile of detritus. "How will we know?"

"If he lives."

Wordlessly, they washed their hands in the same basin. She must have looked as spent as she felt, because Philemon dried her hands for her, then untied her apron. She could barely hold her arms out in front for him to remove it.

"Why do I feel so exhausted?" she asked. "What we did went quickly."

"I never understand it, either," he replied as he removed his apron and tossed both aprons in the corner of the washroom. They started down the stairs. "No teacher of mine could ever explain it." He tugged her down to sit with him on the bottom step. "Don't laugh, but maybe it has something to do with playing God." He glanced at her.

"I'm not laughing," she assured him. "Please go on."

He nudged her with his shoulder, maybe trying to lighten his own mood. "There's something almost, well, spiritual about holding a life in your hand."

He took her hand in his, turned it over, kissed the palm then put it back in her lap. "How did the Lord do it in six days, Laura? No wonder he took Sunday off. I wish we could."

It was good to laugh and go the rest of the way downstairs by herself, because she didn't feel alone.

Chapter Fourteen

Philemon had said he would sit beside Gunner Small for the rest of the night. Laura walked slowly down the stairs, wanting nothing more than to go to sleep until the war was over.

Since her encounter with Billy, she never approached the kitchen late at night without a quickening of breath. She looked around; no one was in sight. She opened the door, knowing there was less reason for silence than usual. Mrs. Ormes and Pierre had returned to Taunton for what Philemon nicknamed a "punitive expedition" against the linen presses and kitchen there. The place in Block Four was practically hers, if she discounted Lillian, the scullery maid.

Laura did not light her lamp because the moon shone brightly enough through the bars on the window. She left her clothing in a pile and crawled into bed in her chemise, her eyes on her pillow. She thought worrying over Gunner Small might keep her awake, but she knew he was in good hands with Philemon.

Laura pillowed her cheek on her hand. *I need to explain*

to Philemon why I have been so remote, she thought. *He probably thinks I am angry at him, and nothing is further from the truth.* She sighed, knowing she would have to explain how Billy frightened her, and reminded her of Sir James, and that would never do. She knew it was time to say something. "Tomorrow," she murmured, "if the damned jetty bell will be silent."

She slept, but not long. She wasn't sure what woke her. She had not pulled the draperies, and the moon shone into her room, but it wasn't the first time she had forgotten. It was something more. She listened. Someone else was in the room.

She wanted to scream, but she knew only the scullery maid would hear, and she was only eight. Suddenly, a hand snaked under the covers and grabbed her ankle. Terrified, she screamed and jerked back, as Billy rose from the floor by her bed and pinioned her to the mattress.

How could an invalid be that strong? She struggled, trying to kick him with her free foot, but in a second he was kneeling on her legs, trapping her. She tried to push him off, going through every nightmare imaginable, re-living moments she thought she had forgotten, so frightened that she feared her bowels would turn to liquid.

Her struggles only caused her chemise to ride up to her waist. Billy looked down as she thrashed. "You've made this so easy, mum. Do you give the bumpkin surgeon such a hard time, or is that what he likes?"

"Damn you," she managed to say, before he slapped her, then leaned closer and pressed his arm across her shoulder and throat, making her light-headed, and at the same time, giving her fingers nothing to grasp.

"Open wide, mum," he said, then laughed. "Not yer mouth, you stupid cow! We can do that later, if ye prefer."

She sobbed and pleaded, not even sure that she was saying words, in her agony to get away. Horrified, she stared as he fumbled with the buttons on his trousers, kneeing her legs farther apart as she fought to keep them together. He raised his arm to slap her again. She closed her eyes, turning away from the blow she knew was coming, and the nightmare to follow.

Before he finished with his buttons, something heavy clanged against Billy's skull. He catapulted off the bed, leaving her free to leap away from the bed.

"Lillian!" she cried, knowing it couldn't be anyone else, but horrified because the scullery maid was in as great danger as she. Lillian stood in the doorway, her eyes huge. Confused, Laura looked around, then grabbed Lillian to push her away. Billy tried to rise, as Davey Dabney, breathing hard, clubbed him again with the pan.

"Davey, you'll hurt yourself!" she shrieked. "Lillian, run to D Ward and get Lt. Brittle!"

Lillian darted away. Laura pried Davey's fingers from the pan and put her arm under his good shoulder, pulling him into the servants' hall. She sat him down and ran to the knife drawer, where she yanked out one of Pierre's wickedest tools. She handed it to him, then grabbed another knife for herself. Her hand shook so badly that she set it down, thinking herself more menace than help.

"Mrs. Taunton, are you all right?" Davey's voice, with its rusty whisper, was the most wonderful sound she had heard.

She nodded as she stared at the open door to her room,

wondering when Billy would rise. "Davey, you're my hero for ever and ever."

"I owed you, mum," he said simply.

She came around the table toward him, trying to see his neck in the gloom. She touched it, dreading to feel blood, but there was nothing except adhesive under her fingers. "Oh, Thank God! Let's get you…"

His face grim, Philemon ran into the servants' hall, gripping one of his capital knives like a seaman boarding an enemy vessel. Matthew was right behind, and all the ambulatory men on B Ward. She sat down, relieved, then suddenly conscious of her torn chemise. Her right eye was already closed and her cheekbone was starting to throb.

True to his training, Philemon looked first at Davey, calm and composed, his hand in Laura's.

"I'm fine, sir. Just tired."

"Thank you from the bottom of my heart," Philemon said, not even trying to mask his emotions. He ran his hand over Laura's arm. "Anything broken?"

She shook her head. "Will I get a black eye?"

"You have one now." He fingered her cheekbone, wincing when she winced. "Anything else?"

She shook her head again. "No, thanks to Davey. Philemon, it was Billy from the second floor." Her breath started to come in short gasps. "He tried to…"

"I know," Philemon said, looking around. "Where is he?"

"I bashed him with a pan Lillian handed me," the foretopman said. "*She's* your hero, Mrs. Taunton. She was ready to clobber him." He blew out the breath in his cheeks. "No telling what he would have done to her, too."

Laura glanced at the scullery maid, who blushed and slipped farther into the shadows.

"I suppose I had better look at him," Philemon said, not even hiding his reluctance. His glance took in the other patients crowded in the room. "Two of you who can walk the farthest, rouse the Marine guard. Matthew, I think that's you and Delaney. Don't rush if you feel light-headed."

He went into her bedroom, coming out a few minutes later with a blanket, which he draped around her bare shoulders. "You don't need to go in there."

"I couldn't."

He rested his hand on her shoulder, while he quietly instructed the men to go back to their beds. "Slow on the stairs, lads," he said. "I'll be up to check on you soon." He shook his head in disbelief. "What a puny phrase 'thank you' is."

Davey Dabney sat still. "Beg pardon sir, but I'm not leaving until that villain is in the brig."

"Not the brig," Laura said.

"The brig," Philemon repeated. "I'll recommend he be flogged around the fleet and I'll start it."

"He'll die!"

"If he's lucky," he said, tightlipped. His expression changed. "Davey, how did you know?"

"It was something Billy said a month ago on his ward. One of the men in my reading class told Matt and he told me. Just threats, but we started watching out for Mrs. Taunton. Seems he's been coming down here and just standing in the shadows. We just sat on the stairs."

"No wonder you're so tired," she murmured, ashamed she had not said something a month ago. "Philemon, it's my fault."

He shook his head wearily. "Don't take the sins of the world on your shoulders."

When Matt and Delaney came into the room, helped by two Marines, Philemon jerked his head to indicate her room. One came out immediately.

"Lieutenant, he doesn't look so good."

"No, he doesn't," Philemon said drily. "I might wander over to the brig later for a look. Or I might not, depending on how I feel."

Laura tugged on his arm. "You can't mean that!"

"I most sincerely do. I doubt Hippocrates would argue." He followed the Marine into her bedroom. "Take him under his arms and by his legs, men."

"Aye, aye, sir," one Marine said, making no attempt to hide his doubt.

"Turn your head, Mrs. Taunton. He's not a pretty sight."

When the Marines left with their prisoner, Philemon put his arms on Delaney and Matt's shoulders. "Help Davey to his bed. Tell the orderly to watch him closely. I hope you didn't do yourself any damage, Davey."

"I'd do it again, sir," was the quiet reply.

"I know you would." He watched them leave the room, then called after the powder monkey. "Matthew, tell the orderly on D Ward to sit with the gunner, then come back down and make yourself comfortable here until morning. I'm taking Mrs. Taunton to my quarters, but I won't have Lillian left alone. Can you do all that?"

"Aye, aye, sir!" Laura heard the pride in Matt's voice.

When the room was quiet, he just sat there for the longest time. Laura's heart sank. *I have been so foolish*, she thought, berating herself.

"I'm sorry, Phil."

"Stop apologizing for what's not your fault," he snapped.

She could see he was instantly sorry for his outburst. He held out his hand. "Let's go home, Laura. You're not going to stay here."

"I must. How can I earn my twenty-five pounds?" she asked, trying to lighten the oppression in the room.

"It's over. The Marines will make their report and it will go directly to Sir David Carew, as it should. It's the last excuse he needs to sack you. I don't think he'll find out about how you saved a life tonight. I wish he could know, because you're easily as talented as my mates."

"But we were right to try."

"Aye. Trouble is, men like Sir David don't think large." He sighed. "Maybe no one does."

When Matt returned, Philemon made sure Lillian was tucked in her bed off the scullery. He took Laura's pillow and made Matt comfortable in the chair where Mrs. Ormes usually sat.

He wrapped the blanket tighter around her, and walked her to his quarters, his arm at her waist. He took her directly upstairs and into the bedroom she had occupied before she moved to the ward block. He went into his room briefly and returned with a nightshirt. He slid her chemise down and she dutifully stepped into his nightshirt, acres too large.

He pulled the coverlets back. "Get in."

She did as he said. He went slowly down the stairs and returned with warm water in a basin. Sitting on her bed, he dabbed at her cheekbone, then told her to lie down so he could place a compress over her eye. When he finished, he stood up, but she tugged him down. "Don't leave me."

She could tell he was surprised. "Are you certain?"

He took off his shoes when she nodded. "We did this before, didn't we? That was the nicest sleep I ever had."

"I'm tired of being alone. I'm tired of being afraid," she said, as he slid in beside her and lay on his back, gathering her close to his heart. "May I talk to you?"

"As a doctor?" She could almost hear him thinking, hesitating. "As someone who loves you?"

It was her turn to pause, wanting to put her arm around his neck, afraid to.

"Talk to me as someone who loves you," he whispered. "I've watched my parents through the years, and I know how a good man acts. Da wasn't always at sea."

That was all she needed. She put her arms around his neck and cried until his shirt was soggy. He did nothing more than hold her close.

"Why am I crying?" she asked, when she could speak.

"Well, for starters… Damn that man!"

"Which one?" she asked, and he pulled her closer.

"You've seen so much in the past few months," he said, when he could trust his voice. "It overwhelms me, and I've been at this business for nearly twenty years. It's not just Billy, is it? Maybe you're crying because people are valuing you as the excellent woman you are, and you don't quite believe them." He put his finger to her lips when she started to protest. "It's true, Laura. We all know it, but until you believe it, it won't matter."

She nestled closer and he obligingly pulled her into the hollow of his shoulder. "I know it is childish to wish something away, but I wish none of this had ever happened."

"So do I." He propped himself up on his elbow, the

better to see her. "There is something impressive in all this, Laura. Let me point it out to you as both your doctor and as Philemon Brittle. In all the hell that men have put you through, no one ravaged your goodness or your character. They wounded you, but there was no fatal blow." He kissed her. "I'll stay with you until you're asleep, but then I have to go back to Building Four."

She closed her eyes. There was something else she had to say, and in the dark with her eyes closed, she might find the courage. "I know I have been distracted in the past month, and I know you have been wondering if it is because you told me you loved me."

He nodded, then kissed the top of her head. "Philemon might think so, but Surgeon Brittle suspects there is more involved."

"The surgeon's right. You haven't proposed to me yet, but if you do and I say yes and marry you, I'm not sure I have enough courage to...be much of a wife," she finished in a rush.

He kissed her head again. She strained to hear any hesitation in his voice when he finally spoke, but there was none, not even to ears listening for it. "What irony. Time either kills or heals. If we surgeons can get to the problem soon enough, time heals. If we can't, it kills. As for you, dearest, you're on the mend. I know it, but it remains for you to discover it. As a husband, I'm ready to give you all my love, but only on your time. Marry me, Laura. We have time."

It was her turn to prop herself up and really look at the man next to her. "I should say yes, shouldn't I?"

"I think so, considering that I love you and have a suspicion that you love me."

"I do." She touched his face, pleased with the way he automatically kissed her hand. "You're telling me the truth?"

"Dearest, I only lie to hospital administrators, and only when it's for their own good."

"Then I say yes," she said, and kissed him. "Or aye, aye."

Chapter Fifteen

Philemon was back in the morning while she still lay in bed, hugging her knees to her chin in a tight ball and shivering, even though the room was sunny and a pleasant fire crackled in the hearth.

She heard him in his room, opening and closing drawers, trying to be quiet, but failing utterly when he stumbled over something and muttered a pithy oath she had heard a time or two in the ward block. She smiled in spite of herself, and gradually relaxed.

She sat up, but wanted to lie down again to stop the throbbing in her cheek. When the pain subsided, she draped her blanket around her and padded next door. She raised her hand to knock, then thought better of it, and backed away.

He must have heard her anyway, and opened the door, a clean shirt in his hand. "I was trying to be quiet," he whispered.

"Is someone *else* around here still asleep?" she whispered back, which made him laugh and pull her inside.

He sat her on his bed, which had not been slept in.

"Close your eyes if you can't bear the sight of a goose-flesh back," he warned her. "Lord, it's cold in this room." He took off his shirt and put on the clean one, keeping his back to her while he unbuttoned his trousers and tucked in his shirttails. "That was simple," he said, turning around. "With the addition of one clean shirt, Lt. Philemon Daniel Brittle has successfully managed to eliminate sleep entirely from a typical day. I think I shall write a paper for the Royal Society, if I can stay awake long enough."

"This is for my benefit, isn't it?" she asked with a smile.

"Certainly," he replied, sitting beside her. "I would do just about anything to hear you laugh. Now, the good news—Gunner Small is still on this side of the topsoil."

She leaned her head against his shoulder, closing her eyes in relief.

"No, it's not funny," he said, his arm around her. "There was nothing amusing about last night."

"Must I go to Torquay?"

"Aye. I'm afraid for your safety. You were lucky last night."

She couldn't argue with that, even though the events seemed to lose their focus, cradled in the arms of a man she adored. "It's better if Davey Dabney doesn't feel obligated to watch over me."

He went back to his clothespress, hunting for a neck cloth this time. When he found it, he held it out to her. She put it around his neck and tied it, then handed him his waistcoat from the chair.

"Can't you take a few minutes to sleep?" she asked.

"No. Walk me downstairs."

She did, not wanting to let him out of her sight because

she did not know when she would see him again. He sensed her reluctance and sat with her on the bottom step.

"I'll certify Matthew for release this morning. Take him with you. Nana wants to see him, and he can convalesce in Torquay. I already arranged for a post chaise for noon. You'll be with Nana by nightfall."

She clutched his hand as he started to rise. "You'll come and see me soon?"

"How could I do otherwise?" He gently pried her fingers from his. "Captain Brackett is trying to arrange for two more surgeons. We're far too busy, thanks to our Corsican friend."

"Mrs. Ormes and Pierre are due back today," she told him as she walked him to the door. "I know she will be happy to continue her work here, as long as you feel she is needed. And Pierre and Lillian, of course."

He nodded. "I won't say no." He opened the front door, then closed it quickly, taking her in his arms and kissing her as she clung to him. "Dear, dear lady," he crooned. "I'll come as soon as I can."

She was sitting on her bed later, staring at her open trunk, when Aunt Walters came upstairs with her freshly washed linen.

"Lady Taunton, things are looking up," she said as she put it in the trunk. "Think what help you'll be to Mrs. Worthy."

The tears started then. "When will I see Philemon again, and him so busy?"

Aunt Walters hugged her. "My nephew won't be a stranger at Torquay."

Laura dried her eyes, grateful for a task as prosaic as packing. As a consequence, when Sir David Carew knocked on the door later and demanded to see her, she was calm and ready for anything.

It was a brief interview. Barely looking her in the eye, he railed at her over her dangerous course in trusting seamen who were little better than felons and not worthy of her attention, in the first place. As he blathered on, she thought of David Dabney, weak but determined, standing over Billy, and Matthew and the others watching out for her when she didn't even realize it. These were no felons.

She had heard enough. She stood up, which had the felicitous result in stopping the flow of words. "Sir David, I am returning to Torquay to stay with my sister, Mrs. Captain Worthy."

"Not to Taunton?"

"No. It was never a home to me, Sir David," she said simply. "I prefer to be with my relatives."

He looked at her, as if trying to decide what to say. "Lady Taunton, isn't Mrs. Worthy the granddaughter of an innkeeper?"

There it is, she thought. *The old hypocrite has probably been wondering how a baroness is related to someone as common as Nana Worthy.* Since she was leaving, why keep him in the dark?

"Nana and I are the natural daughters of William Stokes, Viscount Ratliffe, late undersecretary of the Admiralty and now in a Spanish prison. I believe he is thought to be a hero. Nana and I are his bastards."

Sir David stepped back as though she had shot him. *"You?"*

"Yes. When I wash and put on a good dress, it's hard to tell, isn't it?"

"Lady Taunton!"

"Don't be shocked. It happens in the best of families."

She thought he would leave then, but he had more to say. "This must explain Lt. Brittle's odd attraction to you. Considering your origins now, and his, of course, it's hardly surprising."

She held her breath, far more concerned about mention of her surgical assistance last night that went beyond the bounds of any matron, than the aspersions he was throwing about. "Come, sir. I have surrendered my position at Stonehouse. What Lt. Brittle does is his business."

"No, madam, it is not," Sir David shot back. "He belongs to the Royal Navy."

"And you are lucky to have him," she replied, just as quickly. "His private life is his own, though. Even a warrant from the Navy Board can't take that away." She smiled, which only made Sir David turn redder than he already was. "We're both quite common, probably as common as the seamen you are forced to endure."

Sir David glowered at her, and she gazed back serenely, even though her insides churned.

"I see I have overstayed my welcome."

What welcome? she thought. "I'm leaving, Sir David," she reminded him gently. "Let me go in peace."

Laura and Matthew arrived on Nana Worthy's doorstep after dark, with a howling autumn wind to blow them up the front steps. Nana, visibly much more pregnant, was only two steps behind the housekeeper. She flung her arms open wide for Laura, then laughed as she stood sideways so they could embrace.

Cares don't melt, Laura told herself as she reached for her sister. *Do they?* She kissed Nana, then indicated Matthew. "He will be useful, because Lt. Brittle told him he is the captain's steward-to-be and on duty the moment he signed his release papers from Stonehouse. Yes, Nana, Matthew signed his own papers. He can write."

Nana beamed at the powder monkey, who clutched his knit cap in his fist, eyes proud. "You will be an excellent steward, Matthew. I will show you how the captain likes his coffee. Come in, you two. I have been hungry for you both."

Philemon was not prepared for the sadness that gutted him when he knew Laura would never ward walk with him again. Never before had he been less content in what most men would have considered an odious occupation, but one that ordinarily gave him deep satisfaction. He knew how much he wanted Laura Taunton. He also wanted no one to know, because it would ruffle his usually sanguine composure.

Or so he thought. Comfort came from an unexpected corner. A week after Laura's departure, when October blew itself into November, he was sitting by Gunner Small, who was alert now and looking around for breakfast.

Captain Brackett wasn't due on deck until hours later, but suddenly there he was, pulling up another stool and joining him beside the gunner's bed. Brackett looked with interest at Small's abdomen, no longer red and swollen, and pressed on it gently, as pleased as Philemon to see the drainage pale now and not full of infection.

"Gunner, you have more lives than a cat," Brackett commented.

"Dunno about that, sir, but I'm fair hungry enough to eat one."

Philemon handed Small's chart to the orderly. "I've pre-scribed a moderate diet that does not include cat. Let's see what your bowels will do in the next few days." He turned to Brackett. "What's the matter? Are you tired of sleep?"

The surgeons walked into the corridor and leaned their elbows on the railing, their typical consultation pose. Brackett just looked at him for a long moment. Philemon felt his heart sink.

"Owen, tell me Sir David isn't on your case, too, about what happened?" he asked softly.

"No, that's your purgatory. I hear he scraped you over like barnacles on knuckles for allowing Lady Taunton into a post mortem."

Philemon winced. "He swore to put a letter so big in my file that not even the most nearsighted member of the Navy Board could overlook it."

Brackett frowned. "He's a bastard, is little Davy."

The surgeons contemplated the view of the stairwell again. Brackett spoke softer. "I hear Lady Taunton removed the detritus from Gunner Small. Just a rumor, mind."

"She had the surest hand. He's alive because of her. Not a word, though."

More contemplation over the railing. Philemon couldn't think of anything to say to his colleague that would begin to express his own misery, without reminding the newly widowed captain of his own loss.

"I've requested two more surgeons and four mates," Brackett said. "Little Davy moaned about expenses, but he agreed. When the first one arrives, I'm putting you on leave for two weeks, but you'll be lucky to get one. Marry that lady."

Philemon glanced at his superior, then looked down the stairs again. "You're the one needing leave."

"I had mine, thanks to you, Phil," was Brackett's quiet reply. "You gave me two weeks to bury my wife and make arrangements for my son, when affairs here were at their busiest."

"You take the leave," Philemon urged.

"No. Keeping busy helps." Brackett started down the stairs. "No argument, Phil. Go home and come back a happier man. That's an order."

He had no desire to argue. That night he wrote a long letter to Laura, telling her of Gunner Small's improvement, Davey Dabney's continuing recuperation, and about others he knew she would want to hear of. He told her he loved her, and that he was coming to Torquay as soon as he could. Signing it *All my love* seemed inadequate, but he had never signed a letter that way before, so it took his breath away, all the same.

Laura read the letter over and over. Philemon had been right. As much as he missed her, he knew she was needed in Torquay, buoying up her little sister.

"Keep me busy," Nana ordered her, and Laura did, walking with her down to the harbor, even though Nana was shy to be seen. Arm in arm and well-cloaked against the misty coolness of November on the Devon coast, the sisters walked and talked.

When she felt brave enough, Laura asked Nana about making love. "Maybe I am an idiot to ask these things," she confessed, as they sat at quayside one sunny afternoon before beginning the climb up steep streets to the Worthy home. "I was married for years."

"Not to anyone who cared about you," Nana reminded her. She smiled and covered her mouth, shy for a moment. "As much as I miss the Mulberry Inn, I admit to enjoying my own home, where Oliver doesn't have to shush me when I get excited about what we're doing." She turned her face into Laura's shoulder. "Oh, sister, I love him so much. When I make him happy, he returns the favor. Did you never..."

"Not yet," Laura whispered, her eyes on two children trailing after their mother. "Will I know when it happens?"

"Heavens, yes," Nana said, her face rosy. "Don't be afraid to enjoy every single second. Right now, our men are on loan to us from King George, but it won't always be this way." Her voice was wistful. "Oliver tells me..." She lowered her voice. "He says he can't wait until peace is declared, and he can spend an entire day in bed with me, wearing nothing but a day-old beard! He is a rascal."

"So are you," Laura teased. She grew serious then. "I only hope I am not afraid, when the moment comes. Philemon says he is a patient man."

Nana got to her feet. "I think you will be in excellent hands. And other parts, too. Don't look at me like that!"

They walked slowly to the house, only to have Nana stop, put her hand to her mouth, and sob out loud. Oliver Worthy sat on the front porch, his long legs propped up on the railing.

"Thought I'd have to leave a memo with my regrets, tacked to the door," he said, as Nana hurried toward him. He laughed and grabbed her, carefully lowering her to the bench beside him. Then he was kissing his wife as though it had been years instead of months, gathering her as close as he could. Laura hurried past them into the house, hardly able to contain her own delight to see a sister happy.

She was reading in the sitting room when the Worthys came inside, Nana's face red with whisker burn and her arm around her husband's waist. Oliver kissed Laura's forehead.

"That's from your surgeon." He reached inside his uniform. "Here's a letter." He hefted it. "Not very heavy, but he said he wrote a longer one last week."

"He did," Laura said, shy suddenly. She took it, and glanced at the Worthys, who weren't paying her the slightest attention. "I know I hear an ax murderer in the book room. Should I alert the Sea Fencibles?"

"By all means," Nana murmured, her eyes on her husband.

Laura laughed and took her letter upstairs, reading the sparse note.

Captain Brackett has allowed me two weeks' leave when another surgeon arrives. Still ready to be spliced?

That was all. She thought of all the reasons why it was a supremely stupid idea, but went to her desk and wrote "Yes," then sealed it with a wafer. She gave it to Oliver in the morning when he came downstairs, his face a mask of pain.

"It's back to Plymouth?" she asked, unsettled by his expression.

"Aye. Walk with me to the quay, Laura."

She grabbed her cloak and turned to see Matthew ready, too, his eyes as serious as his captain's. He had slung his seabag over his shoulder, anchoring it casually with the hook Philemon had commissioned. *You're so young,* she thought, as the sight of his hook jolted her. *And you belong to King George, too. This war must end.*

It was a silent walk. When they arrived at the dock, Oliver sent Matthew ahead to the coasting vessel.

"I hope you told him yes," he said, a smile playing around his lips now.

"I couldn't do anything else," she replied simply. "I love him."

He tucked her letter inside his peacoat. "He'll have this before noon. I'm off to Admiralty House then, and when I return, back to my station off Spain." He looked up the hill toward his home. "Nana needs you more than ever." His eyes filled with tears and he made no attempt to brush them away. "This is harder than anything I have ever done."

"She'll be fine, Oliver," Laura said, her hand on his arm, "and you'll return when you can."

"It's the deuce of a business." He kissed her cheek and left her alone on the dock. When she walked back up the hill, Nana stood at the sitting room window, the palms of her hands pressed against the glass.

Philemon was changing a dressing when Oliver dropped the letter in his lap. Surprised, he looked up at the captain, who didn't look inclined to move until he opened it. He left bloody fingerprints on the paper as he pried off the wafer.

"She's a woman of few words," he commented, holding it up for Oliver to see. "So we are to be brothers-in-law?"

"It would appear so." Oliver clapped him on the shoulder. "The sooner the better, too. Since you've never done this, and I have, I recommend a special license."

"That's out of my league," Philemon said.

"Not at all, considering that is my wedding present to you, brother. I have pounds sterling rolling around and up to no good, and the lenient ear of Lord Mulgrave, who knows how to grease matrimonial wheels for Channel men."

"Is it legal if I am not there to sign the document?" Philemon asked.

"Philemon is spelled with one *m* or two?" Oliver grew serious immediately. "I'll mail it to you from London, because when I return to Plymouth, I do not have time to come here or to Torquay." He crouched beside Oliver's stool then. "Brother, do me this favor. Be there when Nana has the baby. I know Mr. Milton is an excellent accoucheur, but I prefer you there. Please."

"Consider it done if humanly possible," Philemon said. He took a deep breath. "And my…my madam will assist. This is all provided you jab Boney wherever you can."

"I always do. Goodbye, Philemon."

Chapter Sixteen

Oliver was as good as his word. The special license arrived from London the same day the *Tangier* sailed with a fair wind to Spain. Philemon had earlier signed the medical releases of Oliver's men who were fit for sea, and felt a momentary pang. His father was on board, and his future brother-in-law. For just a moment, he wanted to sail with them. Then he remembered his own admonition.

"We all fight Boney the best way we know how," he told Davey Dabney.

"My war's over, isn't it?" Davey asked him. "Don't be afraid to tell me."

"Yes, it is," Philemon said frankly. "You no longer have the range of motion that a foretopman needs, even though I am delighted with how well you have healed."

"I'm going to miss that view from a hundred and sixty feet up," Davey said, his voice wistful. "What am I fit for now?"

"My notion and potion room," Philemon said with a gesture.

"Good God, sir, I could kill someone down here!"

Philemon could not help his gallows laugh. "I manage to kill them on all floors, Davey, so don't limit yourself." He sighed and passed his hand in front of his eyes. "I wonder if we will ever know enough…" He let the thought resonate, then looked at the foretopman. "Davey, you can be trained to do this work."

"No money, sir."

"I can find it." Philemon perched himself on a stool. "In fact, I am about to leave for Torquay to marry Mrs. Taunton. Before she left Stonehouse, she was wondering what she could do about your future."

"She cares that much?" Davey said. "I…I was just returning the favor she showed me."

"I am ever in your debt for that, too. Davey, Mrs. Taunton stands ready to pay your expenses to become an apothecary."

"Good Lord!" he exclaimed, and it sounded almost reverent. He looked at the stoppered glass bottles with their murky contents and Latin labels. "You think I could learn all this?"

"I am certain of it. You are bright. You also have a facility for ciphering. The mere fact of your survival tells me of your determination. You could go to the University of Edinburgh and survive my old professors with more facility than I did, probably. Think about it, Davey."

The seaman nodded. He looked around again, sitting on the other stool as though measuring himself in such a place. "How many years would it take?"

"Two years, followed by written and oral examinations that one of my colleagues swore rendered him bald and sterile," Philemon said. "You're a man like me, with no proper background or gentility. This job requires neither, although you will have to prove yourself better than those of higher degree."

They both looked up to the sound of someone calling for Lt. Brittle. Philemon started for the stairs. "Think about it," he said again. "Close the door when you leave."

Philemon was impatient to be away to Torquay. He longed to lie down with Laura, draw her close to him, and tell her of his day. She would offer advice; she would tell him what had happened in her world, during the time they were apart. Maybe they would make love, an activity that smacked so much of leisure time that he could barely imagine it.

He wanted to pack his duffel to be ready to bolt when another surgeon arrived and Brackett gave him the high sign. He didn't, out of lack of time and some superstition that if he did some supernatural event would change everything and leave him still at Stonehouse nursing a powerful heartache.

Nights became harder than days. He suffered through a nightmare where Napoleon Bonaparte bricked up all exits from Block Four and trapped him in his notion and potion room. The walls started to move together, and he began to choke on magnesium sulphate, funneled down his throat by a gleeful Sir David Carew.

Nothing so dramatic happened. After his morning ward walk, Brackett met him with the new surgeon, a well-seasoned man Philemon knew from Haslar Hospital in Portsmouth.

"Walk Captain Bedwyn around, introduce him to your

mates, and make yourself scarce," Brackett said with a smile. "Come back here leg shackled."

Fair enough. Bedwyn was soon conversing with his mates, and Philemon left on a coasting vessel before noon. Other than being royally seasick and enduring the ribbing of others bound for Torquay, he arrived on his doorstep long after dark. He stood a long moment looking at the lights from the Worthy house next door, but he knew better than to slight his mother.

She received him with a firm embrace, Cornish pasties and a tot of rum. After he ate and just before he started to yawn, she pushed him toward the side door.

"Mama, it's too late. Tomorrow."

"Now," she insisted. "Lady Taunton spent most of this afternoon looking out the window."

That's encouraging, he thought, as he crossed between the two houses, noting as he did so that there was a well-defined path now. *Maybe I should gravel it while I'm here,* he thought.

There were lights on, so he didn't hesitate to knock. Tired, but not too tired to kiss Laura Taunton within an inch of her life, he knocked again, then waited, listening for footsteps. Nothing. He leaned against the door and knocked again, trying to subdue the clammy feeling that started crawling out of his stomach.

As he waited with growing alarm, he reminded himself that his mother had said she had seen Laura looking for him all afternoon. He touched the special license in his pocket, and her response of *Yes!* that she had sent only last week. He thought he heard footsteps, but the sound stopped, and he could not be sure. He debated another moment whether to try to open the door, then ignored his own cautions and did precisely that.

The corridor was dark, with lights at the end by the staircase and the sitting room opposite. His eyes became accustomed to the gloom, and he could make out a table and chair in the hall, and there, next to the chair, gathered into a huddle, sat Laura Taunton, her face turned down into her updrawn knees.

During his first year at the University of Edinburgh, one wag masquerading as a student—he didn't last long— had the effrontery to ask the professor if anyone ever died of a broken heart. *It is possible,* he thought, as he stood there, his hand on the doorknob. It might be her heart. *Maybe it's mine,* he thought. *What do I do now?*

Then another thought yanked his hand from the knob as though it burned and sent him running to her, to kneel beside her and raise her face. "Tell me there is nothing wrong with Nana," he demanded, wishing he didn't sound so peremptory, but tensing himself to take the stairs three at a time if she nodded.

She shook her head. "Nana's fine," Laura whispered, then lowered her head again. "It's I," she managed to gasp out before dissolving into wrenching tears that sent more terror through him than any epidemic or surgery gone wrong.

He had no idea what to do, even though he had an inkling of her anguish. How can people be so cruel to their children? he asked himself as he sat beside her in the dark hall and gradually worked his arm around her shaking body. She tried to draw away, but he wouldn't let her.

"Don't hold me so tight!" she exclaimed.

He was barely touching her, but he released his slight grip, praying she wouldn't bolt from the hall. *She is going to take such a light touch,* he told himself. *I hope I am equal to it.*

To his immense relief, she did not move, but crouched, huddled inside herself, breathing as though she had been running hard. He knew she had to stop that.

"Laura. Laura. Just let your breath in and out slowly," he counseled, trying to sound more like a surgeon than a deeply concerned lover.

She did as he said, slowing her breathing until it was almost normal again. He felt her begin to relax, then slowly release herself from her huddled position. Soon her feet were stretched out in front of her as she leaned against the wall. She let him take her hand, but he made no effort to grasp it tightly.

After a long moment he asked, "What's wrong?"

She withdrew her hand from his, then put it back again. He didn't think it was his imagination that she leaned toward him, even though they did not touch.

"I had it in my head that you were coming today."

Her voice was so soft he had to lean closer. "You were right, obviously," he said, his lips close to her ear.

She flinched and moved back slightly, and he held his breath until she settled down again.

"I knew the mail coach was due around five o'clock, but you did not come." Her words ended in a sob. "I knew you had changed your mind. I just knew it! I told Nana she was wrong, and that no one would want to marry me, not a bastard. A used one, in the bargain."

He winced at her words, but knew he did not dare try to tell her she was wrong, or she shouldn't feel that way, because she so heartbreakingly did. He took a deep breath of his own.

"Captain Brackett found me a replacement. I had to show Captain Bedwyn around before I could leave. By then, the mail coach had gone, but I knew the coasting vessel would get me here."

"You came by water?" she asked. He could hear just the slightest bit of hope in her voice.

"I did. Good thing you couldn't see me. I haven't vomited that much since my first post mortem! I had my sea legs, but not my sea stomach, obviously."

She didn't laugh at his weak humor, but he thought a smile played around her lips. When he took her hand again, she did not object when he twined his fingers through hers. He wanted to talk to her, reason with her, but she was not being reasonable. He said nothing.

She cleared her throat. "Philemon, I am not ready."

A capital knife slashed across his gut could not have felt worse. It was his turn to remind himself to breathe slowly. *At least you did not call me Lieutenant,* he thought.

"I'm not certain anyone is," he commented, keeping his voice light, even as he writhed inside. "I know that I love you, and that I don't feel entirely comfortable when you are not around. I'm also starting to get preposterous ideas of a home and children, and mouthing sentences that start with, 'When this war is over we are going to…'"

"We?"

"It's never just me. It's always we."

She made a small sound in her throat at that, and to his ineffable pleasure, rested her head on his shoulder. "Nana tells me I am wearing a path in front of the window. Then I tell her that's impossible because she has already worn the path."

He chuckled, feeling on firmer ground now that his dear one seemed to be relaxing. "Ten years from now, when you're holding your breath over little boys in trees and scolding me when I track mud in the sitting room, you'll wonder what the fuss was all about."

She turned toward him. "You're certain of that."

I'm certain of nothing, he thought, *but you'll never hear it from me.* "Positive." He rubbed his cheek against hers briefly; she did not draw away. "What happened just now, Laura?"

"I honestly don't know," she said, releasing his hand. "I heard you knock and came downstairs. The closer I got to the door, the more frightened I became. Finally, I couldn't even stand up."

She let him put his arm around her this time. "I am asking you to trust me, Laura," he said softly. "It's a novel experience, because I doubt you've ever trusted a man in your entire life. Who can blame you?"

She nodded. "Philemon, everything you say is reasonable and logical and I know it's true. But…"

"…when push comes to shove, it's another matter."

She nodded again. "We could get married tomorrow, but what happens then?" She muttered something then that didn't even sound like words, just a guttural sound of fear that was almost palpable. "I…I never knew when James was coming to my bed. He would open the door in the dark and stand over my bed, then jerk back the covers and tell me to raise my nightgown." She turned her head into his shoulder. "I am so ashamed." She started gasping for breath again.

"Laura. Laura. Just breathe slowly," he ordered.

She did as he said, but less successfully this time, as the words spilled out of her. "It always hurt. Does it always hurt?"

He felt himself on firmer ground now. "Laura, love never hurts, when done right. Never. Quite the opposite."

"That…that's what Nana said. She blushed, but that's what she said."

"Don't doubt your little sister for a minute."

He knew what to do. He stood up and stretched. "Laura, I'm going to bed. Let me walk you upstairs and tuck you in. I'll probably look in on Nana, then I'm going home. Think about this—when we're married, we can keep the lights on. No surprises."

She let him pull her to her feet, even as her mood seemed to lighten. "You're serious? Could you sleep that way?"

"I could sleep in the middle of the High Street at noon with wagons trundling by," he told her truthfully. "Oh, you know that."

His heart started pumping again when she laughed. She made no objection when he walked her upstairs, helped her out of her robe and tucked her in bed. Taking his chances, he patted her hip, and she obligingly moved away so he could sit down.

"You need to know this, Laura. I thought Captain Bedwyn was a permanent addition to the staff, but he's just locum tenens. Temporary. He's between ships. I have to go back in four days. Let's get married between now and then. You can follow me when you feel like it."

She considered his words. "You wouldn't do anything to frighten me?"

"I don't have it in me to frighten you, dearest, but I am

a man," he told her, bluntly. "All I want is for you to trust me. Let me be the one man on earth that you trust."

She nodded. "I think I can do that." She clutched his arm then. "But when I don't think I can, will you still love me?"

"Forever. Go to sleep now." He kissed her forehead.

He decided not to look in on Nana, reasoning that any woman as gravid as she was deserved a peaceful night's sleep. He'd see her in the morning. He went downstairs as quietly as he could, going into the sitting room to rest a moment on the sofa and wonder what on earth he was doing.

He must have slept, but only a little. When he woke up, the candle was not much lower and Nana sat in a chair beside the sofa, watching him with that kindly expression he was familiar with in the daughters of Lord Ratliffe. He smiled back, wondering at the quality of females bred of that bad man, and wondering if some quirk of fate could ever turn William Stokes less toxic and more like his offspring.

"I was trying not to wake you, Nana."

"Who said I sleep, these days?" She laughed softly. "You're an anatomist, tell me why babies seem to press so hard on a bladder at 2:00 a.m."

"It's a warning of sleepless nights ahead," he told her. "Wish I could give you more cheerful tidings."

He sat up and beckoned to her, and she came to his side, allowing him to put his arm around her shoulders. What a pretty thing she was, too, even with her belly so big. Her face was more plump, which he knew probably pleased Oliver, who had worried about her slimness.

She frowned now. "I've done what I can for Laura," she told him. "I even told her how your mother got me through my own cold feet at marrying Oliver." Nana pushed on her belly. "If I press in here, the baby presses back here. It's a game we play. Am I silly?"

"Superbly so. I hope all women play this game."

She sighed. "I've told Laura how terrified I was of marrying Oliver—not because I didn't love him, but because I couldn't convince myself that I was worthy. Laura's going through what I went through, but it's harder for her. We know why."

"We do. I told her I only have four days here, so we must arrive at a decision." He gave her shoulder another squeeze, then got to his feet, tugging her up, too. "It seems that all I am doing tonight is telling females to go to bed."

"I should be tired. I spent all day cleaning, and preparing and doing heaven knows what. Laura even told me to slow down."

He gave her a professional look then. "Nana, old wives' tales or not, that's usually a sign that something is going to happen soon."

"I have three weeks," she told him.

"You're so certain?"

"Lt. Brittle, prepare for plain speaking. When a captain comes ashore as rarely as mine, with only one item on his agenda—don't tell King George—you can pretty well pinpoint such things!"

His arm around her shoulder, he walked her to the hall. When she was halfway up the stairs, she looked back at the sitting room. "Bother it," she said. "I came down to extinguish that light."

"Let me."

He turned toward the sitting room, but turned back at a gasp from Nana. She stared down at the tread beneath her bare feet. In the quiet that followed, he could hear the sound of liquid dripping.

"Oh my," she said, then, "Phil, it's a good thing you're here."

Chapter Seventeen

After so recently assuring his love that he would never surprise her, Philemon had no compunction about banging on Laura's door. She was there in a moment, her face white, but opened the door wide when he gently pushed Nana into her arms.

"Find a towel. I'll get my pocket instruments next door. Laura, have Mrs. Trelease heat some water. I'll wake up my mother. She'd snatch me bald if I didn't let her in on this."

When he was whistling down the stairs, as cheerful as she had ever heard him, Laura looked at her little sister and started to laugh. "Nana, he's in his element."

"Handy to have him so close. Sister, that towel, please."

By the time Philemon returned, Laura was dressed, the water heating downstairs and Nana comfortable in a dry nightgown. Laura had spread a thick towel under her, and taken out the other birthing supplies from the chest at the foot of the bed.

Taking his time on the stairs, Philemon looked so calm she wanted to shake him and screech, *This is my sister!* He seemed to know what she was thinking. He pressed his forehead against hers. "I've done this many times, Laura. Steady as you go now."

He sat on Nana's bed. "My dear, you have work to do. Shall we send Joey Trelease for Mr. Milton? I know he's your accoucheur, and I'm not one to poach patients."

"Send him a note when the sun is up," Nana said. "He's not a young man, and he needs his sleep. Besides, Oliver told me he trusts you. Poach away."

"I'm flattered," Philemon said, as imperturbable and conversational as though they discussed the weather. Laura felt herself under his spell again, as she had during those racking days at Stonehouse, when he seemed the only calm in a terrifying place. "Here is Mrs. Trelease with hot water. Come Laura, let us wash."

The housekeeper poured the water and stood back as the surgeon added enough cool water to the basin to suit him. He handed Laura his apron and she put it over his head and tied it behind, as she had done on several occasions. He rolled up his sleeves and washed his arms to the elbows. "The water is fine," he said. "You'll be assisting."

She gulped and joined him, their hands touching in the hot, soapy water.

"We've done this before, haven't we?" he commented.

She nodded, suddenly too shy to speak.

"Let's do it again," he told her. "You're the best mate I ever had."

She looked at him, loving him with all her heart and realizing he had given her the greatest compliment possible. "You really mean that?" she asked.

It was his turn to nod, then turn the moment into a laugh.

"Besides, I still have trouble with Aitken's brogue." He ducked when she splashed him.

He shared a towel with her, then went to Nana's bed, where she still lay on her side. He knelt on the floor beside her. "Nana, my dear, it's time to toss aside modesty with great abandon. Laura will help you onto your back. Raise your knees, then drop them open. I want to feel what's going on inside, if I may. Will you let me?"

She nodded. Laura helped her into position and Nana did as Philemon asked. He checked quickly, then covered her again. "You have some time," he told Nana. He handed his watch to Laura. "You'll probably want to throw a pitcher at my head, Nana, but I'm going to lie down in Laura's bed. I've barely slept in two days. Laura is going to time your contractions, and keep you company, and walk you around the room, if you feel up to that. Laura, when they get to three minutes apart, wake me. Ladies, good night."

"When he returns, I'm going to order Oliver to shoot you dead," Nana said. "I will laugh and scalp you like a Mohican."

"I don't doubt that for a minute," he replied with a smile.

Laura took his watch in her hands and lay down beside Nana, hiding her smile.

"Rub her back, Laura," Oliver said as he left the room.

Laura did, gratified to hear Nana's even breathing in a few minutes. The peace lasted for ten minutes, then Nana grunted softly and relaxed as Laura reminded her to breathe slowly.

After an hour of dozing and waking, Nana sat up and asked Laura to help her walk. "Like only yesterday," Nana said. "Down to the quay and back."

Arms around each other, they paced the room.

"What do you think Oliver is doing right now?" Nana asked.

He's sound asleep, Laura thought, amused. "He's thinking of you," she said.

"No he's not, silly. He's asleep."

They walked until Nana stopped and clutched her. "That was stronger," she said when she could straighten up. "Let's keep walking."

They walked some more: Nana stopped more frequently now as Laura timed her contractions. When they were four minutes apart, Nana asked to lie down, and Laura helped her back into bed, where she lay on her side again, grunting softly.

When the contractions were three minutes apart, Laura kissed Nana's forehead and went to her room, where Philemon slept in complete comfort, his hands relaxed and open. She looked at him, wondering how it would be to see his face on her pillow every morning for the rest of her life, at least, as often as Napoleon would permit. She barely touched his shoulder.

He grasped her hand before he opened his eyes. "Three minutes?"

"Yes. She's straining more but not complaining. My sister is an angel."

"She knows what she is doing and why," he told her, tugging on her hand until she was sitting on her bed beside him. "Don't worry, Laura. She'll be fine."

She gave him a thump. "Get up!"

Another hour passed, with the contractions not budging beyond three minutes. Philemon dozed in the chair, his stockinged feet propped on the bedside table. Mrs. Brittle came over when the sun rose, bringing with her some ice in a glass. She gave a piece to Nana. "I've been setting out a pan each night, and this is the first morning it was cold enough."

Nana rolled her eyes with the pleasure of it and smiled her thanks, just before the next contraction took hold. She chewed relentlessly through three more contractions, each one closer than the others. Laura patted Philemon awake.

It was as satisfactory a birth as he could ever remember, and more comfortable than most. Red-faced and pushing hard when the time came to bear down, Nana would never have appreciated the stories he could have told of delivering a baby on the gun deck during battle—where was it decreed that babies come at most inopportune times?—or tending to the harsh women in the Stonehouse laundry.

But here they were in a warm room, with early December battering the windows outside and reasonable people within, ready to do what he asked, as Nana labored and delivered.

The hardest moment came right before the birth, as Nana struggled then sobbed for Oliver to comfort her. Philemon had to look away for a moment, as tears came to his own eyes, followed by the deepest hatred of war he had ever felt. It was even stronger than the moment on the *Victory* when Admiral Nelson died. This moment in the Worthy bedchamber was more awful, because it showed him the implacable power of war to mock and harrow the innocent.

All eyes in the room were on Nana; only Laura left her perch on the bed and came to his side to put her hands on his head, kiss his cheek and pull him against her body. She wiped his face, and he looked deep into her eyes, which showed complete understanding of his feelings. There was love, too, from the lady he adored, also a harrowed innocent.

Then came the matchless moment he knew he would never tire of. Protesting her dislodgment from a cozy nest into an uncertain world, Nana and Oliver Worthy's daughter made her appearance. *I love this,* he thought, as he caught her slimy body expertly, cleared her mouth quickly, gave her toes a flick and flopped her on her mother's belly.

Here's to the ladies, he thought, as Nana, weary no more, reached for her baby, crooning to it, trying to pull her close. He gently brushed her fingers aside with his scissors, tied a knot and handed the scissors to Laura, who cut the cord binding mother and daughter, who were already firmly bound in that way of mothers and offspring.

He finished his work below while the women in the room took charge. His mother wrapped the infant in a dry towel and handed her to Nana, who smiled her thanks. She gazed in utter rapture at her daughter, who stared back solemnly.

"We're naming her Rachel, after my mother," Nana told him. She looked at Laura then, her eyes filling with tears. "I want Oliver *here!*"

"So do we all, dearest," Laura murmured, kissing her sister's sweaty hair. "I'll write him before the hour is out."

Taking Oliver's assignment again, Philemon held Nana and her child in his arms while the women changed the bedding, then tucked her in. A word to his mother passed on his next assignment. When he left the room, she was showing Nana how to coax the baby to her breast. He watched a moment, satisfied, then glanced at his time-piece: half past eleven, seven bells in the forenoon watch. The Royal Navy had another dependent.

He watched as Nana tugged her sister down to the bed and whispered in her ear. Laura looked at him and nodded. Nana gave her a push, then turned her attention to the demands at her breast. The room was warm and smelled of birth. He could have stayed there all afternoon. Too bad most surgical duties were not as pleasant as this one.

Laura joined him at the door, and closed it after them. She took him in her arms, and he closed his eyes in satisfaction as the dear woman tended to his needs. How was it women did this?

"Nana ordered me to marry you tomorrow," she said speaking into his neck. "She said I deserved to be as happy as she is."

"You do," he told her, kissing her.

"She told me to trust her. Everyone wants me to trust them."

"When are you going to listen to us?" he chided gently.

"Now," she said, her voice decisive. "I hear you have a special license."

"It's in my uniform inside pocket."

"Do you know any vicars?"

He had to be sure. "Are you certain of what you are doing?"

"Of course I am not," she replied honestly, "but it does not follow that I do not love you. I do. And you have already pledged to sustain me during moments when I do not."

He swallowed several times, trying to speak. He would have thought his heart turned over, except that he knew such a phenomenon was medically impossible.

"Produce that license, Philemon. I believe it entitles us

to be married whenever and wherever we choose, and I choose the Worthys' bedchamber tomorrow morning."

His arms were around her then, gathering her as close as he could, but it was his turn to temporize. "Let's give Nana another day and a good night's sleep. If you send a timely letter to Bath, Polly will come, and I have a little sister in Portsmouth who will come, too." He held her off to look at her face. "Do you need to send to Taunton for your late husband's certificate of death?"

She blushed, which only made her more endearing, a thing he could not have thought possible. "No, actually. When Mrs. Ormes went back recently, I asked her to fetch it."

"You've been making plans," he said, in a voice soft with wonder. "Yes, I do know a vicar." He opened the door. "Mama, is Mr. Matheson still holding forth at St. Mary's Church, railing against sailors and other evils?"

"He is," Mrs. Brittle said. "You know where he lives. Hush now!"

"Laura, write Gran," Nana said, her voice drowsy and distant.

"You're supposed to be asleep!" Laura said, not leaving his embrace. "Philemon, let me go so I can write some letters."

"You're the one who grabbed me," he teased.

"And you're the one who has to find that vicar who has such umbrage against the Royal Navy. Will he be amazed?"

"No, indeed," Philemon said, stepping away from her and untying his apron. "He had high hopes I would not spend my entire life with a capital knife in one hand and a finger on someone's pulse."

Quickly, she raised her wrist to him, and he placed his lips on her pulse point. "A bit too rapid for my ease, Laura."

"You two!" Mrs. Brittle scolded. "How are the Worthys to get any rest if we are all in such an uproar?"

"Look behind you, Mama," Philemon said. "They're asleep." He returned his attention to Laura. "Will two days from now suit?"

"Yes. Let us make it at…at four bells in the forenoon watch. Is that right?"

"As rain, my love."

It was a quiet wedding, each guest crowded into Nana's bedroom a friendly face. The vicar's homily was taken from the Book of Ruth, which made Philemon squeeze her hand tighter.

Laura was amazed at her own calm, which far exceeded that of her husband. When Nana started dabbing her eyes, she knew she did not dare look at Philemon, or she would cry, too. She kept her eyes on their hands, looking up finally to give her responses and look into deep blue eyes swimming with unshed tears. If there was a better place to be in all the world, Laura couldn't imagine it.

He had told her the ring once belonged to his Grandmother Brittle, nothing more than a copper circle, such as an illiterate wife of a pig farmer in Yorkshire would wear. "When I have a minute in Plymouth, I'll find something much better," he had assured her. "Still, that was a good marriage and we could do worse."

He warned her it would turn her finger green, as sure as the world. Looking at the ring now on her finger, she could hardly wait for that to happen. From this moment forward, green would always be the color of love to her, and not the diamonds and rubies in her last ring. She couldn't even remember where she had left that bauble.

There were hugs and kisses from all present, even Captain Brackett, who looked fine in his best uniform. He had brought her former dresser with him from Stonehouse. Laura couldn't help but notice Amanda Peters darting glances at Brackett. *Well, well,* she thought.

Samantha Brittle Wyle greeted her as a sister, with her embrace taking in Laura and her brother, and the admonition not to be a stranger to Portsmouth. And there was Polly, eyes lively in her excitement.

After a professional look at Nana, Philemon shooed everyone downstairs to a wedding breakfast. "You're looking a tad finely drawn," he told Nana. "Let me guess— It's been two days. Your milk is in and you're wishing us to the devil."

She nodded, wasting no time in pulling back the shawl around her shoulders, unbuttoning her nightgown and putting her baby to her breast. "My goodness," she said, as Rachel began to gulp, her eyes wide with wonder at a superabundance of milk. Nana leaned back in relief. "Pardon my rag manners!"

"No pardon needed. Remember, both breasts per feeding, or you'll be lopsided. That's the last wisdom from me, except to keep Captain Worthy at arm's length if he arrives home sooner than four weeks from now."

"You told me six weeks!"

"I am a realist."

Nana blushed. "I wish him here tomorrow."

"So do I," Philemon said, "except that I distinctly remember you telling me he would shoot me dead."

"That passed," Nana replied, with some dignity. "Go on, both of you."

Not until late afternoon did they bid goodbye to the last guest. Gran had come from Plymouth on the last mail coach, stammering her apologies. It was nearly impossible to get away from the Mulberry these days, what with all the business, she said, already on the stairs.

Laura knew better than to stop her with conversation. "You may have my room tonight, Mrs. Massie," she said.

"And that is that," she told Philemon. "We are sleeping in your house tonight."

She had second thoughts, when she came into the room under the eaves an hour later. It must have showed on her face. Her husband sat her down on the bed.

"You're frowning, my love. Let us just sleep tonight. You get the side closest to the wall." He took off his uniform jacket. "Turn around. I will unbutton you."

She did as he said, closing her eyes when his fingers touched her bare skin, feeling her heart race a little faster, even though he had frankly declared there would be only sleep in the attic. What he said had intrigued her.

"Why should I be next to the wall? I would think a wife would be on the side closest to the door. You know, to get up when children cry, and…and those kinds of things."

"Not in the Brittle family," Philemon replied. He took off his neck cloth and draped it with the uniform, then pulled his shirt over his head. "I'm not sure why he told me that several years ago—I had no matrimonial prospects then. Papa said, 'When you marry, let your wife sleep next to the wall. You can protect her that way.' Absurd, isn't it?"

"I think it's lovely," she said, as she let her dress drop.

"That's my father. You'll come to love him, too." He took off his trousers and reached under the near pillow for his nightshirt. "After you, Laura."

Too shy for words, she finished undressing. She needed his help for her corset, which he unlaced expertly, then retied much looser. "From now on, please don't wear it any tighter than that," he said. "You don't need it, and it's harmful." He loosed the strings again so she could remove it.

She touched his cheek tentatively. A second later she was clasped belly to belly in his arms, not sure if she had reached out first or he. He rubbed her back, then his hands went lower, as he pulled her closer.

She felt her breath coming faster, until she felt light-headed and unable to stop the shudder that went through her. "I cannot," she cried out.

Philemon pulled away immediately and sat her down. "Calmly, Laura," he said. "Just breathe. You'll be fine."

She could not help the tears that filled her eyes. "I'm so sorry," she whispered. "Forgive me."

He dabbed at her eyes with his sleeve. "Nothing to forgive."

Miserable, she crawled into bed. He joined her, then reached over and opened his timepiece, placing it by the candlestick. "I have to be up early to catch the mail coach. Laura, don't cry. It's been a long day. I revise that—it's been a long week. I expect you to stay in Torquay until you are quite resolved to come to Stonehouse."

He dabbed at her eyes again, and she made no objection when he pulled her close enough for her head to rest on his chest. "I've left my spare house key on the bureau over there. Aunt Walters went home to Yorkshire last week for a visit, or she would have been here today. If she is not back by the time you come home, you'll need the key."

By the time you come home. He could not have said anything kinder. She nestled closer to him, and he gave her shoulder an answering squeeze.

"I'll have the extra bedchamber made up for you, and there will be mine down the hall, of course. Choose either one." He kissed her cheek. "Good night, Mrs. Brittle. I'll try to be quiet in the morning."

She wasn't sure when she finally dropped off to sleep—it was long after Philemon—but she woke at some point, aware that she had snatched most of the coverlet and bundled herself into it. She turned over to look at Philemon, who should have been shivering, but who seemed oblivious, so deep was his sleep. *My apologies for being a blanket thief,* she thought, looking at him. His nightshirt had ridden up to his waist, as those garments generally did, and there he lay, exposed and relaxed.

In the last few months, she had seen many patients' privates. It was a necessary part of nursing, and fazed her not in the least. This was different; this was her husband. The sight of him intrigued her and she wanted to touch him there, something she had only done to Sir James when he was invalided and needed her help for every function. This man sleeping beside her was a young man in his prime, and she wanted him.

It was an odd sensation for her, one she had never experienced. She felt her own body grow warm as she watched her husband. *Maybe Nana is right,* she thought, as she carefully covered Philemon and settled against him again. His arm went around her, and she wondered, red-faced, if he was awake. It must have been a reflex; his breathing was as measured as ever.

He was up in the morning before the room was fully light. She lay there quietly, her eyes closed, listening to the homely sound of him washing his hands and face, and smothering an oath when he bumped his head on an overhead beam by the washbasin. She started to laugh, and kept laughing when he grinned at her, made a rude gesture and sat on her. Her laughter turned into a shriek when he suddenly growled into her neck.

She gave him a push. He landed on the floor, then tipped his head back to gaze at her. "I hope your mother didn't hear that," she whispered, trying not to laugh.

"She's two floors down," he said cheerfully. "Kiss me. It will make up for what I declare are splinters in my ass. If the Brittle buttocks get infected, you will be removing the splinters, and not my mates or, God forbid, Owen Brackett. There are some things I will not explain."

He dressed quickly, ordering her to stay in bed. She sat up, rumpled in sleep, and watched him, her arms clasped around her knees. She had never thought of him as handsome, but in the growing light, he was precisely that: solid as a road mender, with character in his profile, and his hair that pleasing brown that would look even better if he had more of it.

"Would you grow your hair longer for me?" she asked.

"Not even for you," he told her as he put on his uniform jacket. "I work with too many louse and flea-bitten patients and don't like little visitors in my bed. You'll appreciate that someday."

I expect I will, she thought, *when I am brave enough to share your bed, and all that should mean.* The thought stirred her body again, and she wished she had been brave enough to hold out her hand to him and ask him to stay awhile, to let her try again.

But there he was, dressed and already shouldering his duffel bag. He came to the bed and kissed her. "Don't stay away too long, madam," he said. "Please don't."

Then he was gone, treading quietly down the stairs, as he had probably done many times, heading to sea or to hospital. She lay back in his bed, supremely unsatisfied with herself. She rolled over and tucked her hand under his pillow, where she felt a small piece of paper. The sheet had been torn from his prescription book, with its printed lines.

You're welcome to look all you want, madam. You can even touch me anytime you want. What's mine is yours. Lovingly, P.

Good Lord, he does have eyes that never close, she thought, mortified and amused at the same time.

Chapter Eighteen

Somehow, when he had told Laura to take her time in coming to him at Stonehouse, Philemon had not thought he would be spending Christmas alone, not to mention New Year's. As 1809 faded into 1810, he began to dread the sight of his empty house after a long day or night of work.

At least it wasn't day *and* night of work, he had to admit. He was discovering that winters were slower at Stonehouse. The season of active military campaigning was at a lull, and the beds were filled more often now with pneumonias, catarrhs that developed into the lacerating kind of bronchitis that only deepwater men seemed to suffer, and accidental injury.

The rain. The sleet down the back of his overcoat. As much as he hated himself for it, he started to remember Jamaica's constant warm weather, then—God help him— the amazingly compliant women of all colors that seemed to drift about the island like lovely butterflies. More than once every few days he woke up with an ache relieved bracingly by cold baths, which led to a tendency to snap at well-meaning colleagues.

Throughout all this, he continued to write encouragement to Laura in Torquay. The result was to create in him a duplicity totally foreign to his nature, one that made him as uncomfortable as the cold baths that lowered his sexual temperature. He left his house with a frown and returned at the end of his working day with a scowl.

There was one bright spot he yearned to share with Laura. It was the day he signed Davey Dabney's release papers from the hospital, and put him on a post chaise to Edinburgh. Davey had argued about the post chaise, but he only had to hand him a letter from Laura, directing precisely that.

"She won't have you uncomfortable, all the way to Edinburgh," he told the former foretopman. "God knows Edinburgh is uncomfortable enough. Only Scots thrive there—the rest of us count the days."

He knew better than to approach Sir David about his idea to turn Davey into an apothecary, but climbed right over his administrator's head and directly to Admiralty House, then the Navy Board. The way had been greased for him by Oliver Worthy, who, on Philemon's request, had written his own lengthy letter to Lord Musgrave, detailing the plan.

It was innovative, to be sure. Davey would be maintained on navy rolls for the duration of his studies, with his salary supplemented by Laura Brittle's generosity. Oliver expressed his own praise with a return letter from Ferrol Station off Spain, which was balm to Philemon's eviscerated esteem.

Lord Musgrave said it was a brilliant idea. Why should not the navy find a way to use seamen unfit for the fleet, but capable in every other way? And considering how short the supply of able surgeons and mates, this is pure genius.

He doubted his genius, flogging himself mentally. He couldn't even get a bride into his bed.

When February loomed on the calendar, and he knew he could not stand another minute of this misery, he received help from a surprising source.

He made few trips to the administration building, the sting of Sir David's earlier tongue-lashings before he married Laura still fresh in his mind. He was fully aware that Sir David knew of the wedding, and probably also knew Laura had never left Torquay. Philemon did not feel able to cope with a smirk from Sir David, should he chance to see him in the hall.

There was no avoiding this visit to admin, though. His chief mate was busy, and his two assistants were on well-earned leave. He was already late with his proposed *materia medica* budget for the next fiscal year. If he went in the side door of the building, he could drop it on the matron's desk and do an about-face.

He brought the budget over at the end of the noon break, when he expected the office might be empty, and left it on the outer desk. He would have made a silent retreat, except he stumbled over a dustbin some unseen imp must have shoved into his path. He kept his oath to himself, but the damage was done.

Miss Peters came out of the inner office and gave him one of the few smiles he ever saw in admin. He smiled back, wondering again why Laura had thought Peters intimidating. True, her eyes were a frosty blue that seemed to penetrate the back wall of his retina, but he had only found her unfailingly kind. Resolute, too. Like Laura, she never flinched from jetty duty, when the world was a screaming, moaning, bloody froth. He liked her, but he wasn't up to conversation today.

She had him, though, and from the look on her face, she meant to keep him. "Do you have a minute, Lieutenant?"

He wanted to invent simultaneous amputations, but couldn't lie. "Certainly, Miss Peters. How may I help you?"

"I can help you, actually," she said. "Come this way." She seated him in a hard chair and sat opposite him, not behind her desk.

She hadn't worked in a naval hospital long, but she already knew better than to waste a second of his time. "Chief surgeon Brackett told me how miserable you are."

There was no gilding a lily in Miss Peters's life, apparently. He could be as honest.

"Aye." He couldn't even look at her. "I had hoped I wasn't so obvious. We all try not to bring our problems to work."

"Owen tries, too," she said sympathetically, then realized what she had said. "Surgeon Brackett, rather." She gathered her thoughts. "I hardly know how to tell you this, except to explain it this way. When I look in a mirror, I know I am plain. When your wife looks in a mirror, she knows she is plain, too."

"She's not...she's beautiful. I've never seen a more beautiful woman," he protested.

"I agree. She was treated so poorly by her—I will not

even call him a husband—by Sir James that she sees defects that aren't even there."

"I've told her that," Philemon said, trying not to sound exasperated. "So has her sister."

Miss Peters put her hand on his arm, steadying him. "We are rational. She is not. Let me give you one reason why, so you may see how deep this runs."

Miss Peters rose to pace the floor, then paused to stare out of the window at the rain. "As you know, I was your wife's dresser. There was no intimate detail of her life that I did not know about. I knew how many nights Sir James came to her room. I listened to her cry each time he left, and sometimes before."

Philemon joined her at the window, unable to sit still.

"After a few months, he took me aside and demanded that I tell him immediately when she finished her monthly flow. I had no choice. He would call her into his bookroom then, stare her up and down, and demand that she do better next month—that she become with child. All the servants could hear."

"Good God."

"When each month passed and she did not increase, he would scream at her, demanding to know what was wrong with her, reminding her how much he had paid Lord Ratliffe for her, and what he expected."

Philemon turned away, sickened. "It wasn't her fault!"

"I know that, you know that, Laura knows that. But after enough months of cruelty, you begin to doubt even what you know."

He thought about this, and came to the conclusion Miss Peters wanted him to make. "I think Laura would be quite happy in my bed, and I think she knows that. Miss Peters, allow me to finish this intimate thought. In addition to all the trauma I know of, she fears she will not be able to produce a child? Sir James pretty well convinced her, didn't he?"

"Precisely. It's poppycock. There's every reason to think you two will have many children, but she is not reasonable about this."

He nodded. "Thank you for speaking to me. Maybe I shouldn't feel so sorry for myself."

"Good," she replied, returning to her desk, where she flipped through his tardy budget. "Lieutenant Brittle, you have enormous capacity for everything except the written form. When Mrs. Brittle comes—and she will—beg her to take over this aspect of your work. Get on your knees, if it will help. The navy will thank you."

He knew he had been dismissed, and in the only way Miss Peters could do so and maintain their dignity. *God bless the ladies,* he thought, especially this one. "I couldn't agree more. Tell me, Miss Peters, do you really think she will come?"

"I know she will. At the risk of piling on more praise than any man probably deserves, you're an excellent fellow. If your hair were a little longer, you might have found a wife much sooner."

He laughed and was pleased when she joined in. Then he was serious again, looking into her eyes. She gazed right back.

"How can I get her here?"

Miss Peters began to smile. "I recommend a bad cold, maybe even bronchitis. You know Laura is a champion nurse. All she needs is the smallest excuse to get her over what must be an enormous hump. Let me know when you are sick enough, and I will send a letter."

Thoughtful, he went to the door. He coughed. He pressed his hand to his forehead and coughed again, then quietly closed the door behind him.

As it turned out, he didn't need to pretend. Maybe he could blame his self-inflicted cold baths and the rain down his neck, or more particularly, the visits he paid to tend the laundresses' sick children. By the end of the week, he ached everywhere except his earlobes and had to prop himself up at night to get any relief from coughing.

Owen wanted to relieve him from most of his duties, but several mates were on leave and it was impossible. Philemon dragged himself to work, wielding his knives and lancets only when he had to. Sleep was torture, his appetite nil, his throat putrid.

After nearly a week in utter agony, Philemon was finally banished by Brackett. Brian Aitken, only just returned from ten days' leave in Dumfries, insisted on helping him home.

He didn't notice the small light in his bedchamber, mainly because rain plummeted down and he had given up hoping. Brian saw it, remarking that it wasn't safe to keep a candle burning while he was not there.

"It's my madam," Philemon said. "She came."

Laura opened the door. He felt like falling to his knees in gratitude, but his mate would only have interpreted that as a reason to turn him around and plop him into a proper hospital bed in Stonehouse, the last thing he wanted now. He let Laura help him up the steps, enduring her soft scolding because he loved her.

"I'll take him, Brian," she said. "Please tell Captain Brackett that he will not leave his bed until he is better."

"Laura, we are shorthanded," he protested, but in vain. He tried to crane his neck around for a glare at his mate, but only caught the corner of the traitor's smile. He was too sick to care. "Aye, aye. Do your duty, Aitken."

"And I will do mine," Laura said, smiling at him with the generosity of heart that had attracted him to her in the first place, right after her lovely surgeon's hands.

He knew better than to protest as she took off his overcoat—a sodden thing that never dried out, not in this weather—and handed it to Aunt Walters, who muttered and scolded all the way back to the kitchen with it.

"Bring me some broth, my dear," Laura called after her, "and that wheat poultice from Gran."

She took his hand and led him up his own stairs, then sat him in a chair while she removed his clothing, layer by layer. He was happy to rise and lean on her as she unbuttoned his trousers and stripped him bare. She toweled him so vigorously he knew she removed at least one layer of his epidermis. She had him into a nightshirt and tucked in bed with a warming pan before he started to shiver.

He shook his head over food, and she didn't press him. She propped him up so he could breathe, then draped his neck with the wheat poultice.

"Nana swears by these and so does Gran. By the way, Oliver is home. Nana is over the moon, and Rachel has a fearsome frigate commander as a new conquest. He is porridge."

He muttered something. He wanted to tell her how

grateful he was for her presence, and how much he loved her, but nothing came out except babble.

She was kind. "Shut up, Philemon," she murmured in his ear. "You're pathetic and I love you. You must stop shivering."

His ears were barely working, but he knew he did not imagine the rustle of clothing. In another moment she was in bed with him, naked and warm and holding him close as he shook. In a gesture he thought altruistic beyond belief, she put her bare legs on his cold ones. She even pulled him onto his side until they couldn't have been closer. He wished he had enough energy to do what he really wanted to. No, not that. What he really felt like doing was pulling grave dirt over himself.

Not that, either. Gradually, she warmed him. For the first time in days, he abandoned himself completely to sleep.

When he woke in the morning after a complete night of rest, Laura still stuck to him like a barnacle. Again, he yearned to put her on her back and make love to her, but there was no way any such sport would happen, not while he still felt nine-tenths dead. The fact that the thought even flickered in his brain gave him hope. Maybe he would live, after all.

He opened his eyes. Laura, her expression kind, gazed back at him. He kissed her neck, pillowed his head there, and went back to sleep.

He didn't wake up again until afternoon. The wheat poultice was gone, and so was Laura. He didn't want to open his eyes. Maybe the whole thing had been a dream.

He wasn't sure how many days passed; it hardly mattered. He enjoyed the best nursing care of his life. No wonder invalids in Block Four never wanted to get well. He was content to be waited on, fed, cleaned and tidied by his beloved wife. "The only thing you haven't done is burp me," he said one afternoon, which made her laugh and throw a pillow at his head.

He caught it and tossed it back. He wasn't sure what happened then, but in record time she was in bed with him, after locking the door, shucking her clothes and divesting him of his nightshirt, too. *What a talented woman,* he thought, as he ran his hands experimentally over her breasts, enjoying the heft of them and their warmth.

His warmth, too. A man of science, he was not surprised that his illness in no way affected his urge to make love. There was not a thing he could do about his erection, but Laura didn't seem to object. She looked at his body with interest. She touched him, and then was gently running her hand up and down his growing shaft as he explored her body, so beautiful in the half-light of a drizzly afternoon.

She froze for a moment when he rose to mount her. He stopped right where he was. "Just breathe, Laura," he whispered. "Deep breaths, actually. You're about to surprise yourself." He couldn't resist. "Be gentle with me. I'm not entirely recovered."

She gave him such a look. The fear left her face and she smiled. "Is there anyone like you in the world?" she asked as she allowed him to enter her.

She couldn't have been more ready, he noted to his gratification and increasing ardor. She was like liquid silk. Her eyes, which she had squinted shut in anticipation of pain, were open now and looking directly into his. She sighed, then raised up to kiss him, pulling him down, his mouth on hers.

From her breathing and movements, he knew she would climax, even if this was their first time together. Again, she seemed to startle herself, then give herself over to another wave of pleasure as he climaxed, too. Her legs were tight around him, then raised as she made up for years and years of lost time. She gave him everything she had, and he returned the favor.

Finally, there was nothing to do but lie side by side in a coma of pleasure.

"I had no idea," she said finally, her words practically slurred. "Why on earth did I stay away so long? And you're in a weakened condition."

He laughed then, even if it did make his stomach hurt. "Just think of the possibilities," he told her, a little surprised that his mouth had trouble working, too.

"I daren't," she said. "We'll be finding niches in the linen closets of Block Four or that table in surgery."

He laughed again. "The linen closet will probably be more comfortable."

Only the fact that it was nearly March and chilly made her finally reach down for the coverlet, letting it drop and resuming her boneless state at his side. "I told Aunt Walters I would go down to help with dinner," she said. "Do you think she knows what we're doing?"

"Probably." He caressed her breasts. "This room was throbbing and glowing. There might even be a crowd gathered outside, wondering what the hell."

It was her turn to laugh, then roll to her side and look into his eyes, as serious as he had ever seen her. "Why did I not trust you?"

"Laura, we've barely scratched the surface in medicine.

I doubt there is a practitioner alive who would presume to understand the human mind. I don't."

He kissed her, and slept again.

Laura left him to his peaceful sleep an hour later, taking her time about washing herself, lingering over her own body as though it was a new acquisition. *Nana, you were right,* she thought, as she touched her breasts and smiled at the red marks where her husband—how good that sounded!—had taken a nip. She rested her hands on her genitals, where all was calm now, and wondered at the majesty of it all.

As she dried herself, she gazed down at her husband, unshaven and gaunt, but obviously enjoying the most restful sleep of his life. *I feel that way, too,* she told herself, *and all because we have spliced ourselves together.* She wanted him again, but knew she could wait, at least until the room quit throbbing and the crowd dispersed.

"Philemon, you are so funny," she whispered. "And brilliant, and kind and a lover with no equal, I am sure. How did I ever get so fortunate?"

Her good fortune only increased. Captain Brackett came to see his subordinate the next morning and told him on pain of death not to leave his bed. "Tie him down, if you have to, Mrs. Brittle," he told her, as he thumped Philemon's chest and listened for a long time. "He might need a poultice for his chest, but he can be the judge of that."

"Thankee, sor," Philemon whined, in imitation of the invalids they both served. "Can I chaw tabackee? Have a tot of grog?"

Brackett left the room laughing.

"Roger my madam until we're both bug-eyed and hollow?" Philemon called after him.

Laura put her hand over his mouth. "He is not down the stairs yet! My God, he is laughing harder!" she protested, then forgot what else she planned to say when her husband's hand went under her dress and stayed there until she started to breathe heavily and slid in bed beside him, dress and all.

She knew what followed that week was a conspiracy from the chief surgeon down to the lowliest orderly at Stonehouse. If Owen didn't drop by to check on his subordinate, then Philemon's chief mate did; both pronounced him still unfit for duty. One afternoon she did find his chief mate perched on the bed, poring over his notes as her husband made suggestions. She could see he was tempted to get up and back in uniform, but cooler heads prevailed. Brian shook his head.

"The chief said no, sir. Stay in bed a few days more."

"If I must," Philemon said, then started to cough.

He coughed until his mate left. With a wink, Philemon motioned her closer. "I thought he'd never leave," he confided, as he unbuttoned her dress.

Even when he was sitting up in bed, hungry, and starting to look bored, the conspiracy continued, to Laura's delight. Owen refused to pronounce him well; Aitken clucked over him, and even Miss Peters dropped by to purse her lips in that forbidding way Laura remembered, and shake her head. "Don't you move," she ordered, and he looked meek and did not move.

That afternoon when Laura was bare again, and pillowed against his chest, ready to drift into postcoital slumber, Philemon had the honesty to confess Miss Peters had told him the best way to get her to come to Stonehouse was to feign illness.

"She knew you would come to nurse me," he said, stroking her shoulder. "I swear on Bibles I was sick for real."

"I have no doubt of that," she told him. "And now you're better." She wrapped her arms around her husband and kissed his chest. "Miss Peters hinted that Captain Brackett wants some time off before the spring campaigns begin."

He nodded. "I'm returning to work on Monday. Owen already asked for leave, and he's planning to take Miss Peters with him to visit his son in Gloucester." He pulled her closer. "He seemed embarrassed to tell me that, but I understand. His baby needs a mother, and his late wife had been ill with consumption for years. Only Owen's excellent care pulled her through her confinement. We knew she could not last."

She could tell he had more to say. She closed her eyes when he ran his fingers through her hair. "What is it, my love?" she asked quietly.

"Owen also told me what he heard from a surgeon through here a few days ago. Apparently Wellington is planning a spring campaign that will take him farther north into Spain."

"Good. This war must end. Perhaps he is the man to do it."

He raised up on one elbow. "Do you see what might happen, Laura?"

Her heart plummeted into her stomach. "You will have to go to sea?"

"No. I'm far more useful to the navy here. Come closer."

"It's not possible."

He managed to pull her closer, as if he thought she would move away when he spoke. "Your father was in a Spanish prison just over the border, not so far from Oporto, which as you know, Wellington captured last summer."

"How could I forget? I think I still hear that jetty bell. So many wounded."

He kissed her shoulder. "I know, Laura, your father must have been spirited away to a different prison, because he wasn't found when the British army liberated that area. The farther Wellington maneuvers in Spain, the more likely that Lord Ratliffe will be found and returned."

She froze, then felt her heart beating faster. "I don't want to see him. Not ever. My God, Philemon, he schemed to leave Nana in prison in his place, when he had promised to be a guaranty for a prisoner exchange! What kind of unnatural parent is that?"

She tried to move, but Philemon held her there. "What are you doing?" she demanded.

"Holding you until you calm down," he told her, with just an edge of command in his voice. "I'll never let him hurt you—God's oath, Laura—but there is a strong possibility that he will disembark here, and you must prepare yourself."

"I won't see him," she insisted, shaking her head.

"You might have to do something else, something that sounds so hard and yet is so necessary, if you truly want to be free of him."

She couldn't bring herself to ask.

"You might have to forgive him."

She sucked in her breath. "How can you even suggest

such a thing, after all he has done to me, and not only me, but what he tried to do to Nana? I thought you loved me."

Her words hung on the air like a bad odor, but Philemon did not flinch.

"It's because I love you."

"I wish I understood that!" she said, unable to stop her tears.

"So do I."

Chapter Nineteen

~~~~~~~~~~~

Philemon returned to work on Monday, after a strange weekend of silence from his wife. She denied him nothing in bed, but there was a distance in her eyes that told him he had spoken too soon. He could tell she was trying not to worry about seeing her father, but in quiet moments when he pretended to sleep, he watched her stare at the ceiling.

Even when she slept, she was restless, her eyes moving behind her closed lids in that way he had noticed in men shattered by combat or storm at sea. He berated himself for not noticing that sooner, the way she could look through a wall and not see it. He did it himself, but he had seen too much pain on sea and land. Maybe he had teased himself into not seeing it in his beloved wife, because he knew in his heart that no woman should face what men faced.

The only cure he knew was time and love, two staples in short supply in a naval hospital, but pray God, not in his own home. He cursed the war that sent him off to the wards and the work he loved, when he knew acutely how much damage remained to be repaired in his madam, that time-honored term married naval officers used.

Once he walked through the double doors of Building Four, he knew there would not be a spare moment to think about his wife. He did have a moment's pleasure, late in the afternoon watch, when Oliver Worthy strolled onto Ward C.

After a quick glance to make sure his fingers were not gruesome, he shook hands with his brother-in-law, who looked well-fed but not good-humored. *Why should he be happy?* Philemon asked himself as they stepped onto the landing, that place for conversation. *He has probably just left his wife and baby and is heading back to the war.*

"What do you think of Rachel Worthy?" Philemon asked.

"Are you referring to the princess who must be fed and changed and coddled?" he joked. "I never saw a bonnier baby." His eyes expressed all he could not say. "Thank you for being there."

"All in a day's work," Philemon replied, pleased. "I give Nana most of the credit. She was a trouper."

"I wish I had been there."

"So do we all."

His invitation to dinner was accepted with alacrity, although Oliver admitted he had already visited Laura and given her the same answer. "By the way, your father accepted, too. He is visiting with Laura now."

Philemon felt his eyes well up this time. "Thank you for taking care of *him*."

"He takes care of all of us on the *Tangier*." Oliver straightened up. "I am keeping you from work, but brother, do we have even the smallest inkling how lucky we are?"

"We do, Oliver. We do."

The orderly was calling him. Philemon nodded to his brother-in-law and returned to the ward.

Dinner was an unalloyed delight. Laura had put aside her own qualms and had obviously been captivated by his father. A long embrace with Dan Brittle and he felt like a boy again, looking up to the man he most respected, let alone loved. Although, he told himself over coffee, Oliver ran him a close second.

Laura had started the discussion. "Oliver, you must hear of something Philemon has in mind."

"It's too soon to talk of it," he protested, but not much, especially when she put her hand on his arm and skewered him with the kindness in her eyes.

Encouraged, he told Oliver and his father about his idea to maintain a satellite hospital in Oporto. "Maybe even farther north, when that region of Spain is ours again," he added. "We could save so many of the seamen who now are tended aboard ships where there is little room and less time to provide more than rudimentary care."

Oliver leaned forward, interested. Philemon's father sat back, proud.

"We have such hospitals already in other parts of the world. Why not one near the Bay of Biscay, and perhaps another in the Mediterranean? Why not make them flexible enough to disband, when the danger is past? Or near?"

"Why not, indeed?" Oliver answered. "And you would be in charge."

"Someone would," he said modestly. "That's not why I'm suggesting it. Oh, you know that. For every Davey Dabney or Alexander Small where we get lucky, there are countless seamen less fortunate. I want to shorten the butcher's bill."

Oliver nodded. "You're busy. Laura, perhaps you could outline Phil's main idea, provide statistics, and send me three copies? I can read it and forward it to Admiralty House, with a copy to the Sick and Hurt Board. I know any number of captains and an admiral or two who would add their endorsements to such a plan."

Philemon couldn't convince anyone to spend the night. His father, also coming off leave in Torquay, was headed back to the *Tangier.* Oliver said his life would be as short as a leaf in a hot furnace if he did not sleep at the Mulberry Inn and tell Gran and Pete everything about Princess Rachel.

"She's a game goer," his father told him as Philemon walked the sailing master to the gates of Stonehouse. "Your mother said I would be impressed, and I am, son. Take good care of her."

I aim to, he thought, as he went upstairs, after extinguishing the lights below and bidding Aunt Walters good-night. Laura was already in bed. Wordlessly, they made love.

"Forgive me for being such a trial," she whispered, as she still lay on him.

She seemed disinclined to move, so he pulled the coverlet over them both and they slept, until he woke her later with an urge for more love. Even more gratifying was another round after the sun was up. He was still asleep, but she was stroking him, which filled his whole body with delight because it was solely her idea and she was not shy to act upon it. *One ghost gone, perhaps?* he thought, when they finished and she sat up and stretched, prepared to meet the day on little sleep but a wealth of good cheer.

He watched her wash and dress, admiring the bones of her back and the flesh of her buttocks, so smooth and so his. *I know her inside and out,* he thought. *I just wish I knew her mind.*

Next morning, Philemon had no trouble convincing Laura to tackle his paperwork, especially since Miss Peters had recommended it before she and Owen Brackett left for Gloucester. Maybe she was still a little afraid of her dresser, and feared to cross her.

"What about Sir David?" she asked timidly. "Do I dare say anything?"

"I already have, Mrs. Brittle," Peters said. "I told him you would handle everything for Ward Block Four and he should not cut up stiff about it." She unbent enough to smile at her former mistress. "Even he is a little afraid of me!"

The dining room became her office. The month passed quickly as she sorted and organized, and devised a system of records and reckoning that no one could argue with because it was so efficient. Afraid to take it to Sir David by herself, she allowed Miss Peters—Brackett now— returned from Gloucester and quietly married, to accompany her to the admin building.

What could he do? Everything was organized and in place, from victual budgets and all receipts, to post mortem notes, to records of surgical procedures and items of discharge. Sir David could only nod and accept it, then swallow his pride and ask her straight out if she could organize all his surgeons and mates as effectively. She could, and did. They never spoke more than necessary, but at least she had the courage to go to the administration building by herself.

Sir David even unbent so far as to suggest she set up an office in admin. She assured him her dining table would do. No need for him to know how easily distracted Philemon could make her when he came home during his odd hours and she was happy to follow him upstairs. There wasn't any way she could do that in admin.

Philemon never spoke to her again of forgiveness, but the thought remained like a bolus lodged in her throat. When no word came of her father's whereabouts, she began to hope he had died somewhere in Spain. She resolved not to think of him.

Letters from Edinburgh provided needed diversion for them both. Deep in pharmacopoeia studies, Davey wrote that even the renowned Niall McTavish had looked at his neck and allowed that perhaps Lt. Brittle had learned something during his tenure at the university.

"High praise," Philemon told her with some satisfaction, when he read the letter to her in bed. "Don't look so doubtful! There was a backstairs rumor that the only compliment McTavish ever paid his wife was when she managed to satisfy them both in twenty seconds flat. Economy is everrra-thing, lass, when you are a Scot with a second-hand watch."

"Philemon!" she exclaimed, shocked.

"That is medical school. Our amusements were—are— minimal." He looked at the letter again. "Davey is doing well." He patted her bare rump. "That was the best money you ever spent, my love."

"I can do it again," she assured him.

"In twenty seconds flat? Ow! Have a care with the jewels, dearest!"

In all the paper-shifting, she found time early to organize her husband's ideas about a satellite naval hospital in the theater of war. Some evenings she nabbed him long enough to sit down and describe it in more detail, and give her a rudimentary list of supplies she could convert to budget items. More often than not, those sessions ended with her on his lap. She still blushed to think about the time they never even got upstairs. Amazing what two people of like mind could do on a dining room chair. And thank goodness Aunt Walters had gone to Torquay to visit her sister-in-law.

The report, in triplicate, went to Oliver on the *Tangier,* who wrote a note to say he had forwarded the copies, with his endorsement, to Admiralty, Sick and Hurt, and the admiral of the Channel Fleet. "And now we wait," Oliver concluded.

Nothing else waited. The season of campaigning began with ferocity as Wellington moved inland again, up from the Torres Vedras lines, and unleashed himself and his lieutenants on Masséna this time, that Old Fox, the marshal Napoleon trusted. Beresford, Craufurd, Daddy Hill, Picton and the marquess himself pounded, followed, harried and attacked, and so did their Spanish and Portuguese allies. She and Philemon both listened in amazement to Oliver's stories of guerilla warfare, led by patriots nicknamed The Garrotte, The Needle and The Lash.

The *Tangier* and its counterpart, Captain Virgil Denison's sloop of war *Goldfinch,* darted in and out of Plymouth. When the captains sailing under Admiralty Orders could not afford time-eating trips to London, the semaphore arms of the telegraphs up the coast moved from dawn to dusk.

She saw more of Nana and Rachel, simply because Nana, over Oliver's feeble objections, moved her little family back to the Mulberry, the better to glimpse her husband on his speedy trips in and out of Plymouth. A day spent in her sister's company, playing with her charming niece, was balm to Laura's soul, second only to love in Philemon's arms. He never failed her in any way.

She asked him timidly one afternoon if maybe he should just sleep when he came home during his odd hours. "I prefer both," he told her, his lips on her breast. She did not argue with him again.

When the jetty bell seemed to ring day and night, she had returned to the landing to help. There were literally days when she did not see Philemon or Owen Brackett, or any of the mates, except as they hurried the wounded and dying into the overflowing buildings at Stonehouse. There was even talk of setting up tents in the large courtyard, until the army regimental hospitals began to take more of their wounded sooner. Sir David had seen her there. After a long look, then a sigh that she could practically hear over the moans of the wounded, the administrator had shrugged his shoulders and returned to his own patients. Even he came to the jetty now.

By July she knew she was carrying Philemon's child. Her first instinct was to shout the news to the rooftops in utter bliss because she had never been happier. How strange that in the middle of the wracking trauma that was her life at Stonehouse, she could wake up each morning in her husband's arms (when he was there), and know that their baby was peacefully growing inside her, immune to war and danger.

She wanted to tell Philemon, but she wanted it to be the right time, and not when he came home, fell asleep upright at the dinner table or paced the sitting room, well-thumbed medical text in hand. There had to be a good time, and she intended to wait for it.

There was a certain pleasurable selfishness in keeping the news to herself. She woke each morning with her hands on her belly, relieved beyond measure that her first husband had been so wrong. Even when he had berated her for failing to produce a Taunton heir, she had known it was never her fault. Now she understood, and, understanding, took another look at herself. *I am better than I know,* she told herself. *Much better.*

Easy to say, she discovered, the morning the jetty bell started ringing just before noon and would not stop. Sorting a mountain of records in the dining room, she thought to ignore it, except that Philemon sent an orderly running up her front steps. He burst into the dining room. "Hurry!" he said. "There are so many!"

Grabbing her apron, she ran after him, appalled before she even got to the landing at how many jolly boats stood off in the stream behind Stonehouse. As inured as she was by now to the carnage, she stared at the sight before her.

The lawn was littered with men, the grass turning red before her eyes. "What happened?" she asked a passing stretcher bearer.

"Wounded as usual, but the ships ran into a French fleet that mauled them worse," he said, breathless from running, too. "One of the ships' magazines blew up."

She grabbed his arm. "Was the *Tangier* among them?"

"Don't think so."

Willing herself calm, she looked for Philemon and knelt at his side as he labored, his hands deep inside a boy too young to shave.

"Laura, put your finger on the artery and press it to the bone."

She did as he demanded, moving her finger at precisely the right moment as he twirled the ligature around the offender and stopped the blood. He wrapped a tight bandage, then marked the man's forehead with a number and shouted for the stretcher bearers.

"Trouble is, they are all numbered one or two," he muttered.

He wiped his hands on his apron and reached for the familiar canvas bag. Laura thought he would just indicate where she should start, but he took her by the hand and threaded through a lane of wounded, pushing her to her knees beside a quiet figure with a leg off and a powerful stench.

Lord Ratliffe sprawled before her. She gasped, then vomited before she could control it. She tried to leap up, but Philemon held her there. "Do what you can, Laura. I fear it will not be much. Don't touch his leg."

She struggled under the restraint of his bloody hand, angry now. "I won't! You cannot make me touch him!"

"I will hold you here until you do," he said, and there was no mercy in his eyes. "Tend this man."

He would not relent, even when she began to cry, which made her father stir and moan, calling for water. With his free hand that shook, Philemon wiped her chin of the vomit.

She could not even look at her father. "I will hate you until I die," she told Philemon. "Maybe beyond."

She knew she had lacerated him, wounding him more than the men around them. *Hit me,* she thought then, *shake me, scream at me, do what men do to women who cannot defend themselves. I understand that. Just don't make me tend this demon.*

She could not take her eyes from Philemon. She watched him visibly force himself to calmness, even as he continued to bear down on her. As she glared at him, his expression softened.

"Do you remember when you asked me if I would love you even when you did not love me?"

She nodded, ashamed of herself.

He suddenly released his hold on her, stepping back to free her. "This is that moment, Laura. You have to love me—trust me!—even though you do not." He left her beside her father.

Her first instinct was to run until she was back in Taunton, hiding in a closet as she had done once, when the demands of Sir James exceeded her power to function. She rose, ready to bolt, determined to do it, except that she could not. All around her, surgeons and mates and orderlies worked swiftly, their faces grim and set.

Will no one relieve my *pain?* she cried inside. She glanced at Philemon, who was kneeling beside another sailor now, one terribly burned. He looked at her and nodded encouragement.

"How can you be so kind to me?" she asked.

She knew he could not hear her, but he cupped his hand to his ear, then nodded again as he returned to his hopeless task.

She could do no less, even if she despised the man at

her feet. She reached for one of the tins of water orderlies were placing on the grass at intervals, and took a cloth from her bag, wetting it, and wiped Lord Ratliffe's face. She put her ear to his slightly open mouth, and listened to him breathe. His pulse was thready, but at least he had a pulse.

She wiped his neck and upper chest, which made him stir. She sat back on her heels as his eyelids fluttered and he returned to consciousness. "Hello, Father," she forced herself to say.

Stupified, he stared at her, trying to figure out who she was through a film of pain that she had seen in other wounded men. Davey had described it to her once as looking up from the bottom of a pond, with people wavy and disembodied looking back.

He recognized her then and began to breathe faster. She forced herself to remember what Philemon had taught her, and just rested her hand on his chest. "It's all right. Just breathe easy."

He closed his eyes, did as she said, then opened them again. "Laura?" he asked, disbelieving, then, "Laura," as the pond cleared.

She continued to wipe him, the cloth more grimy than bloody. *Where have you been?* she wanted to ask. *What happened to your leg?*

When she turned him on his side, she noticed the bullet wound, angry, weepy and infected as badly as what remained of his leg. She grabbed another can of water, and quickly washed him until the wound was clean. She held a compress over it, ready to apply adhesive, when she stopped. *I could probe it,* she thought suddenly. *Maybe I can remove the ball, for it obviously has not exited.*

She looked around for a probe, then realized what was happening to her. She swallowed, trying to remember how much she hated Lord Ratliffe, except that it wouldn't come. He was a dying man in pain, and she wanted more than anything to ease his passage. "Why do I not hate you?" she whispered. "I should, you know. I have every right."

She attached the compress to the wound and made herself comfortable on the grass beside her father. He was unconscious again, so she lifted the blanket covering his amputation and stared at the trauma. Maybe the surgeon on land or sea had been overworked. Maybe he had tried to perform a miracle on a leg that should have been tended weeks earlier. She closed her eyes against the red streaks that snaked nearly to his chest. *And I wanted to probe a bullet,* she thought. *I might as well spit in the ocean to fill it.*

She covered him, washed her hands in bloody water, then grasped his hands. The touch woke him. He looked at her with surprising interest, perhaps wondering how she came to be there, or maybe just accepting it.

He tried to speak and she leaned closer, holding his hands tight against her chest now, where her heart seemed to jump out of her body. "Tell me, Father," she urged softly.

"I regret," was all he could manage, but it was enough.

She thought she wanted to tell him she was glad he regretted, glad he suffered, but she could not. She glanced at Philemon, who had moved to another man close by, this one less seriously burned. He worked, but took the time to watch her, too. *Husband, you are so determined not to abandon me,* she thought in wonder, *even though you are busier than any mortal I know.*

She returned her gaze to her father. "It is this way,

Father," she said, amazed at herself. "How can I be small, when I have so much? I accept your regret."

Lord Ratliffe nodded. She released his hands to wipe the tears on his face, then clutched him again. She was still holding his hand when the stretcher bearers came.

"Take him to Block Four."

Philemon was beside her now, helping her to her feet. "Brian is there. I will attach a note on Lord Ratliffe and tell him to probe for that bullet. It'll relieve some of his suffering." He kissed her forehead, although she couldn't imagine there was a clean spot on her face. "Can you tend some more here?"

She nodded, then took his arm when he started away. "Philemon, I am so…"

"We'll talk later, madam."

"You need to know something."

"And you will tell me."

Chapter Twenty

Laura stayed at the jetty until nearly dark, tending to the less wounded, joking with some of them, listening to others tell of the fight at sea. Philemon and the other surgeons and mates had long left the landing and were working indoors.

Exhausted, she went home only long enough to wash, put on another dress, and write a note to Nana, begging her to come to Block Four as soon as she could, and bring Rachel. She began the letter to Nana as she always did, with the underlined words, "Oliver is safe and well." No sense in terrifying her. "It is our father," she wrote, after stewing over the matter.

Nana could decide whether or not to come. After his last visit with them, Oliver had said he had warned Nana, just as Philemon had done, with the reality that Lord Ratliffe might be recovered anytime now. "If she hadn't been nursing Rachel, I think Nana would have thrashed me with a poker," Oliver had joked. Laura sent the note with a passing carter and a generous sum. Nana could make up her own mind.

Her father was on Ward B, according to the chart by the main door. She went to the familiar ward and looked for him. The orderly indicated he was behind the screen, which told her everything. *No hope at all,* she thought, and felt her own regret.

He was clean now, but smelled as abominably as ever because of his rotten stump. Still in bloody apron and stained shirt, Philemon sat with him. She kissed her husband and went for a basin of warm water and a cloth. She wiped Philemon's face, and ran the cloth inside his shirt, because she knew how much he liked that.

"Forgive me for what I said," she told him when she sat beside him.

"I know you didn't mean it." He put his hands on her neck and massaged it. "What a day. I am ready for this war to end."

"How is he?"

"He won't last the night. Brian removed the ball, so he's easier, but there is nothing we can do for him."

"Do you know what happened?"

Philemon nodded. "There was another prisoner with him, a soldier captured during the retreat to Corunna. He said the colonel in charge of the prison was moving them north to France when they were attacked by guerillas. Your…Lord Ratliffe's leg was broken and left untreated for too long."

She put her hand on her husband's knee. "It's all right if you call him my father. He is. Has he been able to speak?"

Philemon moved her hand higher on his leg, telling her volumes about his own need for comfort. "He told me over and over how sorry he is for the way he treated you and

Nana. I don't think he knows who I am, though." He chuckled. "I told him I am married to you, but he can't seem to grasp the idea. Hardly surprising, considering his toplofty ways." He patted her hand. "He just keeps saying, 'I regret,' over and over."

"I don't hate him."

"I know. You're far too big in spirit for that."

"I didn't think I was. How did you know?" she asked.

He only shrugged.

She sat with her father all evening, giving him sips of water when he drifted into consciousness. Philemon came and went, tending to others. Just when she thought Nana was not coming, she heard light footsteps on the other side of the screen.

Paler than she had ever seen her, Nana joined Laura, sidling along the screen and keeping as far from the bed as she could. She carried Rachel, clutching her daughter.

"He can't hurt you, Nana," Laura whispered.

She told Nana of his injuries, and his words of regret. Gradually, the frown left her face. In a few more minutes, she sat beside Laura, keeping as close to her as she could, which warmed Laura's heart. I *am* the older sister, she reminded herself.

Laura took her father's hand. He was hot to the touch, and she knew infection was waiting to claim him. She ran her hand over his fingers, long and shapely as her own, then twined her fingers through his.

"How can you bear to touch him?" Nana asked. "He did you so much wrong. Me, too, I suppose, but I had an ally."

"I did, too," Laura said. She turned to her sister. "I didn't know it until this afternoon. It was I. All along, it was I.

There was something inside me that refused to break. I don't understand, but I can live with that."

Nana started to cry then, handing her baby to Laura as she covered her face with her hands and sobbed. "He tried to do us such mischief! I should hate him, shouldn't I?"

Laura closed her eyes in relief at Nana's question and pressed her face into Rachel's curls. "It's not worth it to hate him. I wish things had been different, but if he had not been who he was, we would never be here. Captain Worthy would sail in and out of Plymouth, and Surgeon Brittle would tend patients, both without us. *That* is what is too awful to think about."

Nana sucked in her breath with the enormity of it, and let it out slowly. She picked up her stool, and carried it around to Lord Ratliffe's other side, where she could hold his other hand.

He regained consciousness around midnight, looking at them both clearly. Laura got up to call for her husband, who came quickly, sitting on the bed. "Sir?" Philemon asked. "Can you hear us?"

Lord Ratliffe nodded, looking from one daughter to the other, then at the sleeping baby.

"We named her Rachel, Father," Nana said, her own voice firm as she spoke to her father. "After my mother."

"Rachel was so lovely," he said. "We?"

"Yes. I am married to Captain Oliver Worthy of the Channel Fleet. Hold her, Father." Nana looked to Philemon for reassurance. He took Rachel and tucked her close to Lord Ratliffe's chest.

"He's not feeling any pain now, sister," Laura said. "Neither should we."

Lord Ratliffe tried to raise his hand to his granddaughter's head, but he could not. Taking a deep breath, Nana picked up his hand and guided it to her daughter's head. He sighed and smiled, then looked at Laura. "Do you…"

She shook her head. "Not yet, although I am with child. I…" She stopped when Philemon put his hand on her shoulder, and ran his thumb gently along her neck. She was suddenly too shy to look at him or respond to Nana's delighted laugh. "Sometime in the spring."

He seemed to understand, looking at Philemon and then at her, something of the viscount in his tone again. "Daughter, he is so common."

"So am I. We're uncommonly happy, though."

Lord Ratliffe nodded and closed his eyes. Nana reached across him to grasp Laura's arm, too excited to speak.

Philemon was called away a few minutes later. He took Laura by the hand and pulled her after him around the screen. "I'm needed in Block Two. Stay with him until he dies, then pronounce him, Laura. Write the time in the log and initial your name."

"Not yours?"

"No. Yours."

He took her in his arms and held her close. "My family, my family," was all he said, before he left for another block, a longer night.

Lord Ratliffe's daughters sat with their father until he died. Laura closed his eyes gently and looked at the timepiece Philemon had left. With a firm hand, she wrote time of death in the log book, and led her weeping sister back to her home, her arm tight around her.

She saw Nana and Rachel upstairs and settled, then

peeked in her bedroom. Philemon was not there. She went downstairs and into the dining room, certain she had heard him come in when she was upstairs. There he was, head forward on his chest, asleep. She touched his shoulder, unwilling to startle him, but certain he would sleep better in bed with her beside him.

He stretched, then pulled her onto his lap. "What time did he die?"

"Half past two. I recorded it." She leaned against him, secure in her love. "I don't think the news of our baby surprised you."

"It didn't." He chuckled. "I've been wondering when you were going to summon the nerve to tell me."

She settled herself more comfortably on his lap. "How did you know? I've only missed one flow and you couldn't be suspicious of my queasiness this afternoon. I wasn't alone in that."

"Too right. We all took our turns hugging the basin. Even I." He cupped her breast. "See there? You've been flinching lately. You're a little tender. And I keep a mental calendar of your cycles. Face it, Laura, I'm a man and I crave my pleasure. I also like to know what's going on inside my nearest and dearest." He started to unbutton her dress. "Besides, have you taken a good look at your breasts lately? I have. It's one of my favorite pastimes."

"My blushes, Philemon," she said as he untied the string holding her chemise together.

He pulled back her chemise. "The areola around your nipples has changed color. See?"

She would have looked, but he was kissing her then. "I love you," she told him.

"Well, what a relief," he teased gently. "Any idea when this event might have taken place? Springtime is too vague to suit a surgeon."

She didn't answer him, but straddled him on the dining room chair. He threw back his head and laughed.

"My God, Laura! I promise never to tell anyone."

Lord Ratliffe's three natural daughters were not invited to his funeral at Stokes Manor a week later, but they attended anyway, sitting close together in the back row of the parish church. The vicar eulogized their father, England's hero, as a vicar might, who owed his living now to Ratliffe's heir—a distant cousin—who was taking in every word.

The interment in the family vault was also a private affair, so the sisters stood in the cemetery, watching from a distance.

"Does our cousin know who we are?" Nana whispered to Laura.

"Probably. From those black looks he's been darting our way, he must think we've come here to make demands on the vast family fortune." She smothered a laugh. "He's probably prepared to shoo us away, but we know better than he does that Stokes is mortgaged to the rafters. What a jolt that will be, when the solicitor reads the will."

"Goodness, you two, have some dignity!" Polly Brandon said, then ducked when Nana grabbed her by the neck and started to laugh.

They dropped off Polly in Bath, but Laura felt less than inclined to go inside. "Miss Pym can wait," she said to Nana. "Where is it written I must forgive *everyone*? Let us go to Taunton."

They did, Nana's eyes wide with the grandeur of the place, even though Laura knew Oliver had made enough money from prize taking to buy it without a blink.

"There are no heirs. I think I will sell it," she said, as they walked arm in arm through the rooms. "Or perhaps I will turn it into a naval convalescent hospital. Philemon will guide me in this."

She dropped Nana and Rachel in Torquay with the promise to visit soon, barely containing her impatience to be home again, when the horses seemed to be poking along.

Philemon was not at home, even though it was late, but that was no surprise. When he came dragging upstairs hours later, she didn't mind being wakened. There was much to tell him. When she finally finished, he held her close, careful not to press against her tender breasts.

"I have some news of my own," he said. "There is a document downstairs in our favorite dining room with all kinds of stickers and seals on it."

She thought a moment, then sucked in her breath and pounced on him. "The satellite hospital?"

He didn't try to contain his own excitement. "The very one. It's to be in Oporto. I have been promoted to senior surgeon and charged with relocating me and my mates there as soon as possible. Last week would be better, according to the Sick and Hurt Board. You know how they are."

"I am coming, too."

"Certainly. I am to find a hospital matron if I can, but that will not be you. Your task will be to keep my records shipshape and birth our baby. My chances of being there for that event are far greater than Oliver Worthy's, poor man. *When* will Boney cease his meddling?"

"When Wellington thrashes him soundly, I suppose."

They composed themselves for sleep.

"You're the only surgeon I trust," she told him, her eyes closing.

"What a relief," he replied, equally drowsy.

He tensed then, and groaned.

"What?" she asked.

"I hear someone running along the walk. Wait a minute. Here comes the knock. No, a pounding." He sat up, and patted her hip. "Laura, I could have been a pig farmer. It was good enough for Grandda."

She blew him a kiss and snuggled into his warm spot, then listened as he whistled down the stairs.

* * * * *

*Celebrate 60 years of pure reading
pleasure with Harlequin®!*

*Harlequin Presents® is proud to introduce
its gripping new miniseries,*
THE ROYAL HOUSE OF KAREDES.
*An exquisite coronation diamond, split as a symbol of
a warring royal family's feud, is missing! But whoever
reunites the diamond halves will rule all....*

*Welcome to eight brand-new titles that unfold
to reveal the stories of kings and queens, princes and
princesses torn apart by pride and power, but finally
reunited by love.*

Step into the world of Karedes with
BILLIONAIRE PRINCE, PREGNANT MISTRESS
Available July 2009 from Harlequin Presents®.

ALEXANDROS KAREDES, SNOW DUSTING the shoulders of his leather jacket and glittering like jewels in his dark hair, stood at the door. Maria felt the blood drain from her head.

"Good evening, Ms. Santos."

His voice was as she remembered it. Deep. Husky. Perfect English, but with the faintest hint of a Greek accent. And cold, as cold as it had been that awful morning she would never forget, when he'd accused her of horrible things, called her terrible names....

"Aren't you going to ask me in?"

She fought for composure. Last time they'd faced each other, they'd been on his turf. Now they were on hers. She was in command here, and that meant everything.

"There's a sign on the door downstairs," she said, her tone every bit as frigid as his. "It says, 'No soliciting or vagrants.'"

His lips drew back in a wolfish grin. "Very amusing."

"What do you want, Prince Alexandros?"

A tight smile eased across his mouth and it killed her that even now, knowing he was a vicious, arrogant man, she couldn't help but notice what a handsome mouth it was. Chiseled. Generous. Beautiful, like the rest of him, which made him living proof that beauty could, indeed, be only skin deep.

"Such formality, Maria. You were hardly so proper the last time we were together."

She knew his choice of words was deliberate. She felt her face heat; she couldn't help that but she damned well didn't have to let him lure her into a verbal sparring match.

"I'll ask you once more, your highness. What do you want?"

"Ask me in and I'll tell you."

"I have no intention of asking you in. Tell me why you're here or don't. It's your choice, just as it will be my choice to shut the door in your face."

He laughed. It infuriated her but she could hardly blame him. He was tall—six-two, six-three—and though he stood with one shoulder leaning against the door frame, hands tucked casually into the pockets of the jacket, his pose was deceptive. He was strong, with the leanly muscled body of a well-trained athlete.

She remembered his body with painful clarity. The feel of him under her hands. The power of him moving over her. The taste of him on her tongue.

Suddenly, he straightened, his laughter gone. "I have not come this distance to stand in your doorway," he said coldly, "and I am not going to leave until I am ready to do so. I suggest you stand aside and stop behaving like a petulant child."

A petulant child? Was that what he thought? This man who had spent hours making love to her and had then accused her of—of trading her body for profit?

Except it had not been love, it had been sex. And the sooner she got rid of him, the better.

She let go of the doorknob and stepped aside. "You have five minutes."

He strolled past her, bringing cold air and the scent of the night with him. She swung toward him, arms folded. He reached past her, pushed the door closed, then folded his arms, too. She wanted to open the door again but she'd be damned if she was going to get into a who's-in-charge-here argument with him. She was in charge, and he would surely see a tussle over the ground rules as a sign of weakness.

Instead, she looked past him at the big clock above her work table.

"Ten seconds gone," she said briskly. "You're wasting time, your highness."

"What I have to say will take longer than five minutes."

"Then you'll just have to learn to economize. More than five minutes, I'll call the police."

Instantly, his hand was wrapped around her wrist. He tugged her toward him, his dark-chocolate eyes almost black with anger.

"You do that and I'll tell every tabloid shark I can contact about how Maria Santos tried to buy a five-hundred-thousand-dollar commission by seducing a prince." He smiled thinly. "They'll lap it up."

* * * * *

What will it take for this billionaire prince to realize
he's falling in love with his mistress…?
Look for
BILLIONAIRE PRINCE, PREGNANT MISTRESS
by Sandra Marton
Available July 2009 from Harlequin Presents®.

We'll be spotlighting a different series every month
throughout 2009 to celebrate our 60th anniversary.

Look for Harlequin® Presents in July!

TWO CROWNS, TWO ISLANDS, ONE LEGACY
A royal family, torn apart by pride and its lust for
power, reunited by purity and passion

Step into the world of Karedes
beginning this July with

BILLIONAIRE PRINCE,
PREGNANT MISTRESS
by
Sandra Marton

Eight volumes to collect and treasure!

In 2009 Harlequin celebrates
60 years of pure reading pleasure!

We're marking this occasion by offering
16 **FREE** full books to download and read.

Visit

www.HarlequinCelebrates.com

to choose from a variety of
great romance stories
that are absolutely **FREE!**

(Total approximate retail value of $60)

We invite you to visit and share the Web site
with your friends, family
and anyone who enjoys reading.